HEADING HOME

BOOK 3 OF THE IRISH END GAMES

SUSAN KIERNAN-LEWIS

SAN MARCO PRESS

1

The colors from the setting sun streaked across the summer sky in a vibrant display as Sarah stood in the front room of her cottage. She filled a basket with fresh-baked rolls for the upcoming dinner at Fiona's. The days in Ireland were long and warm in late June. As she looked across the camp, awash with muted reds and yellows from the dying light, her eyes were drawn to the warm glow from inside Fiona's cottage.

Even from a distance, it looked inviting and cozy. Sarah saw Fiona and Papin moving about the interior, doing the little homey chores necessary for putting a family meal together. She watched them until she saw Mike appear on the porch steps and heard Papin squeal her greeting to him.

She saw Mike open his arms and Papin and Fiona both came to him. Sarah would never forget the day, seven months ago, when Mike rode into camp with Papin cradled in his arms, her broken arm folded against her chest, her eyes wide with hope and expectation. When Sarah ran up to them, he dismounted and carried Papin to Sarah's cottage. Sarah held the dear broken girl—and the man who had brought her home—and believed her heart would burst from happiness.

Since that day, Mike had stepped easily into the role of father to Papin, and the girl had responded like a Morning Glory to sunlight. Gregarious by nature, Papin slipped seamlessly into the pace and beat of family life as if she'd been born to it. For the first time ever, Papin had a loving family.

One thing everyone knew for sure: the bad times were behind her.

As Sarah packed her basket, it occurred to her that tonight was a typical evening meal with the people she loved most in the world. The anticipation she felt—hearing them share about their day and laughing with them, as she knew she would—filled her with a sense of wellbeing and security she'd never really had up to now.

The truth of it was they were finally all together—all except for David. A shadow passed over her heart as she thought of him, buried beneath a scattering of wild flowers in the far pasture by Deirdre and Seamus's old cottage. She shook the thought from her mind. Tonight wasn't the time for reflection or regrets or grief. It was a night for celebration and toasts and joy.

Tomorrow was Fiona's wedding day.

MIKE DONOVAN STOOD at the end of the aisle and watched the bride approach. He had to admit he had never seen her look more beautiful, her face flushed with excitement, her eyes sparkling when she saw him. It was all he could do to mask his quickly misting eyes as he gazed at her.

"You ready, then?" he asked gruffly, holding out his arm to her.

"As I'll ever be," Fiona said, grabbing on to his arm.

"Declan's a good bloke," Mike said, turning toward the chapel.

"I know."

They stood at the end of the path as it wrapped around the last hut before entering the camp. It had been Sarah's idea to have Mike and Fi approach the little chapel from the outdoor walkway. Mike had to admit, it felt even more special to take this walk with Fi, at the end of which he'd hand her over to the man who, in the last seven months, had become his closest mate since his school days.

Hard to believe it had been seven months since Declan and his gypsy gang of fortune tellers, goniffs, and grifters had stormed the little Irish settlement Mike had built and helped rescue them from an English assault. Seven months in which Declan had proved himself to be not only a friend and a capable lieutenant in managing the camp alongside Mike—but the one man in all the world that Mike's sister, Fiona, would give her heart

"There's the music," Fi said, squeezing Mike's arm. "I don't know how your Sarah did it, but it really sounds pretty close to *Haste to the Wedding.*"

Mike grinned. *His Sarah.* As much as he loved the sound of that, and he knew Fiona only said it as a private gift to him on this special day, he also knew Sarah Woodson—an American stranded in Ireland with her family after an ill-timed vacation—belonged to no one.

It was true enough, however, that she was just about the most resourceful person he'd ever met. After everything that went down last year he had started calling her the female MacGyver.

"Let's go, Mike," Fi said, tugging on his arm. "I got the bugger to the altar but there's no telling how long he'll stay there."

"He'll stay," Mike said, as he turned his attention back to his sister and her big day. "You're not the only one who's waited a long time for this day."

～

THE WEDDING COULD NOT BE MORE perfect, Sarah thought as she dabbed her eyes, *if it had been privately catered with a limo waiting for the happy couple afterward.* As it was, they cut a homemade wedding cake that, due to the lack of sugar, tasted more like corn bread than cake and said their vows in front of a seriously inebriated justice of the peace in lieu of a proper priest. Just a few more things hard to come by after the bomb changed everyone's world, Sarah thought grimly.

She turned to her thirteen-year-old son, who was whispering loudly to the bride's nephew, Gavin. John was growing tall, like his father had been. His eighteen months of living in a world with no electricity, no electronics and no transportation beyond what a horse could provide had transformed him from an indulged child into a young man mature beyond his years.

Which didn't mean he still didn't need to be shushed from time to time. "John," she whispered.

He turned to her, grinning apologetically and mouthed the words, *Sorry, Mom.*

Sarah turned back to the wedding to see Mike kiss Fiona at the altar in the little chapel that two weeks earlier had served as a granary shed, then go to stand by Declan.

She glanced at the calluses on her fingers. Before coming to Ireland a year and a half ago, she had worked in an advertising office in Jacksonville, Florida. Her major skillset involved the usual office equipment and word processing software.

A lot had changed since then. Nowadays she baked bread and dug in the dirt and milked goats and mended clothes that she wouldn't have bothered giving to the poor once. Back then she'd had a paralyzing fear of horses. Now, she rode nearly every day and couldn't imagine her life without the presence of the gentle, forgiving beasts.

Back home. It was a painful image that never got easier for Sarah. When the hydrogen bomb exploded over the Irish Sea eighteen months ago, it detonated an electromagnetic pulse that effectively flung Ireland and the United Kingdom back into the eighteen hundreds.

Sarah's dreams, her thoughts, her world would always focus on the hope that one day she and John would go back home to the United States.

Papin sat to Sarah's left. A young gypsy girl, a year older than John, Papin had known only abuse and prostitution before meeting Sarah in Wales last year.

"Do they kiss when they marry in America?" Papin asked in a loud whisper.

Sarah nodded and looked back at the ceremony. She felt responsible, in part, for Fiona's happiness, since it was Sarah who'd met Declan and his band of gypsies and urged him to come to Donovan's Lot. It would never have occurred to her then that the rambling, handsome gypsy who lived off the land —and by his wits—and the fisherman's daughter would fall in love. It had been a pleasure to watch it unfold over the last months.

Fiona, at thirty-five, had never married. Opinionated, fiery with a wild mane of curly brown hair, she looked like a gypsy queen, Sarah thought. *Who would have guessed she'd been waiting for her gypsy king to find her?*

As for Declan, his extended family had assumed after awhile that he would not wed and had given him the mantle of the family leader and patriarch—even though none of the many gypsy children that scampered around the camp were his. When it became clear that he and Fiona intended to be together, it was as if Donovan's Lot had engendered its own William and Catherine love story, so eagerly did the people in the community endorse the match.

Declan, in his suede boots and demi-jacket, turned to Fiona and drew her close to him. Sarah watched Fiona turn to her new husband, her eyes shining, mouth slightly open as if to gasp at the wonder of the moment.

When the couple kissed, Papin gave a loud sigh. "So romantic."

Several people in the seats in front of where Sarah and the two children sat turned to smile at Papin.

It *was* romantic. And for sweet, darling Fi to find someone after all this time...Sarah caught her breath at the pleasure and sheer happiness for her dear friend. Her eyes strayed again to Mike, standing solemnly as the couple kissed and the crowd began to clap and cheer.

Were all brothers like this when their sisters got married? Sarah frowned. She would definitely need a word with him as soon as she could get him alone.

THE WEDDING FEAST was well underway. Two long tables stood opposite the cook fire loaded with fruit pies, roast chicken, fried apples, corn fritters and pitchers of buttermilk.

Sarah watched Mike talking with a few of the other men—clearly discussing camp business of some kind from the serious nod of Mike's head as he listened. A natural leader, he had created this community of over a hundred people by bringing together neighbors and family right after The Crisis happened to form a place of security and fellowship.

Where before there had been only pasture and field, an assortment of huts, cottages and sturdy tents now ringed the main campfire. There were rules in the community, but the underlying belief held by all was that there was safety in numbers, and a good life could still be had, even without electricity or cars.

Sarah edged her way to the circle of men and slipped into the center. "Excuse me, gents," she said as she slipped an arm around Mike's waist. "The presence of the brother of the bride is requested on the dance floor. I'm sure camp business can wait one night."

She felt Mike's arm drape around her shoulders. A big man, he towered over her but she was grateful he didn't resort to stooping to accommodate her. She liked his size.

"Jimmy, Iain," Mike said, "we'll sort it out in the morning. Sarah's right. Tonight's for celebrating."

"Without even a glass of beer?" Iain said, shaking his head.

"Well, seeing how we don't have any, yes. Come on, old son, can ya not dance sober?"

"Not anything you want to see," Jimmy said, laughing at his own wit.

Sarah pulled Mike free of the group. His arm felt relaxed around her shoulders, beer or not. Maybe he'd worked himself out of whatever mood she thought she'd detected.

"You okay?" she asked, looking up at him.

"Sure, and why wouldn't I be? Me with my only sister wed to my best mate and the luscious Sarah Woodson all but pulling me into her arms for a dance?"

Sarah grinned when Mike's hand moved from her shoulders to her waist and then to her bottom. She removed it firmly. "None of that, Mike Donovan. Especially as we don't have alcohol to blame it on."

"I don't need to be drunk to want to feel your bum in me hands, Sarah." His eyes glittered meaningfully.

"Mike, behave yourself. This is Fiona's night."

"Nothing I have in mind will take anything away from my sister's night. And did you have to remind me?"

Sarah laughed. "I can't believe how old-fashioned you are! She's not a virgin, you know."

"Blimey! Did I need to hear that?"

"We may live like we're in the sixteen hundreds but we *did* all have twenty-first century lives until relatively recently."

"It might surprise ya to know, Sarah Woodson, that I'm not so keen to be discussing my sister's sex life."

"Alright, settle down. I just want to make sure you're okay. You looked a little grumpy up there during the ceremony."

"Well, that's just daft. I'm pleased as feckin' punch for the both of them."

"Remind me to make sure you don't make any toasts to the happy couple."

"And what would we even toast with?"

"God! Is it really the end of the world for an Irishman to have no alcohol?"

"I think you just answered your own question." Mike pulled up a bench a few yards away from the music and the dancing and pulled Sarah onto his lap.

"Mike!" she squealed, but laughed as he held her firmly on his knee.

"Now we'll just be watching the others dance and enjoy this special day," he said. "And marvel to the good Lord above that it's possible to do that without beer or whiskey. Sure, I'm not positive it *is* possible to do that, ya ken?"

Sarah slid off his lap and pulled him to a standing position. "Dance with me, Mike," she said. "There's no booze, no DJ, no canapés and no bouquet to catch. Dance with me."

He stood up and followed her to the dirt dance floor, the rest of the dancers parting to make room for them. Some even clapped to see their leader—easily the tallest of them—coming among them. He nodded at Declan who was slow-dancing with Fiona and then drew Sarah into his arms. The music was scratchy and repetitive, but it was lively and had a beat.

As she relaxed in his arms Sarah glanced around the camp, taking note of where Papin and John were. Not surprisingly, John was standing with Gavin at the food table. The women of the camp had outdone themselves creating multiple tables of cakes, pies, ham, and devilled eggs.

She could see Papin on the dance floor. Iain, the man who had been arguing with Mike earlier, was methodically two stepping his way through the song, his large hands gripping her small waist. Sarah frowned. At thirty, Iain was way too old to be dancing with Papin. Plus, he was married.

She saw her fourteen-year-old adopted daughter's eyes flash up at Iain as she spoke, the words drowned out by the music. Papin was flirting with Iain. It was practically the only way the girl knew how to relate to men. Half the time she did it to John and Mike, too, although they ignored it.

Iain didn't seem to be ignoring it.

"Mike," Sarah said in a low voice. She felt his body stiffen as she spoke. It hadn't taken long for the two of them to develop an efficient shorthand communication.

"What is it?" he said. By the way he moved in her arms, she could tell he was looking around to see what had upset her. It didn't take him long, either.

"Oy! Jamison!" he bellowed. "We'll not be needing your minding services any longer."

Papin reddened as Iain dropped his hands from her and backed away. "Da!" she said indignantly. "I'm not a baby!"

Mike had stepped up to the role of co-parenting Papin, a virtual orphan when she came to the camp last year, with Sarah. He had seen immediately that she needed a loving and firm male presence—and one who didn't want to bed her.

Mike gave Sarah's arm a squeeze of apology and went to Papin.

"I'll be having this dance, milady?" he said, bowing at the waist.

Sarah held her breath but she needn't have worried. Papin smiled at Mike and held up her hands for him to pick her up and swing her, which he did, to her delighted giggles.

SARAH SAW Fiona sitting on one of the long wooden benches that had been brought out to line the center campfire. She sat holding the hem of her gown away from the dirt on the ground, her eyes wide with exhaustion and joy. Sarah joined her on the bench.

She reached out and patted Fiona's knee. "Are you happy?"

Fiona turned her face to Sarah with real delight. "Oh, so happy, Sarah. I wish you this kind of happiness."

"I had it once, remember."

"Sure, that's right. With your David."

Fiona fanned herself. A light mist of perspiration coated her face, giving her the effect of glowing.

Sarah held her friend's hand. "Declan is a good man. I can't tell you how happy I am for you both."

"Ta, Sarah. As happy as I'd be if you and Mike were ever to stop playing around and get down to being together."

Sarah squeezed her hand and found herself looking for Mike in the crowd of laughing, dancing bodies milling around the center courtyard. She knew Fiona was right. Just seeing Mike, the way his body moved, the way he looked at her, was enough to make her want to grab his hand and take him right back to her cottage with a *Do Not Disturb* sign on the door. He would probably always have that effect on her.

She wasn't exactly sure why things hadn't moved along in that direction. It certainly wasn't for lack of broad hints and downright *trying* on Mike's part.

She finally spotted him, his hand on one hip, leaning down to listen, as an elderly couple seemed to be talking earnestly to him about something. Sarah loved seeing him like this, unaware of her—or anyone—and doing what he did best: looking after the families in Donovan's Lot. His face was kind, his eyes alert as he listened. He was a good leader, Sarah mused. A little given to the *my-way-or-the-highway* type thinking, but possibly that was normal for natural-born leaders.

"I know you're hot for him, Sarah Woodson. A blind person could see that. And you know he's burned for you since the day he laid eyes on you."

"Okay, Fi, let's focus on one romance at a time, shall we?"

Fiona shook her head, but she smiled and plucked at the lace cuff of her wedding dress, a dated cocktail dress that some of the women in camp had fitted to Fiona's slim body. "I just can't believe he's mine, you know?"

"Trust me, Declan's saying the same thing."

"Which is even more amazing to me."

"Well, it shouldn't be, Fi. You were just holding out for the right one."

"That's one way to put it," Fi said laughing. "Oh, here's my husband. I think he's got that 'it's time we're away, wench' look in his eye."

"I think you're right." Sarah stood up as Declan approached, his faced flushed, his gaze focused on the only woman he had eyes for.

"Excuse me, Sarah," he said, "I'll be taking me bride, now. Fi?" He held his arms out to Fiona and she slipped easily into them. The two kissed and Fi pulled him away toward their cottage. "See you in the morning, Sarah," she said over her shoulder.

"Aye, but not too early, mind," Declan called out as the two disappeared into the evening.

Smiling, Sarah pulled her cardigan around her shoulders and turned back to the party, which appeared to be winding down. She could see mothers pulling their children back to huts and tents. While there was no sugar to wire the little ones, the music and general excitement had served to make most of them cranky and tearful.

"The lovebirds call it a night?"

Sarah turned to see Mike approaching with two steaming mugs in his hands. He handed one to her.

"Oh, that's perfect," she said, taking the cup. She sipped slowly and then coughed, her face reddening. She put a hand to her mouth. "Is there whiskey in this?" she whispered around another small cough. "You could've warned me, first."

"I find the sneak attack is often more effective for my purposes. It's some of the last of what we got from that trip to Limerick in the spring. There's only just a dram so don't go broadcasting it."

"Perks of the rank?" Sarah asked, reseating herself on the bench.

"Something like that. Fi and Dec pack it in?"

"Please don't put it like that," Sarah said with a grin.

"Oh, very funny. You just don't quit, do you?"

"Well, not when you make it so easy to tease you."

They sat, shoulder to shoulder, sipping their whisky and hot tea and watching the last of the partiers pick up children, food, and musical instruments. A few of the gypsies—Declan's extended family—seemed to be bedding down around the center campfire, which would burn all night long.

"Papin and John in bed, do you know?"

Mike shook his head. "They're in your cottage but too excited to sleep, I'll wager."

"It was a perfect night," Sarah said, finishing off her drink.

Mike took both cups and set them aside. "The night's not over yet," he said in a low voice.

When she saw his eyes regarding her, so full of tenderness and care, it was all she could do not to climb onto his lap right there. He was so much a part of her world, her support system in this life. So strong, so confident.

So damn sexy.

Her face must have expressed more than she intended because he leaned in and kissed her mouth. A slow kiss she couldn't push away from.

She placed her hands on his broad shoulders and fell into the kiss, feeling him pull her close into his chest. A small moan escaped her lips as he looked into her dark eyes.

"*Yes*, Sarah?" he whispered.

"God, yes," she responded without hesitating.

"I'd pick you up and carry you there," he growled, his voice full of urgent need, "but I don't want to alert the camp to my intentions."

"*Our* intentions," Sarah said, kissing him firmly. "I can walk. At least for now."

"God, woman, every word out of your mouth is making me hard as a brick." He tilted her head back to see her face lit by the firelight, her neck long and bare. He kissed her again.

"Oy, Mike! You still up, son? Is that you over yonder I see snoggin' the Widow Woodson? Mike?"

Sarah stood up quickly, straightening her blouse and pulling her cardigan around her in time to see Jimmy Baskerville waving at Mike from across the campfire.

"Bloody hell," Mike cursed, shaking his head. "Are ya kidding me?"

Sarah would have laughed if she weren't so annoyed by the interruption herself—and if she hadn't noticed that Jimmy was approaching with a stranger in tow.

"Oy, Mike," Jimmy said, walking to stand in front of Mike, still seated. "We got us a visitor and you said we're always to bring 'em before yerself, like, whenever that happens."

The stranger stood behind Jimmy, almost as if hiding, Sarah thought. He looked bedraggled and hungry. He'd clearly been traveling and living off the land for many weeks, if not longer. Camp policy was to welcome all travelers with food and a bed for the night.

"I don't mean to disrupt the festivities," the man said, peeking out from behind Jimmy. "But a bit of grub would be welcome."

Sarah saw Mike work to pull himself together and shake off his disappointment. He nodded to Jimmy. "Go see if Molly is still up and have her put together a sandwich." Jimmy saluted him and turned on his heel.

The traveler stood alone now, his eyes darting from Sarah to Mike like a canary between two cats.

"Won't you sit down?" she said, although the grunt she heard from Mike indicated he had hoped the man wouldn't be staying long.

"Thank you, missus," he said, not moving. He had a tattered backpack on his shoulder, and even in the dark Sarah could see it held very little. She returned to her seat on the bench.

"Please, sit," Sarah said again. "We usually ask visitors if they have any news to share." She was hoping to make him feel less like a beggar by suggesting he had something to offer to the camp. The effect of her words on him was immediate.

"Can I ask you, missus," he said, "if the way you speak is because you're American? I've got nothing against Yanks, mind," he said hurriedly. Not everyone in Ireland shared his tolerant attitude, Sarah knew.

"Yes, that's right," she said. "I'm from Florida. I was on vacation in Ireland when The Crisis happened."

The man seemed to relax a little. He knelt in the dirt and shrugged off his pack and then slowly sat down, crossing his knees Indian-style on the ground. "Well, it's mebbe that I do have news for you, in that case."

Mike, who had been watching the newcomer closely, turned his head to look at Sarah. Had she gasped? News about America —other than groundless rumor—was rare these days.

"Yes?" she said. "You've news about the US?"

"It happens, I do, missus. I'm coming from Rathcoole. Been on the road, I guess, three weeks since but I reckon the news is still fresh."

Jimmy appeared with a ham sandwich. He had a few deviled eggs wrapped in paper, too. "Sorry about no juice," he said. "But we've been dry for months now." He handed the newcomer a flask of water.

The traveler shook his head and took a large bite. He looked at this audience apologetically as he chewed. "Forgive me. Fresh bread...I've died and gone to heaven."

He's starving, Sarah thought. It was sometimes easy to forget that outside the walls of Donovan's Lot there were many who struggled daily just to survive.

"I'm Mike Donovan. You're welcome to stay the night. Jimmy'll find a place for you to throw down a bedroll."

"Ta very much. The name's Randy Paxton."

"English?" Sarah asked.

"No, missus. I'm from up north."

"You've come a long way."

"This news," Mike said, eyeing the man suspiciously. "Where did you come by it?"

"News? He's got news?" Jimmy looked at Mike. "Should I rouse the camp?"

Mike waved him back down into his seat. "Unless the news is that the bloody British are invading, we'll have time enough tomorrow."

Paxton finished off his sandwich and drained the water flask. "Thank you kindly for the food," he said. "I came by my news in Dublin."

"How is Dublin?" Mike asked.

"It's...I don't rightly know how to say it. I was there just shy of three months. It was the three longest months of my life."

"Crime?"

"Aye, and sickness."

Sarah felt her pulse quicken. "Disease?"

Paxton nodded grimly. "Garbage in the streets. And worse."

Mike grunted. "It's not surprising. The wonder is people hadn't started getting sick before now."

"You said you had news of the Americans," Sarah said, tapping her nails against the seat of the bench.

"Aye, missus. In Dublin it was just a rumor, but when I came through Limerick I saw it for myself."

"Saw what? What did you see, man?" Mike asked.

"The Air Lift, they call it. The Yanks have their military in

Limerick and they're coming and going back and forth to the US like nothing ever happened. I saw the transport helicopters and also the big planes. Looked like whole families were leaving."

Sarah gasped and stood up, knocking the two teacups she'd shared with Mike to the ground. She was vaguely aware of his hand on her arm.

Limerick was only a day's ride away.

She turned to look out beyond the boundaries of the camp, her eyes glittering with awe and wonder. "We can go home," she said, her voice a whisper. "Thank you, God, it's finally happened. We can go home."

2
_____

The road home started the next morning with a rock wedged tight against a horse's frog, a steady drizzle, and a morning so quiet not even the birds seemed up for it.

In spite of the bad weather and the bruised hoof, the nine-hour ride to Limerick was uneventful. Mike rode without speaking, and Sarah decided that was probably a good idea—at least until they knew all the facts. If she and the children really were going to be able to go back to the States there would be plenty of time to deal with the emotional fall-out later.

And if they weren't, well, she assumed the ride back to camp would be a little merrier for at least one of them.

Nine hours later they entered the first gateway leading to the center of town. One thing was certain, Sarah thought, as they rode through the city center, now that the Americans had come to town, Limerick was a vibrant, noisy metropolis of controlled chaos. As they passed groups of US servicemen, Sarah couldn't help but think this must have been how it was during World War II when England was damaged, rationed and shell-shocked and the American GIs showed up with their chocolate bars and nylons. The 1940's lament *"over paid, over sexed, and over here"* was accurate *then,* and it looked to be pretty accurate now.

The streets were full of working military jeeps shuttling well-fed American servicemen from one point to the other. Up and down the main drag, food kiosks and makeshift pubs were doing a bustling business, whereas not six months before they had heard news that the whole place had been little more than a ghost town. Sarah's first thought when she saw all the trading activity was that they would be able to get some supplies they needed for Donovan's Lot. Then she remembered they had nothing of value to bargain with. She tried to see what was being used for currency and thought she saw people handling greenbacks.

The excitement in the streets was palpable. The feeling that things were definitely getting back to normal imbued every happy face she saw as they rode down the paved street to the cul-de-sac where the American consulate was located.

Mike took the horses and went to buy sandwiches. He would wait for her in the little courtyard out front of the embassy. Before The Crisis, it had featured a koi pond and a cultivated French garden, with careful, manicured lines of lawn and flower beds. Since then, it had clearly been used as a parking lot for horses and wagons.

The moment Sarah stepped inside the consulate, the sight of the American flag that hung over the main foyer brought tears to her eyes. A young man in a US Air Force uniform sat at the reception desk. He looked up with a smile.

"Afternoon, ma'am," he said. "Can I help you?"

"I'm an American," Sarah said, feeling her throat close up as she said the words.

The young man's face broke into an easy grin. "Well, ma'am," he said with a Texas drawl. "Then I guess you're home now."

The consulate was able to find suitable, if separate, lodging for both Mike and Sarah, as well as boarding for their horses. In the meantime, she met with an adjutant who scheduled the necessary travel arrangements for her return to the States. Later, she shared a largely silent meal at the pub with Mike and fell into her borrowed bed exhausted and too excited to sleep.

The next morning, after an American breakfast of fresh orange juice, steak, eggs, and grits, which Sarah noticed Mike pushed around with his fork instead of eating, they tacked up their horses and left for the return ride back to Donovan's Lot.

A very quiet ride back to Donovan's Lot.

In Sarah's saddlebag were three travel vouchers to the United States.

In the nine hours it took to ride back, Sarah hadn't been able to think of three things in a row she could imagine Mike would want to hear. The thoughts that buzzed relentlessly through her mind were a jumble of giddy excitement the upcoming reunion with her parents, and the growing knowledge of impending loss.

When they finally arrived in camp, worn out more by the tension of all that was unspoken than the actual ride itself, Mike, his face unreadable, took both horses and disappeared in the direction of the stable.

Sarah walked across the length of the camp to its center and her cottage. Papin and John would be sleeping at Fiona and Declan's.

She hesitated on the porch of her cottage and watched the moon dip behind the lacy shreds of remnant clouds. There were a few gypsies sleeping by the fire.

Her glance strayed toward the direction Mike had gone. To be physically so close to him all day long and yet feel so far away from him was not something she was used to. Mike had a bigger-than-life quality that seemed to push down barriers and grab a person by the lapels. She smiled sadly remembering the first time she'd ever laid eyes on him. She had pointed a loaded Glock at him while he stood, regarding her with bemused interest, unarmed and blocking her only escape route.

The truth was the man had always crossed her picket lines—whether she'd been married or not—right from the start.

And nothing had ever felt more right to her.

She sighed and sat down on the porch steps. Whatever joy she felt yesterday when it was confirmed that the Americans were indeed gathering up their stranded nationals for the trip home had long given away to stark practicalities. Witnessing the crushing disappointment of the man who in the last year had become the single biggest part of her life felt like a knife in her heart. It took every ounce of courage she had to remember that as much as it hurt her to see Mike so miserable, it was necessary to endure if she were to stay resolute. And for John's sake, she knew she *must*.

John. She flinched at the thought of her last conversation with him. *Turns out Mike isn't the only one who can't celebrate the good news.* Before she left for Limerick, John had told her flat-out he wouldn't leave.

Sarah rubbed the night's chill from her bare arms. There was no sense in waiting for Mike to finish with the horses. Anything she could have said to him, she'd had nine hours to say. She stood up and surveyed the camp briefly before turning toward her front door, the exhaustion of the day finally settling on her shoulders like a fifty-pound sack of feed.

No, there was nothing for the fact that this wonderful news would bring no joy to the people who mattered most to her. But that didn't stand in the way of the fact she knew it was the right thing to do.

The next morning, Sarah awoke to a pounding on her cottage door. She wore a long tee shirt of David's that she slept in and opened the door to reveal Fiona, fully dressed, her hands on her hips and clearly ready for battle.

"Goodness, you're up early. I don't even have the stove lit," Sarah said, stepping out of the way to let Fiona storm past her. "I don't suppose you brought a thermos of Starbucks?"

"So, it's official, is it?" Fiona strode to the center of Sarah's cottage and whirled around on her. "You'll have your on-demand television and upscale chain grocery stores, and sure, nobody could blame you. Why not? Nice to know this is all we mean to you. A hardship made a little less hard, that's all."

"So I guess that's a no on the coffee," Sarah said as she shut the door. "I haven't gotten the tea started yet." She moved into the kitchen and began sticking wood and kindling into the cook stove.

"I cannot believe you're doing this, Sarah. I cannot believe this is all we mean to you. A stop-over until you could get where you really want to be."

Sarah straightened up and faced her. "And you wouldn't do the same, Fiona? If you could go home again? See your folks again?"

"You can see them and then come back. If you stay there it's because you value convenience and drive-thru banking over your friends. *Over Mike.*"

"That's not true."

"If you don't come back, then it *is* true."

"Look, Fi, if it were just me, I would—"

"Oh, please. Spare me."

"I can't leave John there. Would you ask me to do that?"

"He loves it here! Mike is as close to a father as the lad'll ever have after David. Why don't you ask *John* if he wants to go?"

Fiona obviously knew John was vehemently opposed to going back to the States.

Sarah turned to light the stove. "Sometimes, the best things for our children *aren't* the things they'll thank us for in the moment."

"Got an answer for everything, don't you, Sarah? Why do I bother? Clearly, you want to go. And here's me thinking we were sisters and all."

Sarah whirled around to face her. "We *are* sisters! If you were a mother you'd understand why I can't leave my only child in the US! You wouldn't even suggest it."

"Then *don't* leave him. Bring him back with you."

"I can't. If he has a chance to go to college and live a normal life, which he does back home, then he deserves to have that chance. His father was Phi Beta Kappa, for crap's sake. Am I going to allow David's son to pick pole beans for the rest of his life instead of going to college?"

"Is that what you think we're doing here? Growing pole beans and scratching our bums?"

"Well, you're not doing a whole hell of a lot of reading and writing as far as I can see. And I get it. This life is hard and it's about surviving. How can you fault me for wanting something better for my son? This kind of life can't compare to the opportunities he'll have in the States. Opportunities that are his birthright."

"Well, then I guess we have nothing more to discuss."

"You can't understand why I'm doing this? *Really*?"

"We're done, Sarah. Go to America. We don't need your help for the harvest. In fact, it's bloody cheek, throwing your scraps at us, saying you'll stay to help. Typical bloody Yank, if you ask me."

Sarah could see tears threatening in Fiona's eyes, which felt worse than anything she'd said so far. She took a step toward her but Fiona bolted for the door, slamming it on her way out. Sarah watched her friend stomp across the camp, grabbing up a basket of wet laundry as she went. In their last year together in the camp, the two had nearly decided to move in together until Declan began to stake his claim and it became clear that Fiona would only be a temporary roommate.

As Sarah watched her now, her heart squeezed to think she might never see Fiona again after next month. Sarah couldn't imagine a friendship back home as close. She turned back to her kitchen. Of course, she hadn't depended on pals back home to quite the extent she'd had to with Fiona in the months following The Crisis.

It was a different world. When it came to forging relationships, she had to admit, maybe a better one.

She returned to the kitchen and pulled out a bowl of dough she'd allowed to rise all night. She grabbed the dough and began to knead and shape it until it was satiny smooth before plopping it back in the wooden bowl she always used. It was Dierdre's bowl, the dear old woman who had taught Sarah so much in the weeks right after all the lights went out.

She touched the rim of it, worn smooth after decades of shaping dough. Sarah wouldn't bring many things back home with her, but she'd like to have the bowl. On the other hand, items of function here were valuable, this bowl no less so. She would leave it in camp.

Voices coming quickly closer made her glance out the kitchen window. Papin and John were coming in. She frowned. John should be with Gavin, minding the goats in the north pasture— or mending harnesses or whatever chores Mike had them doing. At midday, it wasn't usual for him to be home.

"Mum!" Papin called as the two entered the cottage. "Da gave John the day off to help you pack." The girl frowned and looked around the cottage. "Cor, we're not bringing any of this shite with us, are we?"

"Watch your language, Papin," Sarah said, wiping her hands on her apron. "Well, that was nice of him, although not necessary. I told him we wouldn't go until after the harvest. That's four weeks yet."

John sat at the table and threw a ball against the wall. It hit with a loud whack and rolled back to him. It looked to be a cricket ball.

"Stop that, John. As long as you're here, you can fill up the wood box. I'm baking all day tomorrow and I'll need at least twice as much as I have in there."

John didn't move or look at her.

"And Papin? Aren't you to be helping Auntie Fi with the wash? I'm sure I heard her say you were."

"She told me not to bother," Papin said cheerfully. "Is there anything to eat? Only me and John haven't had our tea yet, have we, John?"

Sarah sighed. She supposed she couldn't force Fiona to have Papin help her, but the child managed better—even at the best of times—if she was kept busy. Sarah pulled out a piece of bread and spread it with the soft churned butter she kept on the table.

"I have some things you can do for me, in that case," she said, cutting the slice in half and handing one to each of them.

John shook his head. "Not hungry."

It took everything Sarah had not to scold him for his sullenness. But they'd already had all the words that could be said between them on the subject. Nothing she could say was going to make it any easier for him. He had it in his head that his home was here and his friends were here and his family was here, and that's all there was to it.

At thirteen, he wasn't really a child anymore. Except, of course, he was.

"Well then, go ahead and fetch the wood, John," she said, turning back to the stove. "Dinner will be same as usual."

"Except we won't be having it with Aunt Fi and Uncle Dec, I guess."

Sarah's shoulders sagged but she turned back to him. "It's true your Aunt Fi and I are working something out. But mostly it's because she's a newlywed and needs some *alone* time with her new husband. Okay?"

John frowned as if he hadn't thought of that. "Really?"

Papin elbowed John in the ribs. "And you know what she means when she says *alone time*, don't you, boyo?"

"That's enough, Papin. Off you go, now, John."

He pulled himself to his feet and trudged out the door, banging it shut behind him.

"All right, Papin, the dishes won't do themselves. The rag is by the tub."

"It's impossible to clean them without soap," Papin whined.

"It just takes longer. Like everything else in this life."

"But not back in America." Papin grabbed the rag and began polishing a ceramic dish with it. "Tell me more about what our lives will be like back there."

"Well, we'll have automatic dishwashers, of course. But I don't want you to think there won't be chores."

"Work for the sake of work? To build character?"

"Something like that. And school, of course."

"I'm too old for that."

"Well, you're not."

"Sarah, I'll be the class eejit! I'll be in the same grade with the five-year-olds or the half-wits."

"You'll be in a class with people your age and ability. Don't worry, it's going to be fine."

"And you'll teach me to drive, right? Will we have a car straightaway? And all of us with smartphones? I had a mobile phone before The Crisis, you know."

Sarah saw Papin stare moodily out the window, as if remembering her phone.

"It's hard to imagine how different our lives will be," Papin said softly, as if to herself.

Sarah turned back to the chicken she was plucking—a job she loathed and one that always reminded her of three terrible days she spent living in a chicken-processing factory in the Cotswolds—when it occurred to her that *different* might not necessarily be better.

A part of her hated the fact that she'd said they'd stay until after the harvest was in. As upsetting as their leaving was for everyone, it would be so much easier just to rip the bandage off and *go*. But the harvest was a lot of work and three extra hands picking and sorting would make a big difference to the community.

As Papin started to hum, a flash of red outside the window caught Sarah's eye. It was Mike, wearing a red tee shirt, leading his gelding through the camp and talking with Gavin, who was trotting to keep up with Mike's long stride. Seeing him unexpectedly like this gave her a funny fluttering feeling in the pit of her stomach, as it always did.

Watching him, she found herself facing down the barrel of a nascent thought she had kept at bay all these months of living so close to him, the same thought that had been slowly forming through the long, tense ride home yesterday.

I'm in love with him.

As she watched him, knowing for sure how she felt—how she had always felt—and knowing it just when she was about to leave for good was about the sickest, most excruciating feeling she'd had in a long, long time.

And she had felt some pretty sick things in the last eighteen months.

"So WILL we still have *Lughnasa* this year?" Gavin swung down from his horse. He, Mike and Declan gazed at the long line of irregular fence posts jammed into the ground before them.

Declan frowned. "Do ya usually have a harvest fair?" he asked Mike.

Mike shook his head. "What's usual? We've never had a proper *harvest* 'til now."

"Right."

"I meant what with Mrs. Woodson and John and Papin leaving straight after the harvesting," Gavin said.

Declan patted his pony's neck. "Sure, it'll put a damper on things."

"We'll have the festival," Mike said firmly to Gavin, "to celebrate the year's harvest no matter what. Meanwhile, we need to get busy on these defensive boundaries."

"Busy how, Da?" Gavin said. "It's impossible to string wire between all the posts. We don't have it to hang for one thing."

Declan scratched his head. "I didn't want to say anything, but wouldn't it make more sense to use what fencing we do have to strengthen the pastures? Surely, keeping our livestock corralled has to come first..."

"First behind our security." Mike said. "Nothing comes before that."

"But, Da, we can't put a fence around the camp. It's just not...not..."

"Feasible," Declan finished.

"Feasible or not, it's what we'll do. I'd suggest the two of you get working instead of working your gobs."

"But, Da—"

"This is not a democracy, Gavin," Mike said severely. "I have given considerable thought to the situation and I've decided that strengthening our perimeter is the best use of our resources for the now."

"Why not have us dig a moat while we're at it?" Gavin said under his breath as he turned away.

"What's that?"

"Nothing."

"Too right."

As Gavin mounted his horse and rode to the first fence post in the line, Declan turned to his friend. "Fi's right out of her mind over Sarah and young John leaving."

"I know."

"Have you talked to her?"

"Who? Sarah? And what would I be saying? *'Don't go back to your own country where life is still normal but stay here and plant turnips with your new friends?'* Besides, she's made up her mind."

"Fi's practically mental she's so pissed off."

"She'll get over it."

"How are *you* doing?"

Mike shrugged. "It is what it is."

"You're wrong about messing around with the perimeter fencing. It won't keep anyone out who wants in bad enough."

Mike clapped a heavy hand on Declan's shoulder. "Dec, me boyo, I'll tell you what I told me lazy gobshite of a son."

"Yeah, yeah, I know, we're not a democracy."

Mike watched as Declan pulled out a roll of fencing wire from his saddlebag and began unspooling it. It was late July but still not hot, even at midday. By Mike's calculations, they should start harvesting within the week. There was a good crop this second year and they would have much to celebrate.

He went to his horse and rummaged around in his saddlebag for pliers. They didn't work nearly as well as wire cutters would but, like everything else in this new world, he would make do with what he had.

The summer day had a fresh scent to it that filled his lungs with the pleasure of being alive and a part of it all. He caught a glimpse of a butterfly moth inspecting one of the gorse bushes by the closest fencepost.

As he watched it flit through the leaves, he found himself thinking that to his dying day he would remember the look on Sarah's face when she realized she could leave Ireland and go back to the US. There was no conflict, no doubt, no ambivalence at all. Just sheer undiluted joy at the thought of leaving Ireland.

Of leaving me.

Didn't he always know this time might come? *Would* come? Ever since that first US military helicopter showed up last year, wasn't it always just a matter of time before another one came?

Honestly, as he'd told Fiona earlier that morning, he *had*

hoped that his relationship with Sarah would have progressed to the point that she wouldn't *want* to go home. He shook the thoughts away. *What possible good is to think like that now?* He and Sarah had been close this last year, but not in the way he'd hoped. And now there was no more time.

Now she was leaving.

Out of the corner of his eye, he noticed Declan had stood up from his fencepost and was looking down to where Gavin worked. Mike twisted around to see what he was looking at.

"Who do you suppose that is?" Declan said.

Gavin stood a hundred yards in the distance, his hands on his hips, his long hair moving in the summer breeze. He was talking to a tall man with a pack on his back.

Mike swung up into his saddle and put his heels into his horse's side. "Stay here," he said to Declan with more force than necessary as he cantered the distance to his son and the stranger.

3

That night, Brian Gilhooley sat in the seat of honor at the campfire. It was a warm summer's night, with the scent of the evening meal still wafting high above the camp. Having drained him of any news he had, many of the families—with children needing to be in bed—had said their goodnights and left the fireside, leaving Sarah, Mike, Fiona and Declan with a few others to entertain their guest.

Even as an outsider, Brian could tell there were painful dynamics in play around the campfire. He smiled at the American woman, Sarah, as she handed him another mug of tea. She had lost her husband the year before but he could see she was strong. She had sent her own two children off to bed twenty minutes earlier and had spoken more to him than anyone else in the camp, which he found to be very odd.

"Sure, we don't find too many who deliberately walk this way," Declan said to him. His teeth showed bone white in the night, reminding Brian of the man's gypsy heritage. Gypsies—if there wasn't too much inbreeding—were a wily, canny lot. Excellent allies and, having no real code of honor to prevent them from fighting dirty, formidable enemies,

"Well, as I said, I'm looking for a better life for my family."

"And they're safe enough while you're off looking for this better life?"

Brian turned to Mike. The camp leader clearly didn't trust newcomers of any kind. Likely, they'd had some experiences in the past to warrant that kind of suspicion. These days you were crazy not to be suspicious of strangers.

"My father and brothers are looking out for my wife in Dublin. My father-in-law has some health issues so it really fell to me to go out and find a better way of life for us all."

"Is your wife a delicate sort, Mr. Gilhooley?" Fiona asked, looping her arm around her new husband's in a comfortable, proprietary way that showcased her newlywed status.

"I suppose you could say that. Although even eighteen months into this new world of ours, there are many who haven't survived at all. My Katie may not look hardy, but I know she has a strength deep down that will prevail."

"Prevailing out here in the hinterlands is a far cry from prevailing in the city," Mike said. "It's a hard life with hard work that needs doing every day."

"Even so, staying in the city isn't an option."

"We heard there was disease in Dublin."

Brian nodded. "And getting worse all the time. At first, I thought the laws would be reinstated. That some kind of government would resurface."

"But it hasn't?"

"No. And the longer the city goes without leadership, the worse the problems will be to overcome. Already there are gangs who rule neighborhoods through coercion and murder."

"So have you come south to find a new town or to start a new town?" Mike asked.

Brian met his gaze directly. "Whichever happens first, I reckon." He looked around at the shadowed outlines of the huts and cottages lining the perimeter of the camp. "I would be grateful if you would allow me to stay among you so that I could see how things are here. If you were amenable to accepting a new family into your midst, I'd be interested in knowing what that process is. And if you're not..." He shrugged. "It would be valuable for me to see what works in the creation of your community." He looked at Mike. "And what doesn't."

"For building your own community."

"Exactly."

"Well," Sarah said, "I'd have to say one of the things that works at Donovan's Lot is how everyone helps everyone else. It's not a matter of ten families and a few couples living separate lives here. There's a strong sense of community."

Brian couldn't help but notice how pointedly Sarah delivered her statement, not to him, but to the gypsy's bride, Fiona. Obviously, the two women were feuding about something.

"Aye," Mike Donovan said. "But for all that, what works best for us is a central autocratic leadership." His eyes glittered meaningfully at Brian.

"By autocratic," Brian said frowning, "you mean no community voting over central issues."

"Aye, that's right."

"Well, sometimes it's a matter of a decision needing to be made and I understand that," Brian said. "If nobody will step forward, you need a strong leader to make things happen. Is that what you have? A community that can't think for itself?"

"Nobody said that," Mike growled.

"It's what *you* said," Brian said.

"It kind of is, Mike," Declan said quietly. "Like we're your kids or something or maybe just too feckin' stupid to know what's best for us."

"Is that what you think?" Mike said to him, his eyes widening, his mouth pressed together in a firm line.

"It is," Declan said. He gave Fiona a squeeze. "It's what we both think. Hell, it's what half the camp thinks."

"Well, if you want to know what I think," Mike said standing up abruptly, his temper building inside him until he could no longer sit still, "I think I'm bloody exhausted from having to do everything and think of everything and I'm going to bloody bed. I'll see you all in the morning."

"Aw, come on, Mike, don't be that way," Declan said, but he didn't stand up.

Mike knew he sounded petulant and he hated that, especially in front of the stranger—and Sarah—but the truth was he *was* tired. The day had been long and nonproductive with surprises he could've done without.

Maybe the bastards needed to run things without me for a while. Maybe then they'd seen how well their bloody voting on central issues shite worked.

4

M ike pulled back the husks. The kernels were plump and firm, a sure sign that the corn was ready to harvest. He blinked into the morning sun. They could start on the corn this week and leave the cabbage and the potatoes for next week, then finish up the kale and the wheat the following week. He shrugged and tucked the corncob in the pocket of his vest.

His second real harvest at Donovan's Lot. The first one hadn't been miserable, but had fallen short of actually supplying the camp with enough food for the winter. If it hadn't been for reserve supplies in abandoned root cellars, it would have been worse than it was.

Except for a simple garden plot Ellen had tended when they were first married, he had no real experience with growing food before last summer. Moving away from the coast—and fishing—was the one and only concession he'd made when he created Donovan's Lot. Everyone else knew next to nothing about farming or fishing. At the time it seemed the learning curve on an inland homesteading experience was the least daunting.

"Well, Da? Are they ready?" Gavin nodded at the rows and rows of tall green corn.

"They are. Tell the others. We'll pick this field this week and start on the south field when we're done."

"Starting today?"

"Yes. Tell the others to stop what they're doing."

Gavin was trotting away toward the camp before Mike even finished his statement.

Why do all the young run everywhere? They're always in such a hurry.

Turning back toward camp, Mike saw Sarah coming toward him. He should have expected this. It had only been a few days since she'd announced she was leaving—a few days when a lot else had happened in the interim, not to mention that bogger, Gilhooley, taking up residence practically in the middle of the camp. But he hadn't had much time to talk to Sarah—or rather he had but preferred not to—and he should have expected she wouldn't put up with that for long.

So American, he thought, as he watched her stride purposely toward him. He could almost hear her voice in his head: *What are you thinking, Mike? Are you feeling okay, Mike? Is it something you'd like to talk about, Mike?*

Bloody woman. Yet the sight of her growing ever nearer filled his heart with an aching sense of peace, too. Like a feeling of a magnet drawing its metal shavings to itself. The innately right feeling of two things that belong together being brought back together.

Such fecking rubbish.

"Mike? Do you have a minute?"

It was daft to think he could avoid her until the moment she climbed on that military transport copter. He arranged his face into a smile.

"Sarah." Her face was flushed with color, her breath coming in pants from the exertion of the hike. Except for her daily ride on old Dan, she didn't usually venture too far from the comfort of her cottage and the camp.

Especially not after her last outing, which left her husband dead and her forever changed.

"We need to talk about my leaving."

"What would you have me say?"

"Fiona won't even talk to me and you've been avoiding me."

Well, it was true. He sighed and ran a hand through his hair. "I guess it's just hard to say goodbye."

"Don't you think this is hard for me, too? It's the hardest thing I've ever had to do. Do you think I *want* to leave?"

"You know, Sarah, I don't think I can stand here and listen to outright bullshite. Because if you're going to bang on that same drum that says you're just doing this for John's sake—"

"I *am* just doing this for John's sake!"

"Well, that's just a little difficult for those of us left behind to fully believe, ya see."

"*You* wouldn't leave if you could?" She stood in front of him now, her hands on her hips. Her jeans were snug and fit her in all the right places. Mike looked away from her. Thinking like that wasn't going to get him anywhere.

"Seeing as how this is my home and all I've ever known, I'd have to say, no."

"But it's not *my* home."

"That has been made abundantly clear to me."

"Oh, stop! Really? I'm really going to be the bad guy in all this? All because I want to go home to my own country?"

"What did you need to say to me? Because I think I've heard all this before. You're going. And you don't want anyone to be unhappy about that fact. I guess we should all just work to love you less."

That stopped her. He watched her face crumble into the threat of tears.

"Now, now, Sarah..." He put his hand out to her and she came easily into his arms. It hadn't been his intention to touch her. Nothing good could come of that, but touching her he was. He brought his other arm around and held her close.

Was it only guilt and the thought of missing him that brought her to him like this? He couldn't help enjoying the feel of her in his arms. A piece inside of him relented and he felt his shoulders let go of the tension he'd held ever since she said she would go.

Hadn't he always known she would go?

"I'm so sorry, Mike," she said, her voice muffled against his chest. "It's killing me. You have to know that."

"Aye," he said softly. "I know it."

He tilted her chin to look into her eyes and saw her fighting a battle with herself. Likely it was the urge to tell him, again, that it was all for John. That if it were just up to her, she'd stay... although she'd never even hinted that *that* was the case. Wisely, she held her tongue.

"Walk with me back to camp," he said. "We're ready to start the harvest on the corn and the extra hands of you and the kids will be a big help." He knew she needed to hear it, regardless of how essentially untrue it was.

Back at camp, they parted, but not before she'd made him promise to come to dinner after the day's work in the field. The families of the camp, alerted by Gavin, were milling about the center of camp, waiting for Mike to give them instructions on the corn harvest.

"Right," Mike said stepping up to the elevation of the decking in front of his hut. "It's time and the good Lord has blessed us with enough rain—but not too much—so it looks like we have a decent corn crop this summer after all. I'll be asking the Sullivan family and the Dohertys to start at the southeast corner of the field, and the Mulligans and the Kilpatricks to pick at the northwest corner and work toward the middle. Everyone else will follow me. Now, remember there'll be pickers, pruners, and them to cart the harvest back to camp."

He turned to Fiona, who was standing on her front porch, her hands on her hips, listening. "Fiona will coordinate the processing and storing of the corn once it's transported back to camp."

Fiona nodded, a faint smile on her lips.

"Sarah, Jenny, Maggie and Lyndie will all help Fiona. Every child over twelve is in the field picking. Under twelve will be minded by Papin and Daisy." He turned to the two girls. "Mind everyone gets their kiddies back in one piece at the end of the day, eh?" They grinned and nodded.

"That's it. We'll do the corn this week and the potatoes and cabbage next and finish up with the kale, the wheat and the beets the final week."

"What about the *Lughnasa*?" someone called out.

"We'll have the feast the Sunday after the last cabbage or beet is picked, packed and stored for the winter. Any other questions?"

Brian Gilhooley raised a hand. "Where would you like me?"

Mike forced himself not to wince. *Would Dublin be too far?*

"If you could work alongside the Kilpatricks," he said, nodding to the family of eight already moving into the fields, "that would be a big help, so it would," he said.

His eyes followed Sarah, who was walking over to Fiona on her porch.

SHE COULD SEE Fi was a little calmer since the last time they talked. It had been two days. Two long days where Sarah missed her best friend dearly. Two days of no gossip, no laughter, no advice on the children, the weather, her brother or life in general.

Sarah wondered what in the world Fiona could find to miss about *her* company. She looked up at her. "Well?" she said. "I'm here for my orders."

"Oy! That's what I say every morning," Declan said, materializing from behind his wife and putting both hands on her waist. He leaned in to kiss her on the neck and Sarah blessed him when she saw Fiona smile.

It wasn't in her direction, but it was a start.

"Now, get away with ya," Fiona said, as she turned and returned Declan's kiss.

Sarah waited until Declan had jumped down from the porch, flinging one last air kiss at his bride and giving Sarah a wink as he bounded away.

Fiona turned from Sarah and clapped her hands at the gathering of camp women who were approaching her deck. "All right, ladies," she said. "Let's get set up, shall we now? They'll come in the back entrance to the camp and we'll need every empty box, jar, jug or basket you have in your homes, so if you could collect those we'll be ready for when they come."

The women turned as one to head back to their cottages and tents but Sarah didn't move. Fiona watched the women leave and then, without a glance at Sarah, turned to go into her cottage, saying over her shoulder, "Come on then. I'll put the tea on."

THE WORK WAS hard but the sense of fellowship was something Sarah had never experienced before. Because she and David had lived outside the community during the last harvest, she missed this feeling of family, of working together for the good of the whole.

When the first cartful of corn ears arrived, Fiona had the women create a triage. Two women lifted the crates of just-picked ears from the cart and passed them down the line of woman leading to two long picnic tables.

On either side of the tables, the camp women stood ready to strip the corn and wrap or package depending on its final, intended use. Corn stunted or too badly damaged by insects was tossed in the baskets for the livestock feed. The rest were tediously combed of their fine silks and stored in solutions of salty brine or kept in their husks for eating that week or the next.

"Cor, what I wouldn't give for a working refrigerator," Fiona said, wiping the perspiration from her forehead. "I think it's the one thing I miss the most. It like to kills me the food we waste because we can't preserve it."

Sarah stood next to her friend. Their tea taken together had focused on simple things: Papin's recent sassiness, the pleasures of sleeping next to a loving warm body, and the luxuriant bliss of the summer weather. They had studiously stayed away from any talk or hint of the future, talking only as far as the coming harvest festival and the plans for it.

Fiona was no doubt sorry for some of the things she'd said, Sarah knew, but apologies wouldn't be forthcoming. It was enough that the fight appeared to be behind them now.

"I know," Sarah said. She chose her words carefully since a refrigerator would likely be in her future before the end of next month. "How long do you think the corn will last?"

Fiona frowned and looked over her shoulder at the sound of another cart loaded with corn heading into camp. "Half will probably rot in the root cellar. The other half should take us through Christmas, I reckon. Mebbe."

And then? Sarah felt a heavy weight of guilt for the fast food and easy, cheap groceries in her future. Here, there would be potatoes for awhile—always the vegetable that lasted the longest in the cellars—and then long months of only meat and whatever preserved vegetables in the salt brine was still edible.

"Did I ever tell you about the cheese man what came around last January?"

"Cheese man?"

"It wasn't half bad. Made from goats milk and a nice break midwinter. Only problem was, the last thing we needed at that point were more things to bind us up. We needed something green."

Sarah remembered last winter as a cocoon of indoor living—bread baking and eating preserves and whatever David could pull out of their rabbit traps for the three of them. It had been cozy, if largely uncomfortable. For some reason, she had assumed that the community was faring better than they were.

"Is there any way to keep what we harvest through next February?"

Sarah knew the answer to her question before Fiona answered.

"That's seven months sitting in a root cellar or a jug of vinegar. Whatever good you were hoping for from the green had long since disintegrated, I'll wager. If there is anything left at all."

Sarah knew the rest of summer would be a sumptuous time of plentiful food and delicious, succulent seasonal foods. The fresh corn, roasted and slathered with churned butter, the tomatoes with crisp bacon on baked bread for a BLT that would make you weep with pleasure, and omelets with heaping side dishes of boiled cabbage, leeks, and wild garlic. Even now, the omnipresent scent of berry pies, cobblers and tarts wafted deliciously over Donovan's Lot.

Come fall, the larders still full, the camp would pick the apple orchard bare and add fried apples, apple fritters and apple dump cakes to the daily menus. The fruit was so sweet, nobody seemed to notice they'd run out of sugar six months earlier.

Then, bit by bit, up to then their comfort assured, their bellies continually full, the camp would be jolted back to reality. Come November, the game would leave, the chickens would wilt and stop producing, the hay would grow mold and the root cellars would be scraped clean.

Thanksgiving would feel a long way off, Sarah thought. *And will I be sitting in front of a bronzed roasted turkey with dressing and mashed potatoes and real gravy? And wondering if this is the day Fiona and Mike go to bed hungry again, or maybe the children, because they're trying to make their stores last?*

The thought of Thanksgiving made her cringe in spite of the pleasure she wanted to feel at being with her parents again, John and Papin at the table. The picture just wouldn't gel into anything that felt good, she thought with surprise.

And Christmas will be even worse.

A squeal of laugher erupted from behind the line of huts out of sight. Sarah recognized that squeal and she frowned. She dropped the shears on the table that she had been using to cut the toughest stems that held the husk in place.

"I'll go," Fiona said, a light hand on Sarah's arm. It was so much better for Fi to deal with it, Sarah thought. Papin still found reason to force herself to be polite or mind her tongue with Fi—something she was failing to do more and more with Sarah, and Mike too, she noticed.

"Thanks," Sarah said. "Sounds like a boy's in the picture."

"Just what I was thinking," Fiona said as she wiped her hands on a rag and left the work area, disappearing between two of the closely constructed huts.

Perhaps Papin was just at *that age.* Or maybe it was the thought of leaving to go to America. In the seven months since Papin had come to live at Donovan's Lot, she experienced the first real stability of her life. She had been treated as a daughter by Mike nearly from the moment Mike carried her out of that whorehouse in Wales. In those months of being loved and tucked seamlessly into a family, Papin had appeared strengthened and been restored.

Or so Sarah had thought.

Maybe the idea of being uprooted yet again—even for a place as wonderful as a home with hot and cold running water—was too much for a child used to abandonment and inconsistency. Even paradise, if there wasn't a boundary to hold all the goodness in and keep the evil out, was just another place to live.

Should she have asked Papin if she wanted to come to the States? Sarah had assumed that Papin would want to. She assumed that, as part of Sarah's family, she would simply comply, as all younger members of every family must do.

While she had always known it, it occurred to her that Mike had stepped into the role of father to both Papin and John. And because that had been such a help, and because the children needed what he had to give, Sarah had just accepted the situation.

Only now, without asking anyone's opinion—not the kids, not Mike's—she was splitting up the family.

No wonder everyone was so pissed off.

She eased a kink out of the small of her back and massaged it with a free hand. The corn was piling up to her left and it filled her with relief and pleasure to see it. Even if there wasn't enough corn to last the camp through the winter, it would serve as many months of sustenance. Better than last year, and for some of these families, she knew, better even than life before the bomb went off over the Irish Sea.

As she picked up another ear of corn, she saw Fiona step back through the huts, her hand firmly clamped to the arm of a recalcitrant and belligerent Papin.

Sarah's shoulders sagged. If Papin didn't care to behave even for Fiona, they really were coming to the end of their days. For the first time since the girl had come to live with her, Sarah found herself wondering if she was going to be able to handle her.

"I can walk by meself Auntie Fi!" Papin said, trying to twist out of Fiona's grip. "And we wasn't doing nothing."

"That's just the point, Papin," Fiona said, giving the girl a push toward the corn-shucking table. "You were supposed to be minding the bairns and the wee ones, not snogging with Bobby McClure."

"We wasn't snogging!" Papin said, brushing off the touch of Fiona's hand on her shoulder with much drama and exaggeration.

"Well, now you can shuck corn with us so we can mind *you*,"

Fiona said tartly. "Lyndie, darling, I'm sorry to have to ask..." Fiona gave a helpless shrug to the young mother standing beside Sarah, who quickly took off her apron and headed in the direction behind the huts to take Papin's place watching over the children.

"Papin, what the hell is the matter with you?" Sarah said with exasperation. "You can see we're all working here. You were carrying on with Bobby McClure?"

"A foul lie, Sarah, as sure as I'm standing here," Papin said, glaring in turns at Sarah and Fiona.

Sarah knew the fact that Papin was addressing her by her first name instead of "Mum" was not a good sign.

"A liar, is it you're calling me then?" Fiona said, her hands clapping onto her waist and facing Papin. "Would you care to have your uncle Mike define what it means to call your elders liars—at the end of his leather strap?"

"Da won't whip me," Papin said haughtily. "Go ahead and call him. Bet you he tells me to go pick berries and to think about what I've done." Papin smirked, then turned on her heel and flounced off toward Sarah's cabin.

"Let her go, Fi," Sarah said when she could see Fiona was inclined to go after her. "I'll deal with her later."

"You've got your hands full there, Sarah," Fi said, coming back to the table and shaking her head. "She's wild deep down no matter how tame she sometimes acts."

"I know." Sarah had a memory glimpse of the first time she saw Papin. Dressed in colorful gypsy rags, sitting on the back stairs of a boarding house in Wales, munching on a fried meat pie that she'd earned by selling her body. She had bright eyes, a fast mind, and a quick tongue. A week after knowing Sarah, Papin had sacrificed her body, and nearly her life, so Sarah could find her way home again to her boy.

Is it true we don't always know what our children really need? she thought with a sinking heart as she looked in the direction the girl had gone.

HE WAS sorry now that he had promised Sarah he'd come for dinner. He was too old for these long harvest days, even if he was doing more problem solving than actual picking, himself. He still dragged back into camp, tired and hurting in every joint he had to bend. If a hot bath could be possible, and an early night, he'd even skip the meal.

When he got back to camp, most of the other men had already quit for the day and were back with their families. The gypsy contingency was already in place by the main campfire. The women stirred a set of three large tri-pod black pots that hung in the campfire while the men lounged about the perimeter smoking and talking. The smell coming off the pots reawakened Mike's nascent hunger.

As the leader of the camp—and because he had no real family himself—he and Gavin tended to rotate turns as dinner guests at the other community members' hearths. Gavin had recently been spending all his dinner hours at the family of young Jenna McGurthy. To address the balance, Mike had increased the communal store of foods for the McGurthies. Gavin ate like most young men—ravenously and constantly.

Squinting as he neared his cottage, he could see wee Papin waited for him on his deck. It wasn't the first time he'd found her waiting for him, but lately it was less about greeting her foster da and more about bracing him to hear her side of some disagreement between her and Sarah. The closer he got, he could see she was standing near a steaming pail. His mood brightened. The lass had prepared a bath for him.

"Papin, me darlin'," Mike said as he mounted the steps. "Sure you're a sight for sore eyes, *leanbha*."

"Sarah thought you'd be wanting to clean up before dinner."

"*Sarah*, is it?" Mike said, tossing down his saddlebag and vest onto the porch. "You and yer mum into it again, are ya?"

"Not at all," she said, rising on tiptoe to kiss him on the cheek. "I just know she's a little wobbly these days, what with Auntie Fi being mad at her and all."

"They've still not resolved that?"

"Not so's anyone could see. The tub's out back. I saved the last pail so's it would go in hot for ya, Da."

"Thank you, *leanbha*. I can't think of a thing that'll do this broken down body more good at the moment. Tell yer mum I'll be over directly, eh? And Papin?"

The girl turned and gave him a questioning look before leaving the porch.

"Go easy on her, will ya? This isn't the easiest time for her."

"Nor for none of us, Da," Papin said, shrugging. She turned and left.

THE DINNER that night was quieter than usual. Mike chalked it up to the fact he was so tired he could barely lift his fork. That, and the usual chatter the family could always count on from Papin was not forthcoming.

Whatever fight she had had with Sarah, Mike thought, must have been serious. When John and Papin excused themselves to go to their rooms for the night, he was relieved to be able to talk to Sarah alone. She made tea and brought two cups out to the porch for them. It was a fine night and quiet, only the soft murmurings of the gypsy men still sitting by the central campfire and their gentle guitar strumming breaking the night's calm.

Mike took a sip from his mug and nodded his thanks to Sarah. She looked tired, too, although it could be emotion, he realized. She worked hard on the best of days. Still feuding with Fi and now a row with Papin…

"We're not fighting," Sarah said.

He frowned. "Eh?"

"Papin and me. You acted like you were on eggshells all through dinner. We didn't have words."

"Well, then, what's going on?"

Sarah sighed and looked out at the night camp, as if trying to memorize the images in order to recall them many nights later—air-conditioned nights with the sounds of the telly coming in from the salon, Mike thought.

"Fi caught her making out with one of the camp boys."

"Making out?"

"Do you not have that phrase over here? It means—"

"I know what it means, Sarah. When she was supposed to be watching the bairns?"

"Exactly."

"What's going on with her? Is it my imagination or has she started to act the maggot ever since you announced you were taking her back with you?"

"I don't know. I also don't know how to handle it." She looked at him. "Fi suggested you spank her."

He grimaced. "She's had enough of being hit," he said. "I'd rather make her whitewash the entire camp."

"Like Tom Sawyer?"

Mike gave her a questioning look.

"Never mind. And I agree, I think that's the best way to handle it, too, but what with us leaving in two weeks, well, she doesn't feel like anyone's really in charge of her now."

Mike didn't say anything.

"You know, Mike, speaking of that, it occurred to me that I'm being very unfair to you by taking Papin and John away. You love them like your own and I'm just...*removing* them where you'll never...or... likely never..."

"Whisht, Sarah," Mike said. "It can't be helped. I know that."

But it could be helped.

"I just hate this."

"Let's leave it, shall we? There's nothing for it, so let's stop picking at it. In the meantime, I'll put wee Papin to work where she'll be too busy to get into trouble. And mebbe, by the time you get her back home, she'll be too distracted by the newness of everything and she'll settle right down."

Yeah, sure. But he watched the hope in Sarah's eyes and he realized how tense she was, herself, about leaving. He and Fiona had kept her so busy trying to explain why she was leaving, that he hadn't stopped to think about her having to process her own grief about leaving.

Nothing's ever easy, that's for sure.

If this had been a normal day in their lives, the two of them discussing one of the kids and what's to be done, he'd have leaned over and kissed her to end the day as sweetly as he knew how. They didn't often kiss. He could definitely count the times. He could also tell she wanted him to kiss her, but for reasons he couldn't explain—and he didn't want to hear—she pulled away too.

Now of all times, with her leaving, he knew if he wanted to—*don't I want to?*—he could not only kiss her without worrying about being rebuffed, he could probably take her to bed, something he'd thought of pretty much nonstop since the moment he'd laid eyes on her.

Only the knowing of *why* she'd finally do it, because she knew she was saying goodbye to him for good, well, that pretty much took the desire and the pleasure in the idea of it and nailed it facedown to a bloody tree.

5

She couldn't blame him. As Sarah watched Mike walk across the camp, stopping briefly to talk to a few of the gypsy men still by the campfire, she found a deepening sense of disappointment fill her. If there was ever a night when she wanted, needed, Mike to take her into his arms and help her forget what she was doing, what was going to happen in two weeks, *this* was the night. She had hoped he wouldn't be too tired or too discouraged by the thought of her leaving, that perhaps together they could have shared their grief, finally express their love.

In many ways, it seemed to her that he was always just out of reach. She knew at least up to now she had been the reason for that. Tonight she had given him every silent cue she could to communicate that an overture on his part would be welcome, short of launching herself at him, which she didn't feel she could do. If he wasn't up for it—what with her leaving—she could understand that. As she turned to go back inside the cottage, she found herself thinking, *doesn't he know I want what he wants? How could he spend the last year with me and not know how I feel?*

She closed the heavy cottage door on the creeping chill of the night.

But because I've had to make the decision to walk away, I don't get to feel regret or longing or sadness about what I'm leaving behind.

It's so unfair.

"Mom?"

Sarah walked to John's doorway and peeked inside. "Hey, sweetie. It's late. I thought you'd be asleep."

"Uncle Mike go home?"

"Yep."

"Aren't you gonna miss him?"

"I am, sweetie. Very much."

"What about Dad?"

Sarah moved into John's bedroom and sat down on his bed. She put a hand on his cheek. There had been a time when she wondered if she would need to have a conversation with John about Mike perhaps someday moving in with them if she and Mike were to...but those thoughts had vanished, and the worry about having to have that conversation, too, the day she got the news of the US helicopter in Limerick.

"What about him?"

"Are we just gonna leave him behind, too?"

An image of David's grave came to her mind and tears sprang to her eyes. She leaned over and hugged her boy and kissed his cheek. "Go to sleep, angel," she said. "No room left in this day for any more worries."

"G'nite, Mom."

"Good night, John."

∽

BRIAN PULLED the flap of his sleeping bag over his face and turned his back to the campfire. The nights were fine lately, being summer and all, but it still felt good to have the warmth of the fire to his back. The long day of labor felt good too, as did the warmth with which he was received back at camp when he'd trudged in after the day's work. This place was more than he could have hoped for or imagined finding. It was, in fact, everything he needed or wanted—with a few notable exceptions, of course.

Mike Donovan walked past him on his way back from the American widow's place to his own hut. *So at least he had the decency to keep up appearances,* Brian thought. He waited until the big man had climbed the steps to his hut and shut the door behind him before he closed his eyes.

All in due time, he reminded himself as the distant strumming of the gypsies' guitars began to lure him off to sleep.

All in due time.

MIKE BROKE his fast at Fiona and Dec's the next morning. It gave him a chance to ask Declan's opinion of the animal tracks Gavin had discovered near the north perimeter of the camp. And to intervene, if he needed to, in Fiona's ongoing war with Sarah. He intended to remind her of how long they had been friends and how hard this was on Sarah. He expected her to be open to hearing that Sarah wasn't happy about leaving either. Not really.

"Don't fash yourself, brother dear," Fiona said as she scraped a portion of scrambled eggs onto his plate. "Sarah and I kissed and made up hours ago so you can take me off your to-do list and put your mind to more important camp leadership tasks. Like finding out who's been stealing the whiskey barrels and now us without any decent storage vessels. You know barrel-making used to be considered a skill in the old days?"

Mike dug into his breakfast, concentrating on not noticing how Declan couldn't seem to keep his hands off his sister, even as she was trying to pull hot rolls out of the oven.

"Mind yourself, Dec," she said, laughing. "Let me at least straighten up."

"And let me clear out of the house first," Mike growled.

"Aww nah, the two of yas," Dec said settling into the chair at the table. "I'm just starting my day in rare form. What a glorious day it is, is it not, brother? The corn is high and the sun shines and I have the love of a good woman. Kill me now. I'll not need for anything more."

Fiona tumbled three rolls onto each of their plates, then shocked Mike by plopping herself down in Declan's lap to butter and eat one of the rolls while inside his embrace.

"Oh, get on with you, Mike Donovan," she laughed when she saw him staring. "We're newlyweds, ya wally."

Declan bounced her on his knee, prompting schoolgirl squeals and giggles that brought Mike out of his chair.

"Right," he said, wolfing down the last bite on his plate. "Remind me to have breakfast from now on with old Joe McGillems. Dec, I'll see you in the field."

As he exited Fiona's cottage, a biscuit in one hand, he watched several of the families walking out of camp toward the fields. By his current calculations, they'd finish up sooner than the week, although whether that was because there wasn't as much corn as he'd estimated or because people were working faster than he expected, he wasn't sure.

He spotted Gavin and Brian Gilhooley walking together, both with long raffia bags draped from their shoulders.

"Morning, Da. Heading out, are you?"

Mike nodded to Gilhooley, who slowed his pace as Gavin did as if they were mates and he wouldn't carry on walking if Gavin decided to visit a spell with his father.

"In a bit. It looks like rain later so we'll need to get as much as we can done today."

"Da, Brian here was talking about a way we could strengthen

the camp's perimeter without stringing ten kilometers of wire to do it. He said—"

"While I'm grateful for Mr. Gilhooley's vast knowledge and irrefutable expertise on community defense," Mike said briskly, "I think we'll settle for the sweat of his back to be helping us bring in our harvest. And again," Mike looked directly at Gilhooley, "I'll be thanking you for your efforts on behalf of the whole camp."

"No problem," Gilhooley said dryly. "Come on, Gav. The corn won't pick itself."

Mike watched the two walk off together. Brian was easily ten years older than Gavin, he guessed. Old enough to be considered wiser and more experienced, but not so old as to be irrelevant and clueless. He sighed and walked back to his hut to get his tools for the day's work.

PAPIN WAITED until she saw Sarah run out to grab the wash from the clothesline before the heavens broke open and ruined a hard morning's work. She knew she should help her. Two hands would bring it in quickly enough.

But then I wouldn't have Sarah busy and looking the other way, would I?

Careful not to move too quickly and attract attention, she slipped out the front door and off the porch. *The silly cow was so intent on pulling the shirts and tea towels off the line,* she thought, *I could probably sashay right out in front of her.*

But if Papin had learned one thing in her life, it was that there was never a need to take chances that weren't absolutely vital to take.

She pulled down the bodice of her singlet to force out the tops of her breasts to best advantage and hurried around the back of the cottage. Just one more time, she promised herself. One more time and then she would leave him alone. The randy bastard certainly wasn't able to tell her no, himself. It looked like she would have to be the responsible one. The mature one.

The very thought made her giggle.

She began to trot to where she knew he waited for her.

MIKE SQUINTED at the gray deluge pouring from the skies.

So much for getting in a decent day's harvesting. He closed his legs around his horse, feeling the wet leather squeak in protest. Of the four men out by the fence, he was the only one mounted. Gilhooley, Declan, and Gavin walked the length of the north fence, which was constructed of wood and some remnant barbwire. Mike knew it wouldn't keep anything but cows out of the camp but it clearly stood as a message to the outside world to stay out.

Declan had insisted Gilhooley come with them. The big gypsy and the newcomer walked together, shoulder to shoulder, down the line of fencing and Mike found himself wondering what they saw in each other. By Gilhooley's speech, he was clearly a Dubliner and, if a few of the facial expressions Mike had seen him make meant anything, probably a racist, too.

In truth, there were few in the United Kingdom or Ireland who didn't hold judgment against gypsies.

Mike watched them stop fifty yards away. He could see Declan gesturing beyond the fence and then turn and point to the camp.

Whatever the feck they had in mind, he thought, *they could just forget it.* He'd see the entire camp fenced before the end of the year or know the reason why.

Gavin trotted over to where Mike sat on his horse. He looked winded as if he'd run the entire perimeter. *Silly eejit. He probably had.*

"Da, you won't believe how many breaks there are in the

fence. It must be fifty percent holes and gaps. It'll take a year to plug 'em."

Mike didn't answer. He knew he was spitting in the wind with this argument. But he couldn't help think it wasn't the wisdom of his idea people were having trouble with. It was the work involved to pull it off.

Gilhooley and Declan had turned around and were making their way back toward him. His eye caught the motion of Iain running across the field to intercept them. Something about the way he ran made Mike think he had information. He frowned when he saw the three men stop and confer.

Obviously, information he doesn't feel necessary to bring to me first.

"Da? Did you talk to Mr. Gilhooley about his idea on fortifying the perimeter without having to dig pits or stringing new wire?"

Mike looked up at the sky. It had been raining all morning which was the main reason the men were examining the fence line instead of finishing the harvest. One of the women in camp swore she'd seen a wolf skulking about the edge of the woods. There hadn't been a wolf in Ireland since the late seventeen hundreds.

The gray clouds overhead were billowing high in the sky, forming dark and threatening thunderheads. Mike sighed. It looked like the entire day was going to be a wash. *The wheat for sure didn't need any more damn water. If it kept up like this much longer, they'd start to lose crop.*

"Da?"

"No, Gavin, I haven't talked with Mr. Gilhooley about his idea." Mike watched the three men approach. They looked like they were all of one mind about something.

Gilhooley raised a hand in greeting even though they'd all spent the morning together. "Donovan!" he called. "Declan got something to tell you."

Mike watched Declan approach, his gait unhurried but purposeful.

Something tells me I'm about to hear Gilhooley's words come tumbling out of me good mate, Declan's, gob.

"I'm listening," he said.

Declan put his hand on Mike's horse and patted its neck. Like many gypsies, Declan was good with animals. Mike couldn't help but feel that Dec was physically soothing Mike's horse as a substitute for trying to placate its rider.

"Well, I got the idea," Dec said, "when you were talking about how much wire we'd need to finish the job of stringing the camp, you know?"

Mike didn't speak or nod. He tried not to look at Gilhooley, who seemed to be standing back as proud as a new parent waiting for his bairn to break into a buck and wing.

"And it occurred to me that instead of trying to enclose the camp, we should focus on repelling unwanted guests, you see? Oh, sure, have a basic barrier up..."

"Like we've got now," Gavin said.

Declan nodded. "That's right. Holes and all, it's still a kind of demarcation. But trying to make it do the work of a castle wall is just never going to work. We don't have the materials or the manpower to make it work."

"Is that what you think?" Mike said mildly. He could feel his temper rising and he fought not to let it show. "Is that your big newsflash?"

"No, that's the *reason* I felt it necessary to come up with something different than what we're planning on," Declan said with more firmness in his voice than Mike had ever heard before. "I think we need to form an army."

"*An army?*" Mike's mouth fell open.

Gilhooley stepped up. "Well, really more of a protective force or squad, right, Dec? A group of men whose sole job it is to patrol and protect the camp."

"Aye," Iain said. "Like they did in the Middle Ages, right?"

"Exactly," Gilhooley said. "It worked then because it's a sound idea. Set aside those men in the community not needed for planting and hunting and have them concentrate on our full time protection."

"I volunteer!" Gavin said. "Can I, Da? It's what me and Jamie have been doing sort of all along anyway." He turned to Declan. "How would it be organized, like?"

Declan shrugged. "We're just early days, lad," he said, watching Mike's reaction. "There's lots to talk about before we do anything."

"Mind you," Gilhooley said. "We don't want to wait too long."

Mike shifted in his saddle. He tried to give every appearance of considering this daft idea of making an army from the layabouts and fishermen that constituted the bulk of the community of Donovan's Lot. "Well, it's something to think about," he said finally, before turning to Iain. "Iain, you were tearing up the pasture pretty good and it's not usual for you to actually run if whisky isn't somehow at the end of it. Has something happened?"

Iain looked at him with confusion for a moment and then his face cleared as he remembered. Mike was astonished to see the man actually glance at Gilhooley first, almost as if for approval.

"Yer sister stopped me to tell ya you got a visitor."

"A visitor? What the feck does that mean?"

Iain shrugged. "She said a woman showed up an hour ago, walked all the way from the coast—with a little girl, mind—looking for you."

Mike stared at him for a moment and then turned his gaze toward the camp.

Was it Aideen? Could it be? What the hell was she doing here?

But he knew the answer to that.

6

"How in the world did you get here?" Mike leaned across the small dinner table and handed a cloth napkin to little Taffy, but his words were for her, Aideen knew.

"Just put one foot in front of the other and Bob's your uncle."

"You walked all the way from Wales?"

"Mum said we'd get a ride part of the way." Taffy, a mulatto child with large expressive eyes, pulled her bowl of stewed rabbit with pole beans closer to her. "But we only did the one time. We walked the *whole* way."

Aideen smiled at her daughter. It had been difficult trying to make the journey an adventure, especially when Aideen had been nearly frightened out of her wits a good deal of the time. She'd heard the stories of the terrible things that happened to women in the backcountry of Ireland after The Crisis, especially women traveling alone.

"Did living with your aunt in Wales not work out then?" Mike asked.

It had been a little less than a year since the last time she'd seen Mike and, if anything, Aideen had to admit he looked even more handsome. She knew that was likely because he was happy. He certainly looked happy. And *that* was likely because he'd found that woman he'd been looking for last year.

"You could say that," she said, her eyes trying to express her unspoken words over Taffy's head, silently asking him to reserve any questions until they were alone.

He seemed to understand, because he nodded and looked back to his meal.

"You always made Donovan's Lot sound like Eden." She turned to Declan, Brian and Fiona, who were sitting at the table with them. "He said it was a community of like-minded people, some family, but mostly people brought together by circumstance and that you all lived and worked together. So I thought, why not? Why not start a new life in this new world where I have at least one friend?"

"I'm new here, meself," Brian said.

Aideen thought Brian had interesting looks. He was good looking in a rough sort of way, with a slightly pocked complexion but because his eyes were so kind, the flawed exterior came off rugged and honest.

"It's really as grand as it seems," he said. "Everyone supports each other. Just as you'd think they should."

"Are you planning on joining the community, Mr. Gilhooley?" Aideen asked. She noticed Mike lifted his head from the study of his plate to hear the man's answer.

"I am. That is, if they'll have me. I have a wife and some family back in Dublin. I wouldn't want to bring them out until I had a place for them."

Mike grunted, noncommittally, it seemed to Aideen and she wondered if the two of them were at odds in some way. She knew that Mike was the leader of the community.

"So you'll build a cottage for them?"

"Well, me father-in-law and brothers can build their own homes. They're all healthy and quite capable. They can live in tents until then. The gypsies don't seem to mind living rough, do they?"

Aideen turned back to Mike. "Does everyone have jobs here? I'm a good seamstress and a fair cook."

"Aye," Mike said, turning back to his own meal. "Everyone takes care of their own families and then contributes to the community whatever skill they have to give. Families take turns feeding the bachelors and widows in camp, and newcomers like yourself and Mr. Gilhooley. Then everyone pitches in on the planting and the harvesting since we all benefit from that."

"And security measures," Declan said. "My job is to patrol the perimeter and keep an eye on things."

Fiona turned to Aideen. "We had a terrible incident last year when Sarah...when a few things happened...and we were attacked by a gang from the UK." She put a hand on her husband's arm as it lay on the table. "My Declan and his family came in the nick of time to help us beat the blackguards back."

"Well, true enough, it was mostly me," Declan said, scooping a squealing Fiona into his lap. "But me family helped a bit." The two of them began snuggling, shutting out the rest of the world.

Brian attacked his plate with new fervor but Taffy stared at the newlyweds, her eyes wide, her little mouth open.

"Finish your tea, Taffy," Aideen said.

"Sure, I'm glad you came, Aideen," Mike said suddenly. *Possibly prodded by the infectious display of affection from his sister and her new husband?* "It's good that you're here."

"Is it, Mike?" She made sure that he caught her meaning with no mistake. She'd walked many miles—been hungry more times than ever before in her life—and went to bed each night with terror as her sleep mate—and the one thing that kept her going was the memory of Mike Donovan.

Before she could underscore her meaning to him with anything more, Fiona hopped up and grabbed the pot on the stove behind the table.

"So how old are ya, darlin'?" Fiona asked Taffy as she ladled another serving of food into the child's bowl.

"Seven. Almost."

"Such a big girl." Fiona turned to Aideen. "My brother tells me the two of you met last year on his hunt for Sarah?"

"That's right. In Boreen. He..." She stole a glance at him to see if he was listening. He was. "He stayed with my father a few weeks to earn passage on the ferry to Wales."

"But you said you never made it to Wales," Fiona said to Mike, frowning.

"He didn't," Aideen said. "He gave his passage money to me so Taffy and I could leave."

"Ahhhh," Fiona said and returned to her chair at the table.

"And what's *that* supposed to mean?" Mike growled. "Oh, never mind. I don't want to know."

Aideen took a breath and, affecting insouciance, leaned across the table for the water pitcher and said, "You mentioned Sarah in the altercation you had last year. Does that mean you found her after all?"

"I did."

"But she's leaving now," Fiona said. Implied, it seemed to Aideen by the way Fiona spoke were the words, *after all that effort and worry.*

"Leaving *here*? Why ever for? She found something better than this?"

"She's going back to the States."

"Oh, my. Well, good for her." *And very good for all the rest of us, too.*

"Not that any of that matters," Mike said with clear irritation at the route the conversation had taken. "The point is, you and Taffy are here now and very welcome. Are you thinking of staying?"

"If you'll have me."

"Aye. We'll have you," Mike said spooning into his meal. "With pleasure," he muttered.

Aideen forced herself to say nothing. *Plenty of time to seal the deal later*, she told herself. *Take it slow for now. You've got your foot in the door. The rest will come.*

She let the feeling of immense relief and peace envelop by relaxing her spine deep into her chair. She let out a long breath to help remind herself that her journey was over and she was finally home.

"This stew is wonderful, Fiona," she said, smiling at her hostess.

"Oh, yes," Brian chime in. "It's delicious."

It hadn't escaped Aideen's notice that Mike's sister was incredibly sharp and seemed unusually alert to people and their motives.

That would be important to remember going forward.

THE NEW WOMAN WAS DIFFERENT, Sarah noted. First, even though she was Irish, she didn't sound it. Second, unlike every single other woman in camp—herself, included—she wasn't half-baked from the sun or scrubbed raw with the wind. If Sarah had to conjure up a picture of the perfect English rose, unfortunately, Aideen Malone would come to mind. It was pretty clear the woman wasn't used to physical labor. Whatever she'd done in the months since the bomb dropped had obviously been indoor work.

In Sarah's mind, the first profession that came to mind literally was the first profession. There was just something about her she just didn't like...

Fiona had the newcomer by the elbow and was going down the very short line of camp women clustered around the potato sorting tables. The weather was fine, almost hot, and there had been general rejoicing that the pickers in the field would be able to make up time for the two days earlier in the week when rain had prevented them from harvesting. Sarah watched the camp women giggle and grin as they were introduced to the woman. One of them nearly curtsied, but caught herself in time. Was it just because Aideen was a stranger with a different accent? She knew how the English were about their class system but she hadn't really seen anything like that in Ireland.

Had the camp women ever treated Sarah with this kind of deference?

If anything, the women had always seemed a little resentful of Sarah. Her relationship with their camp leader hadn't helped things. She'd heard rumors they believed she and John enjoyed unfair advantages because of her close friendship with Mike.

Hell, they were probably right.

"And this is our Sarah," Fiona said as she brought the newcomer over to where Sarah waited. "And you'll notice she wasn't with the other women because, being American and all, she thinks she's kind of a special case."

Sarah's mouth fell open. Her friend looked at her with a mirroring startled expression. *Too far?* she seemed to ask.

Aideen held out her hand and Sarah shook it.

"I've heard so much about you, Sarah," Aideen said, her accent clipped and precise, her voice soft and honeyed. Sarah could see why the women were treating her like royalty. She sounded like Princess Diana.

"Have you?"

"Aideen was able to put Mike up last year when he was on the road looking for you," Fiona said.

Put Mike up? What the hell did that mean? If Aideen's sly and self-satisfied expression meant anything at all, it seemed the words meant exactly what Sarah was afraid they meant. She pulled her hand out of Aideen's clasp.

"Well, if Fiona hasn't thanked you enough yet for that, then please allow me. I'm sure it was as a result of your *helping* him that he was finally able to lay hands on me." She could see Fiona jerk her head at her in surprise at Sarah's choice of words, but it didn't matter. All that mattered was that Aideen's smug smile had dissolved from her lips.

"My pleasure," Aideen said, biting off every syllable.

Sarah turned to Fiona. "So, will Aideen be joining us today in the spud sorting department?" She looked at Aideen. "It's hard work here and we don't get many days off, especially not during harvest time."

"So I see," Aideen said pleasantly.

"No," Fiona said, her hand back on Aideen's elbow. "Go on and get started if you would, Sarah. I'm to deliver her back to Mike. He's giving her a full tour of the place today and helping her move into her new cottage."

Sarah watched the two move toward Mike's hut and saw him come out onto his porch. He was holding a small girl in his arms, who instantly ran to Aideen when he put her down. Sarah could hear her excited prattle from fifty yards away although not her words. Even so, she could guess. Mike had that effect on children.

She hurried over to the potato sorting table, smiling broadly at the two women waiting for her—and was met with surprised return smiles. She picked up the first potato from the rag sack of them on the ground and brushed the dirt from it. At the first melodic tinkle of laughter that caught the summer morning breeze and carried back to her, she turned her head to see the figures again in front of Mike's hut.

Fiona was leading the child away toward where the rest of the children were being watched behind the new makeshift school-house they were building.

Mike and Aideen walked toward the stables. Sarah could see he was pointing out something to Aideen that was out of Sarah's line of sight.

He had his hand on the small of Aideen's back as they walked.

"REALLY? She just waltzes into camp one day and she's *in*?"

"Mike vouched for her."

Sarah grabbed two more potatoes and began vigorously scrubbing their jackets with the small brush she was using to clean them. Fiona stood next to her with a paring knife, attacking the eyes and bruised spots or insect damaged areas.

"I'll just bet he did. And where is she staying? Has Mike arranged that, too?"

"Of course. You know Mike. He wanted to give her his hut because it's so close to the camp center, only it's hardly bigger than an outhouse so she'll take Old Lady Mordor's place for now. It's been vacant since she died and it has a pretty setting. Too late for flowers this year, but it gets full sun in the morning when—"

"Okay, Fi, I don't care about the damn sun her new place gets."

"Sure, why am I rattling on? In truth, she won't even be there in the spring anyway."

"So she's just here temporarily?" Sarah's arms dropped to her sides. Was she really getting unglued over nothing? She turned and picked up the small basket of potatoes she'd finished cleaning.

"Of course. Just until you leave. Then she'll take your cottage."

Sarah dropped the basket in the dirt.

"Hey, watch that! Some people have to eat those things. So what did you think, Sarah? That's we'd keep your place as a shrine to you? It's one of the nicest cottages in camp, if not *the* nicest. Two bedrooms, big kitchen, facing the center of camp, and Mike is just two doors away."

"I get it, Fi. She's here to take my place. I get it."

"Oh, I think she can do a little better than take your place, luv. It's pretty clear by the moon eyes she was making last night at dinner that she means to get that big stubborn brother of my mine hitched and in her bed. Oh! I guess that would be *your* bed, now, wouldn't it?"

Sarah turned on her heel and stomped off to her cottage. It was all she could do not to slap Fiona first. She could hear her calling to her, "Oh, come on, Sarah, I was just teasing! Come on, I'm sorry if I went too far…"

She slammed the front door as hard as she could, wishing the windowpanes would pop out and the doorknob would fall off at the impact. A heavy door, it was, nonetheless, solid and slow and only made a small shushing sound when it closed. She had an overwhelming urge to break something or scream at the very least. Trouble was, screaming would sound an alarm that she didn't have the right to sound, and breaking anything when everything was so valuable was just wrong.

She sat down and thought about crying but decided she was too angry for that.

Worst of all, she knew she needed to go back outside and resume cleaning and packing potatoes. She took a long breath and straightened her blouse and smoothed out the lines of her jeans.

I'll go back and do my part, she thought, marching to the door. *And if Fiona Donovan Cooper says one word to me I swear I'll soak her head in the vinegar brine bucket.*

～

AIDEEN WRINKLED up her nose at the smell of the place. Mike had to admit, the Widow Mordor hadn't been the most conscientious of housekeepers.

"It's just temporary, mind," he said to her as he stepped into the cottage. He should have had Fiona air the place out or take a hose to it, more like, but what with the wedding and all—and not needing the place—that had taken a back seat to more pressing things.

"It's fine, Mike. Better than fine," Aideen said. "It's a real roof over our heads and everything else can be made lovely."

"It's further away from the center of camp than I'd like," he said. "But when Sarah moves out, you can move in closer." As if taking his words as an invitation, she turned to him and put her hand on his arm.

"You know where I came from," she said quietly. "You know what an improvement this is over that."

"Aye," he said. He couldn't help the feeling of wanting to protect her from her past, from the people who'd hurt her, as daft as that notion was. There was something about her that made him want to keep her safe. "This camp will be a good home for you, Aideen. And for Taffy. I swear it will."

"I know it will," she said, shifting her weight so her hip grazed his thigh. She looked around the dingy little cabin as if imagining its transformation.

"I'll have Iain bring in food for the rest of the week. We usually parcel it out on Saturday so those wanting a Sunday lunch can have it. You're joining us in the middle of our time of plenty. So that's good."

This tour had seemed like a good idea when he'd suggested it last night but now, with her standing so close to him and the thought of all the work that still needed doing out in the field, he started to feel fidgety. Best he left her to doing her best to tidy the place up.

Because he wasn't expecting it, he didn't think to stop her or push her away when she turned to him and kissed him on the mouth. Because he wasn't expecting it, he automatically dropped his hand to her waist and pulled her to him. And because he had hungered for the touch of another for so long, his body reacted to the moment with instinctive immediacy.

Aideen wrapped her arms around his neck and ground her pelvis into his before he thought to untangle her and hold her at arm's length. When he did, he realized they were both panting.

Her eyes glittered and focused on his lips. He knew that she'd let him take her right there on top of the old widow's dusty bedclothes and broken curtain rods.

And for a minute, he considered it.

"We can't, Aideen," he said hoarsely.

"Sure we can now," she said, her eyes flitting from his mouth to his eyes. She still held her arms out as if he would move into her embrace at any moment. "Your Sarah is leaving."

"Yes, but she's not gone yet," he said before even thinking.

Aideen dropped her arms and turned around to face the cottage interior. "I see."

"No, you don't. It's not like that. I just need a little time to reorganize things in my head, is all."

"Seemed to me your body has already made the leap. Maybe you're thinking too much."

"Maybe. Can we table this discussion for another time? I really need to get out to the field. This is a very big time for us."

"Of course, of course. I'll be fine here."

She smiled bravely as if he hadn't just rebuffed her and then suggested he bolt out the door, too. He put a hand to her face, so pale and the apples in her cheeks like a blush about to happen.

"I can be patient, Mike," she said, her eyes smoldering once more and locked onto his lips. "Take the time you need."

Twenty minutes later he was on his horse and cantering toward the north pasture where the potatoes had been planted. His blood felt racing and alive as he rode. The summer breeze ruffled his hair and the sun pounded on his back. It was truly a beautiful day to be alive, he thought.

Aideen had just taken a shite week and made it shine.

As he neared the field, he could see the kneeling forms of twenty people digging up the potatoes. He was surprised to see how orderly they seemed to be. Two people dug in each row while a runner—it looked to be an older child—carried a small bag of unearthed spuds back to the end of the line where someone else packed them in larger bags and stacked them on the back of pony carts, which were then driven off back to camp.

At this rate, they'd have the field clear by nightfall. Mike stopped his horse at the pony cart and saw that several people were packing the potato harvest onto the cart.

Brian was one of them. In fact, Brian appeared to be the one orchestrating the runners and the packers.

"Morning, Mike," Brian called to him as Mike dismounted.

"Gilhooley," Mike said. "Looks like you've got things well in hand here."

"A hunnert percent," Brian said, grinning. He ruffled the hair of a boy who walked up carrying a bag of potatoes. "Couldn't do it without young Liam, here."

Mike saw the boy beam at Brian as if the man's praise were all the sustenance he could ever want.

"Mr. Gilhooley's figured how we only need so many actual pickers to a row," Liam said. "This way we're not running over on top of each other."

"And we can actually come away with larger yields and fewer damaged spuds," Brian said, patting the boy on the shoulder. "Off you go, now, Liam. Still daylight left."

"Right you are, sir."

"Looks like you've taken over," Mike observed.

"Well, the potato picking anyway," Brian said, his eyes showing no humor as he spoke.

"Brian! You'll be wanting to come see this," a woman yelled from the middle of the potato field.

Mike craned his neck and squinted at her in the distance. Surely it wasn't a snake, although Saint Patrick not withstanding, it wasn't totally out of the question.

"What is it, Maggie?" Brian yelled back. He began to move into the field.

Mike remounted and stood in the stirrups to see what the woman was hollering about. She stood with her hands on her hips, wiping the sweat from her brow from time to time. If it was a snake, she wasn't too concerned with getting away from it, Mike thought, frowning.

As he watched, he could see the problem wasn't in the field but in what was coming across the field at a fair clip. He twisted in his saddle and strained to get a better look, because from what he could see, the thing coming slowly across the potato field looked to be the closest thing to an actual ghost as he had ever seen.

Conor Murphy was coated from head to foot in unbleached flour. The boy wasn't nine years old, but stood in front of Mike without a tremor, the whites of his eyes the only tale-tell hint that he was at all concerned with what was coming.

With the help of a growing entourage, Conor made his way through the potato field with the affect of the condemned man. Maggie gave him a healthy swat on his backside as he passed but he didn't flinch. Just before he reached the potato packing clearing where Mike, now dismounted again, waited, Brian swung around and stopped the boy from proceeding.

Kneeling down, he grabbed Conor by his shoulders and gave him a light shake, resulting in a faint cloud of flour puffing in the air around him. Mike could hear Gilhooley talking to the boy, but his voice was low, his words indistinct.

"Let the lad come on," Mike said, irritation with Brian's intervention making his voice harsher than he'd prefer. He saw the child's eyes looking at Brian Brian gave him a comforting pat and released him, allowing him to go to Mike.

"You'll be explaining yourself, Conor Murphy," Mike said

solemnly, his hands on his hips. The pickers moved in from the field, and while Mike was tempted to send them back to work he knew there was some merit—both for the boy and the community—for the group to be present.

The lad cleared his throat. "I'll take me whipping. I ain't scared of it."

"There's no doubt you'll be taking your whipping, young Conor," Mike said. "I'm asking you *what happened*. No blubbing now."

Conor wiped his face with a grimy fist leaving streaks of caked white across his cheek and was about to speak when John Woodson pushed through the gathered crowd.

"Wasn't all his fault," he said. "Me and some of the lads started it."

Mike looked at John with surprise. First, because he hadn't seen him in the crowd, and second because the boy rarely got in trouble, and he never *started it*.

"Explain."

John shoved Conor to stand by his side and Mike saw the flour rising off the lad in puffs of white. "We were just having some fun on the other side of the bluff, rolling barrels down into the ravine, like." He shrugged as if that was all he needed to say.

"*Rolling barrels down into the ravine?*" Mike knew they were all watching him and he knew he needed to keep his temper in check. Still, the camp had long complained he dealt John with a lighter hand than the other children.

John shrugged again, which served to inflame Mike at his casualness about the crime.

"And what happened," Mike asked with exaggerated slowness, "when the barrels hit the bottom of the ravine if I may ask?"

Conor took a step forward and made a sound of an explosion. When he did, great clouds of flour rose around him, causing many in the crowd, adults included, to titter.

"So, in other words, they broke," Mike said to John. "Is that what I'm hearing? You deliberately smashed perfectly good barrels just to see them break?"

I swear to God if he shrugs now I'll knock their heads together.

"Yes sir," John said.

"And this?" Mike gestured to Conor. "What's this got to do with exploding barrels?"

John glanced at Conor and seemed to fight to keep a straight face. "Conor just got a little creative."

"I put a whole bag of flour in one!" Conor crowed, "and kapow! Even the bushes and grass is white!"

More snickers from the crowd made it clear that the two miscreants were well in the lap of public opinion, Mike thought. *Wonder if they'll still be there when nobody has fresh bread tomorrow...or next week.*

"Where's Dylan Murphy?" Mike asked, trying to keep his voice even.

"Me da's working in the south field," Conor said, his voice not quite as steady as it was before.

"Right. Off you go to inform him of your day's shenanigans. And mind, Conor, I'll be speaking with your da later today to make sure he got the right set of facts."

Conor nodded glumly and turned away.

"What about me?" John said.

"Who are the other boys with you in this vandalism?"

"I forget."

Mike held John's stare and then nodded his head. "Right. You'll whitewash the camp's huts, starting with the one just inside the main gate. Your Aunt Fi can show you where the paint is."

"What do you mean? Which huts?"

"All of 'em. Maybe it'll help jog your memory of who helped you destroy the barrels. Everybody else, back to work, please. We only have other four hours of light, summer or not."

"Before everyone leaves," Brian said, "may I make a suggestion?"

"This doesn't concern you, Gilhooley."

"Well, since I hope to be a part of this community, I'd beg to differ. And it seems to me that since both boys have confessed their sins, it would be more healing for the community if they were allowed to just go on from here."

Mike's posture went rigid. He turned his back on Brian to address John. "So, will you tell your mother or shall I?"

SARAH FELT the exhaustion of the long day seep into her hips, her arms, her every aching joint. She knew she wasn't the only one falling into bed at night so tired she barely had the energy to pull on a nightgown. But like most of the women in camp, she still had baths to organize and a meal to get on the table before then.

She cut into the chicken potpie and placed a large wedge on John's plate. Papin had napped most of the day and was still sleeping.

"Doing this right in the middle of the harvest was incredibly irresponsible, John."

He just shrugged.

"Do you have anything to say for yourself? I mean, this is so unlike you. And young Conor is paying the price—"

"He's old enough to know what he was doing."

"You cannot absolve yourself from this, John! If it weren't for you, the older boy, egging him on—"

"I did not egg him on!"

"Do I really have to tell you how this works? Didn't you get into trouble enough times when you were younger by following *Gavin's* lead?"

"Whatever."

"And now you'll be taken out of the workforce, just when the camp could really use your help in the fields harvesting the potatoes."

"They might as well have me picking potatoes 'til we leave. I'm not going to paint any stupid huts."

Sarah gasped at his audacity. *Who was this boy pretending to be her respectful, compliant son?* "You absolutely *will* paint the huts just as Mike ordered you to."

"Why should I? This isn't our home any more. We're leaving in ten days."

"We are still members of this community until the minute we walk out those gates."

"That's bullshit."

"John! What has come over you?"

"You don't like it, but it's the truth. Everyone's already mentally said goodbye to us, it's just our bodies still hanging around."

"They needed us for the harvest."

"And that's not true either. But whatever."

"Look, I can see you're upset. After dinner, why don't you go see if Gavin wants to play cards or a game of chess?"

"He's busy. Besides, he's already signed off on me. And why wouldn't he? I'm as good as gone."

"But you're *not* gone."

"I am, as far as anyone's concerned. Same as you, Mom."

Sarah left the boy to his thoughts and the two ate in silence. When he was finished, he brought his plate to the sink and went to his room.

There was a time when she would have gotten a goodnight kiss first.

Or at least a goodnight.

Feeling even more tired than when she began making the dinner earlier that evening, Sarah brought her own plate and utensils to the sink and set them in it. She'd deal with them in the morning.

Out the front window she could see a candle flickering in

Mike's hut. As she stood in her kitchen, she could see his shadow moving in the front room.

Was this really how it was going to all end? After everything?

Without stopping to think what she was doing, she grabbed her sweater from the chair in the front room and stepped out the front door, closing it silently behind her.

THE EXHAUSTION of the day couldn't compete with the cacophony of emotions and thoughts spinning inside Mike's head as he tried to settle in for the night. For a change, the gypsies weren't playing their music around the fire and it was quieter than he ever remembered it being—even before they had come.

In the old days, he'd have the telly on and be pottering about his cottage repairing this net or that, checking out a possible new purchase on the computer—that is if Gavin wasn't hogging it. Now, with the lights out pretty much as soon as the sun sets, everyone was in a mind to go to sleep. Unless you had a bed partner to whisper with under the covers there really wasn't much else to do in the dark.

But it still didn't feel right to go to bed at nine o'clock in the evening.

When the knock on the door came, his stomach muscles clenched. He knew it was Aideen and his first thought was, *who's minding wee Taffy, then?* With a groan and the full intention of telling her to go on back to her child, he swung his feet off the bed and lumbered to the door, not bothering to shrug on a shirt.

Sarah stood shivering in the summer evening and pulling her cotton sweater tight around her shoulders. Mike knew the night wasn't cool enough to cause her shivering.

"Is everything ok?" He stepped back to allow her to enter although they'd long had the policy—for the sake of the robust gossipers in camp—never to be in either of their cottages alone. The rule didn't seem to matter much any more.

She stepped inside, glancing briefly over her shoulder as she did. "Yes. Well, except for John today."

Mike ran a hand through his hair. He should have expected she'd want to talk about that. As strange as it was, they were in the habit of co-parenting both John and Papin, almost like a divorced couple might—a divorced couple who'd never actually slept with each other.

He picked up a clean shirt from a chair and shrugged into it. "Well, 'tis not the end of the world, what he did."

"It's just the fact that he did it."

"It's the coming change, most likely."

Sarah went to sit in the chair in Mike's sitting room. "I know. I figured that. So...you moved Aideen into her place today?"

Ahhh, so that's what this is about. He sat opposite her in a lumpy chair that had been tossed in the dump in the days before it became a valuable piece of furniture.

"And how many days is it before you go?"

"I guess I thought you'd wait until I was actually gone."

"Wait for what? To sleep with her?"

Even in the dark, he could see her face flush and he regretted his flip words. This wasn't easy for her either. He'd like nothing more than to pull her into his lap and just hold her. It would do them both good.

Until it didn't.

"It's just that...I won't be getting over *you* so quickly. I guess I'm just surprised, is all."

"What is there to get over? Our friendship? A few snogs? Is the power of my effect on you really so strong? Oh, wait. You're leaving. So I guess not."

"But if I *wasn't* leaving..."

"Do not even say it. Do not even dare to say it." He felt an irrational anger build up in his chest. "We've had this conversation and there's nothing more to say. Is it your concern over John's behavior today that's brought you here tonight?"

"No."

"No. It's jealousy when you've no right or claim to me. Do ye not want me to find happiness, Sarah?"

"You know I do."

"I know nothing of the sort. Or is it just happiness that doesn't involve the love of a woman who can love me back?"

"I love you."

The air punched out of him as if she'd hit him square in the solar plexus. His mouth fell open and he stared at her.

"How can you believe I don't? How could you *think* I don't? Because I'm leaving? Because I'm determined to sacrifice everything I've got—my life, my own happiness—for the sake of my child? You couldn't be so obtuse. Not even you."

She stood up and he could see she was trembling now. When he reached for her, she came easily, willingly. "I love you, Mike," she whispered into his collar, her arms wrapping around his neck and pulling his face to hers. "I love you, I love you. I know this isn't fair to either of us, but I need to feel you next to me and in me. I need to remember that I once had you as close as two people can be."

Not knowing where he got the strength, he swung her into his arms and took the two steps that measured the distance to his bed...and their inevitable goodbye.

8

The sun was full out the next morning, shining down on him.

And life had never sucked so completely in all the days he'd lived so far.

If Mike thought living through the next ten days knowing she was leaving was tough *before* they slept together, it didn't compare to how bad it felt now.

Would they sleep together again? Would they continue to be together right until the moment she stepped onto that transport plane? Or was last night their first, their last, their big goodbye?

As he sat on his horse, he could see Sarah as she spoke with one of the camp women outside her cottage, her hand on her hip —the very hip he had caressed naked just that morning, the very hip he had pulled to himself and claimed as his. After all those months...

"Oy! Mike! There's a ruckus by the gypsy camp. Brian's already there but you'd better come quick."

Mike snapped his head around to see Jimmy and Iain trotting in the direction of where the gypsy families had their tents. Even from a distance of a hundred yards, he could hear the yelling coming from that direction.

"What the hell?"

Two other men from camp dropped their tools and ran toward the sound of the altercation. Mike dug his heels into his mount and launched into a canter. As he approached the furthest point of the camp where it abutted the northeast pasture, he could see that at least three men were scuffling in front of the main tent the gypsies had erected. Declan was in the center of the melee.

Mike swung down from his horse and charged into the fracas. An elbow caught him in the stomach and he grabbed the offending limb and jerked its owner off his feet. He could feel the fight collapsing as he found the man at the center of it, a young cousin of Declan's. He was curled into a ball protecting his face and stomach from the blows and kicks of his family.

"Oy!" Mike shouted. "What's going on? Why are you hammering the lad? Declan!"

When Mike turned to his friend, the tall gypsy's eyes were blazing black with anger. Mike could see he had a small club in his hands. The end was bloody. "Jaysus, God, Dec, what's gotten into you?"

Gilhooley pushed aside a gypsy who had been beating on the boy. He stood over the young man, his booted foot on his leg so he wouldn't rise. "Young Ollie here's murdered his girlfriend," he said tensely.

"What?" Mike turned to Declan, whose face was set in implacable, rigid lines. "Is this true? Is the lass dead?"

"She is," Declan said, spitting in the dirt beside the boy. "And he's confessed."

Mike leaned over the young man and pushed Gilhooley's foot off him. His face was bloodied and streaked with tears and his eyes were clenched shut as if in agony. "Is this true, son?" Mike said, shaking the young man's arm gently.

"His name's Ollie," Declan said.

"Ollie," Mike said. "Open your eyes and look at me." He waited, hearing the sounds of the gypsy families drawing closer, murmuring.

"I wouldn't waste your time, Donovan," Gilhooley said. "He confessed, I told you."

Ollie's eyes opened and in a flash he was on his knees, his hands grabbing for Mike's. "Please," he said. "It was an accident. A terrible, rotten accident. Please don't let them kill me."

Mike shook off his hand and stood up. "So was it murder or an accident?" he said to Ollie, and then to the gathered crowd.

"Cor, they fight all the time," a woman's voice screeched out.

"Too right! Eeny said she was brutal scared of him, so she did!"

Mike turned to Declan. "Do you know anything of this?"

Declan gave him a look of disgust. "He killed her. That's all we need to know."

Mike wasn't sure in what way Eeny was related to Declan or, for that matter, how he was related to Ollie. But his brother-in-law seemed convinced it was not an accident.

"Get him on his feet," Mike said. "Take him to the new barracks." Declan and Gavin were in the process of securing a small hut with bars and a lock on it to be used if needed as a temporary holding cell. "Meanwhile, Dec, talk to his kin, and hers. Get eyewitnesses or anyone who knows anything. We'll convene a panel straight away to hear the evidence against him."

"And then what?" Gilhooley said, turning to Mike. He looked angry, as if the act of bothering to gather proof of guilt was in itself somehow a crime.

"If he's found guilty of murdering the lass," Mike said, his voice loud so that everyone could hear, "he'll be banished."

A brief silence followed and then Gilhooley turned to face the crowd. "Is the family of poor Eeny happy with that judgment?

Banishment for the monster who's robbed them of their daughter? Of future grandchildren? Is that justice?"

The crowd's roar assaulted Mike as he dragged Ollie to his feet and flung him into Declan's arms. "Take him away from here *now*," he said and then turned to face the crowd. "We'll have a trial first because that's the law here and you all know that."

"And after that?" Gilhooley spat. "After your *trial*?"

It took everything Mike had not to slam his fist into the man's haughty, sneering face. "We'll deal with matters once we have all the evidence," he said. He looked over his shoulder to see Declan dragging the boy toward the main camp and the makeshift jail.

Gilhooley stretched his arms out to the gypsies who were gathering in closer, their faces flushed with anger and frustration. "I say what the Bible says...an eye for an eye! If Ollie killed Eeny, he should pay with his life! Not be escorted to the nearest bush outside the camp."

"Escort him to a bush and put a bullet between his eyes!" a voice in the crowd yelled out.

"Hang the bastard and hang his thieving bastard kin while you're about it!"

That prompted the eruption of a fistfight that pushed Mike and Gilhooley to the edges of the crowd. Mike grabbed him by the arm. "What are you trying to do, Gilhooley? This is not how we do things."

"Oy!" Gilhooley raised a hand and the combatants dropped their fists and, with the rest of the crowd, turned to listen to him. "We all know what happens if we let Ollie get away with this, and so we're not going to let that happen—"

"What the feck do you think you're doing?" Mike shoved Gilhooley hard and the man sat down in the dirt with a thud. "This isn't your place, ya little bogger. Shut the feck up!"

Gilhooley scrambled to his feet and put his face close to Mike's. "I figure it is my place," he said fiercely. "This camp has no law that I can see and people are living in fear. Bad enough for what's on the outside wanting in, but to let our own people terrorize us? You're weak, Donovan."

Before Mike could react, Iain Jamison slithered out of the crowd and stood between them. He put a firm hand on each man's chest and separated them. "Now, gents, let's don't get carried away," he said easily. Mike could feel the alcohol blasting off him and he wondered where in hell the bastard had gotten the grog.

"It won't help the situation to start swinging and I'm sure when heads are cooler, you'll agree," Iain said, his voice oily and wheedling.

"I agree *now*," Gilhooley said backing away, his hands up to show he wouldn't be the one to throw the first punch.

Mike turned to the crowd. "Everyone go back about your business. We'll—"

"Hold on there, Donovan," Iain said. "I've a mind to make one wee announcement before we break things up."

"What are you talking about?" Mike saw Iain give a quick glance to Gilhooley who, he could have sworn, gave the barest of head nods in return.

Iain cleared his throat. "As none of us here had any say in the running of this camp we all call home—nor the selection of our leader—it is my..." he gave another quick glance at Gilhooley, as if searching for the right word from him "...suggestion that we nominate candidates to be our leader and vote for who we want to be making decisions on our behalf. All agree, say *aye*!"

Stunned, Mike heard the entire assembly of gypsies chorus their assentation.

"I'll pass it around the main camp, too," Iain said to Mike, as if reassuring him. "You'll hear soon enough," he said, "but I'm nominating Mr. Brian Gilhooley as the candidate who'll be running against you in the election to be held..." He looked again at Gilhooley.

"The day after the Harvest Festival," Gilhooley said, his eyes watching Mike warily. "After which time," he said turning to address the Gypsies, "we will celebrate the fact with the public hanging of one murdering sod."

The crowd cheered, their voices growing louder and louder as Mike turned to locate his horse and make his way back to camp.

SARAH LOOKED around the dinner table and felt the usual flush of fellowship and contentedness she always felt when everyone she loved was gathered around the dinner table, laughing and talking at once. That is until, as her eye traveled around the table and came to Mike and Aideen.

After their night of lovemaking and an intimacy, which turned out to be every bit as exquisite as she had imagined it would be, she wasn't sure what to expect from Mike in the bright of day. Would they pretend it hadn't happened? She assumed they would to everyone in camp, but with each other? Wouldn't they take advantage of the brief time they had left and spend it as intimately as possible?

"Earth to Sarah, luv, pass the corn, if you would," Fiona said from across the table. Sarah looked up, jerked out of her thoughts. Fiona pointed to the plate of corn at Sarah's elbow. She slid it across the table to her, and glanced again at Mike at the end of the table. Aideen was practically sitting in his lap.

And he was not acting like he'd just held another woman in his arms a few hours earlier.

Not at all.

A giggle rose up from Aideen and Sarah caught Mike grinning.

Private jokes? After last night? Really?

"Mum, you okay?" Papin frowned at her. "You look like you've just seen the Devil himself."

"I'm fine," Sarah said, her voice abrupt. She saw Papin's face react and instantly she was sorry for her tone. She reached a hand out to soften her curtness but Papin pulled away, refusing to be mollified.

"So, Da, we'll be having a little democracy at Donovan's Lot after all, it seems?" Gavin looked at his father from over a heaping plate of fried corn bread, sliced tomatoes and at least four ears of corn slathered in fresh butter.

"It's for the best, Mike," Fiona said. "Surely you can see that."

"Well, as it happens," Mike said, sourly, "I can't. But as you're so keen on being able to vote on every little question of how to run the camp, then by all means, have an election."

"I think it's terrible," Aideen said, looking up into Mike's eyes, "after everything you've done for everyone, and all the sacrifices you've made that they should do this."

"Me, too, Da!" Taffy chirped up. Sarah snapped her head around in stunned disbelief that the little mite was already calling Mike 'Da,' but everyone else seemed not to notice. In fact, the table laughed heartily at little Taffy's comment.

I suppose it's not so unthinkable. All the camp's fatherless kids called him Da, and half of the ones with fathers.

"I'll admit to being surprised," Mike said. "I mean, I created this community."

Fiona handed a basket of yeast rolls down the table. "Yes, dearest, you did, but now it's growing beyond the handful of starving families needing a place to lay their heads for a night. We're turning into a kind of village and we need...representation."

"Does that mean I can count on your vote, sister dear?"

"Now, Mike, you know you're always my favorite candidate, after Dec, of course, but I don't think there's a reason not to explore other leadership styles. That's not being disloyal."

"The hell it isn't."

"I think what Fiona's saying," Declan said, "is that it might be good to see if another way might not work better for us. For example," he said quickly, "Brian doesn't get quite as stitched up as you do over little things,"

"It's true you do have a famous temper, brother dear."

Sarah watched with creeping outrage when Aideen put her hand on Mike's arm—like he belonged to her—and actually stroked him as if trying to soothe him.

"And Mr. Gilhooley has some good ideas, Da," Gavin said between mouthfuls. "If you'd give him a chance, you'd see that."

"Oh? And is killing a young lad in front of the whole camp one of those good ideas?"

"Not. At. The. Table," Fiona said.

A brief silence intervened and then Papin stood up. "Auntie Fi, do you mind if I lie down for a tick? I don't feel so hot."

"I noticed you were quiet, darling," Fi said, standing and putting her hand to Papin's forehead. "You're not warm, but you don't look well. Yes, go on and lie down on my bed."

Sarah watched her shuffle to the bedroom and close the door. Her first thought was to wonder if there was a window in the bedroom.

Gavin and John stood up and asked to be excused. There was a new colt in the stable they wanted to check out. When Taffy whined to accompany them, Aideen was forced to go with them. "My, I guess it'll just be the grown ups left," Aideen said, looking at Sarah but smiling haughtily.

I wonder what she'd say if I told her I rode her seatmate there last night like a bronco-busting Amarillo cowgirl?

Sarah flushed with fury when Aideen leaned over and kissed Mike on the cheek before taking her daughter's hand and sauntering out of the cabin. It was all Sarah could do not to trip her on her way out.

∽

"SOUNDS like it was a rough day for you." Sarah sat on Fiona's porch step with Mike sipping an after dinner cup of tea.

"You could say that," he said.

"Do you think we could talk about what happened last night?"

"Are you still leaving?"

Sarah stopped and sucked in a quick breath. "What?"

"Because unless it changed anything, I don't think there's much point, do you?"

"Is that why you and Miss Big Boobs were all over each other at dinner tonight?"

Mike gave her a surprised look. "You think she has big boobs?"

"Fine. Play your games. Whatever." Sarah forced herself to take a breath. She knew he was moody these days and she would just have to let some things go. "I would like to ask you, though," she said, "since we've never discussed it, if you would drive us to Limerick in the carriage after the festival."

Mike frowned. "I might have to ask Jimmy to do that."

"Are you seriously not going to take me to Limerick?" She swallowed hard and pinched her lips together. Was he trying to hurt her? Was he really not going to see her off?

"In case you weren't listening, Sarah, that tosser Gilhooley is attempting a hostile takeover of the community. Or do you in fact think it's all about you?"

Sarah held onto her temper. Was this really the same man who held her naked in his arms just this morning, stroking her back and kissing her neck? "Right," she said, "well, then, if you'd arrange it with Jimmy, I'd be grateful. Thank you."

"No problem."

"Is something bugging you, Mike? I mean, something more than usual? Because I'm not really used to all the monosyllabic responses from you lately and I hope I'm not being all egocentric here to ask." She silently cursed herself for the sarcasm. She really was trying to be understanding.

"What could possibly be wrong, Sarah? I'm losing my leadership in the community *and* you all in twenty-four hours. At this rate, I'm expecting to come down with cancer any minute. No, Sarah, things are brilliant. Thanks for asking."

Sarah softened and reached for his arm. "I'm sorry, Mike," she said. "I just hate feeling so far away from you. Especially after last night."

He grunted.

"And along those lines," she said quietly, "how about if I knock on your door again tonight after the children are in bed?"

She stiffened when she saw him look away from her and pause.

"I'm not sure that would be such a great idea," he said.

"Really?" She forced her voice to sound normal and calm. "Why not?"

He sighed. "It would upset Aideen if she knew."

"Aideen?"

"She says she's the future and there's truth to that. I'd be hurting her needlessly and for what? Another memory to put away in me memory book?"

Sarah couldn't help the feeling of jealousy, sharp as glass, which raked her skin. She removed her hand from his arm as if it burned her. "I see. So you two are still an item, I take it?"

"Are you asking me to hold off with her until after you leave, Sarah? Because it's not like you to be indirect."

"Oh, yes? How about *go to hell*. Is that direct enough for you?"

"WELL, YOU HANDLED THAT WELL." Fiona came out of the shadows. "I would've told you I was here except the two of you started going at it before I had the chance."

"And we all know how embarrassing that would have been for you."

"Okay, brother dear, do catch me up on what's happening because I think I've missed some important episodes."

"Fi..." he said warningly.

"If I heard correctly, you and the Widow Woodson finally did the deed? I only ask because I promised the camp I'd run the flag up the pole once it happened and I'd hate anyone not to make the money on their bets."

"You're pissing me off, Fiona."

Fiona laughed. "I'm sorry, but you do see the funny side of this, don't you?"

"Really? Is there one?"

Fiona took one look at the stark misery on her brother's face and the laugh fell from her lips. "Oh, Mike," she said. "I'm so sorry. I know this sucks."

"And then me own sister is voting for the plonker. Feck, he's probably English underneath it all."

"Maybe you declined Sarah's offer for a midnight visit too hastily," Fiona said, her eyebrows twitching impishly. "Sounds like you could really use a little relaxation technique or two."

"You know, what I could use is not hearing about sex from me own baby sister, if you don't mind."

"Suit yourself," Fiona said, picking up an empty fruit basket and heading back inside the cabin. "I do find it works wonders for Declan, though, after a frustrating day of dealing with camp yobbos and gobshites." She grinned as he groaned and turned back to his hut across the camp center.

THE MINUTE MIKE pulled open the door of his hut, he knew someone was inside. He braced himself for an attack, although he knew it was just as likely to be Aideen lying in wait.

Which it was.

She emerged from the darkened recesses of the room where she'd been sitting in the only chair in the hut and slipped into his arms. Although he didn't hold her, he didn't push her away either.

"I thought something had changed," she whispered into his ear. "At dinner. You were different with me."

"Was I?" Mike was tired but he had to admit the feel of Aideen in his arms, pressing against his hips, felt good. "Where's Taffy?"

"Still with the boys. So what made you change your mind?"

"Who says I have?"

She put a hand to his face and peered into his face in the half gloom. "Were you flirting with me at dinner to take the piss out of Sarah? Was that it?"

He pulled away from her. "I don't play games."

"Maybe not knowingly. But I picked up on the difference and I could see that she did, too. Is it because you finally realized that she's really leaving?"

Should he tell her he slept with Sarah last night? Wouldn't it just hurt her and what did it matter now? Was he trying to start with a clean slate with Aideen? Did that mean he *wanted* to start something with her?

She turned and maneuvered him easily into the armchair and slid onto his lap. She was light but substantial in the places that counted and Mike could feel his body reacting to her without his permission.

"She's *going*, Mike. I am here. She is yesterday and I am now." She lifted his chin and kissed him. He felt the heat shoot up his loins and his arms moved to capture her. When the kiss was done and she pulled back to look at him with obvious satisfaction, Mike felt a rush of guilt.

On some level, he'd been expecting to see Sarah's face. He

patted Aideen on the back to signal she was to rise and then he stood.

"I'm interested, Aideen," he said gruffly, not looking at her. "But not until Sarah's gone."

He finally looked at her to see the hurt in her eyes. But she nodded. "That's fine," she said. "But I'm not talking about a one-night stand, mind. I need a father for Taffy and a man to love and stand by me. I'm not playing games either, Mike."

He nodded. "Then we understand each other,"

DECLAN EASED himself through the broken slats of the milking shed. He figured it was a little after midnight although nowadays it was never easy to tell for sure. One of the cows made a deep lowing noise but settled down quickly when she acclimated to Declan's presence. At first he hadn't felt good about this. *Shite, I didn't even tell Fi. Now what does that tell you?* But he had to come. Not just to hear what the bugger had to say—he already knew Gilhooley's spiel front and back. No, he came because he was already on board.

"That you, Cooper?"

Declan grimaced. "Aye, it's me."

"Let's move away from the cow shite, eh?" Gilhooley slipped past Declan and led the way to a windowless anteroom on the other side of the line of stalls. Normally, Declan knew there was no need for this kind of secrecy. Each candidate would be well within his rights to meet publicly with his campaign advisor.

It just wasn't so straightforward when the campaign advisor was also the brother-in-law to the other candidate.

Gilhooley settled himself on the corner of the feed table and rubbed his hands together. "What's he thinking? All of this is bollocks to him, right? Am I right?"

"I told you," Declan said. "I won't spy for you. We'll win this right and proper."

"Of course, of course. I just wondered how much of a fight he intended to give me."

Declan shrugged. Mike hadn't made it much of a secret that he would do little to win the election. He supposed he could reveal at least that much.

"He won't campaign."

"Very good. We're as good as in, Coop. You know that, right?"

Declan hated when Gilhooley called him by a shortened version of his last name. Seemed a very American thing to do. He wasn't sure why it hit him wrong.

"Likely. Yes," he said.

"I need you to get your boys started on the new clink."

"Before the election?"

"That's right. We're wasting time as it is."

"But you're not in yet."

"I will be, you said so yourself. Get three men started. They can work at night. Donovan never goes in that direction after hours, does he?"

"Not if everything's quiet around the camp."

"And you always make sure it is."

"Well, he trusts me."

"As he should. Without you, he'd have to patrol the damn perimeter himself, wouldn't he?"

Declan had to admit he sometimes wondered how Mike had handled things before Declan came to the community. His job was to patrol the perimeter—or assign men to do it—and secure the camp. It was an unpleasant and fairly thankless job. And come to think of it, that was especially true where Mike was concerned.

"Coop?"

Declan looked at Gilhooley.

"The men?" Gilhooley pressed. "Can you get them on it? Quietly?"

The hell of it was, Declan thought Gilhooley's plans for securing the camp made sense. The fact that Mike wouldn't even listen to a different way of doing things was worse than arrogant, in Declan's opinion, it was irresponsible. He hated going behind Mike's back like this but Gilhooley had been right about that too: *sometimes you have to do things you know are wrong for the good of the community.*

He nodded.

"Good man," Gilhooley said, hopping down from the table and giving Declan a hearty clap on the shoulder. "Between you and me, we are going to have a community to be proud of."

9
_____

The man had both hands around the woman's neck. As Mike ran toward them he watched her claw at the hands, her mouth opening and shutting like a fish starving for breath before Mike could reach her. He gave the man a hard clout against the base of his skull and the woman fell at his feet with an elongated groan. When her husband turned to Mike, clearly ready to take him on until he saw who it was, his eyes went from murderous intent to shame in seconds.

Mike turned to the woman, Annie, who Declan already had in his arms on the ground. One of her eyes was blackened and the crimson red imprint of her husband's hand could clearly be seen against the stark white of her cheek. She looked at Mike and shook her head, her voice still too raw to be anything but a rasping whisper.

"Not his fault," she said.

Mike looked at her husband who now stood, his head hanging, his arms limp at his sides. If he had his way he'd take him out behind the tents and the huts and beat the living bejesus out of him. But it would only make himself feel better.

It wouldn't make one bit of difference for next time.

"All right, Annie," he said, holding out a hand to help her up. "Go see Fi for something for that eye. Go on, now. Me and Dec are going to have a word with Padraig."

"It wasn't his fault," she said again, more clearly, her eyes going from Mike to her husband.

"I heard you. Go on now."

He watched her as she stumbled down the gravel path toward Fiona's cottage. She looked back once, then turned and ran.

"You're a right sod, aren't you, O'Connor?" Mike said, fighting to keep his calm.

"She fell," Padraig said. "It was an accident."

"Dec, take this miserable piece of excrement to the holding hut. Pray he doesn't have an *accident*, himself, along the way, only I'll not fault you if he does. Things happen."

Declan nodded and took Padraig by the elbow then drove his fist hard into the man's stomach. Padraig groaned and bent over double retching. He fell to his knees.

"Oh, sorry, mate," Dec said. "My hand slipped."

Padraig struggled to his feet but he was looking at Mike as if expecting him to intervene or at least chastise his deputy.

Maybe I have been too lenient, Mike thought incredulously. *If this sod thinks I'll raise a hand to pull Dec off him, he must think I'm fecking soft in the head.*

"Don't look at me, arsehole," he said, roughly. "Blokes who beat women deserve every *accident* that comes their way."

Padraig looked at Declan with real fear and moved quickly ahead of him holding his stomach. Mike watched the two move toward the makeshift jail. *Bullies are always the biggest fucking cowards.*

He slapped his gloves against his thigh in frustration. *What was he supposed to do?* Maybe Gilhooley *should* take over the camp. Mostly it was just a huge pain in the arse babysitting operation anyway. He watched Declan's retreating back and could hear Padraig's beginning verbal protestations at being treated this way.

He'd be well and bloody happy to be rid of every whiny, cursed one of them.

FIONA WATCHED her brother come across the main courtyard of the camp. He looked like he had the weight of the world on his shoulders, she thought. At only forty, he looked old.

Annie O'Connor had left only moments earlier, a piece of cool liver on her eye and a cup of tea under her belt. Fiona liked Annie. She'd helped deliver her last bairn—one of the first to be born after The Crisis hit. Her husband was a different story altogether.

Fi stood in the doorway of her cottage with her hands on her hips as Mike climbed the porch steps. "That Padraig is a right bugger," she said. "But she wants him released."

"Aye, I know."

"He should be punished, Mike! This isn't the first time he's hit her."

"But the family needs him. He's a hard worker."

"When he's not hitting on her."

"What can we do? She married him. She's got three kids by him." He sagged into a kitchen chair and dumped out a leather roll of carving tools and a sharpening stone. She went to the kitchen to fetch another mug and poured tea from the pot on the table.

"Just makes me sick," she said.

"I know. But if I fine him or punish him in some way..."

"He'll just take it out on her."

"Exactly. Her only option is to leave him, if she will."

"She won't."

"Well, there you are then."

Fiona walked over to the window, paused and then waved. "You know Brian has been kissing babies and taking tea with every single family in the compound."

"I heard," Mike said with disgust.

"Might not hurt if you were to get out more."

"I'm not prancing about, Fi. If they want me, I'm right here."

"If you don't campaign, it'll just be Brian out there making promises and smiling all friendly like."

"These people know me. There's nothing new I can tell them about who I am."

"That's just it. Maybe they need to hear something new."

"Seems to me everyone was fine with the way we were doing things."

"That is true," she said carefully. "And it's also true that since the Middle Ages every village had its lord."

"I never acted too grand!"

"I'm not saying you did." Fiona turned from the window and sat down at the rough wooden table across from Mike. "And you've done immense good for all of us. There's not a man, woman or child who'd say different, but we've grown too big to be governed by one person without having a say."

"I always listened."

"And then went ahead and did what you wanted to do."

"Yes, I made decisions. Unpopular ones, sometimes."

"Mike, we need a voice in how we're governed, not a loving but firm despot. Now you can come to grips with that and campaign your arse off telling folks how things'll be different with you in charge...or you can step down. Continue on this way and you won't have a choice."

Mike grunted but didn't answer. "Who were you waving to? That bogger, Gilhooley?"

Fiona stood up again. "No, I saw Dec walking back to our place. I wanted him to know I was here."

After three sharp raps on the front door and before Fiona could reach it, the door swung open. Mike looked at his friend and frowned. It was unusual for him to come into the camp by day, unless it was to eat lunch with Fiona.

"Everything okay?" he asked.

Dec leaned over and gave Fi a kiss. "It is," he said. "I put O'Connor in the brig. Was all I could do not to drill a new hole in his head. He'll do it again, you know."

"Anything else?"

"I finished the inquiries on young Ollie. You were right. Sounds like he lashed out in a fit of anger and she zigged when she shoulda zagged."

"It was an accident?" Fiona asked.

Declan frowned. "Well, let's just say he didn't *mean* to kill her, but if he'd had better hold of his temper none of it would have been an issue."

"So it's manslaughter, not murder," Mike said.

"Whatever the difference *that* makes," Dec said with disgust. "Eeny is just as dead."

"Her family?"

"Wants his gonads nailed to a tree."

"They're devastated," Fiona said, sighing.

"Aye, but so is Ollie," Dec said. "And not just because his neck's in the noose either. He's beside himself with grief and guilt. He loved her."

"If you say so."

Declan turned to Mike. "We're lucky our two jailbirds aren't interested in busting out. The hut isn't secure. We need a better place of detention."

"We don't have the available men to build it."

"We would if we took them off plugging holes in the fence."

"No way," Mike said. "Our security comes first."

Declan sighed. "That's what I thought you'd say." His eyes turned to Fiona. His look was inscrutable. She knew he wouldn't argue with Mike any more on the topic. She also knew he wouldn't go along with it much longer either.

. . .

THE HEATHER WAS vivid and thick around Sarah as she rode Dan down the narrow path that led to her old cottage. The shades of mauve and purple seemed to move and meld into each other from both sides of the trail.

It had been too long since she'd saddled up just for the pleasure of riding. With so much to do in camp, taking a pleasure ride around the pastures and fields seemed like an extravagance she couldn't afford. That was especially true now that she was leaving within days.

But she was glad she'd forced the issue today. Not only would she be saying goodbye to all her friends—and Mike—but also to the big mixed thoroughbred, Dan, who had seen her through almost every important adventure of her life since The Crisis.

Seen her through and carried her through.

If there was any way she could take him with her, she would. A tall bay of nearly seventeen hands, Sarah had been literally terrified of him when she first realized he was her only form of transportation after the bomb dropped. Her fear—as a result of a riding accident in her teen years—had taken months to overcome. And Dan had done that for her.

Now, riding down the Irish country lane, feeling the slow rocking movement of his gait beneath her hips, she was reminded of how soothing it was to ride him. How, in almost every case of stress and panic she'd experienced in the last eighteen months, a long ride had almost always made things better. She looked over her shoulder at John, now nearly too big for his pony, Star, but too loyal to give him up, and Papin—never one for horseback riding but always open to doing whatever was necessary to please.

Well, almost always.

Sarah frowned as she watched Papin sit on her polo pony. She spent more time clutching the pommel than the reins but it didn't matter. Her pony, Jack, would take care of her. Something was wrong with Papin, that much Sarah knew. She just didn't know if it was teenage-girl-everything-blown-out-of-proportion wrong.

Or *really* wrong.

And with Papin's horrific childhood pressing in on her, that could be a pretty big distinction.

"Are we nearly there?" Papin asked in a bored voice. "Me bum's dead and I'm feeling queasy again."

"It's right up the road," John said. "Past those stone pillars there."

"We'll cut across the pasture here," Sarah said, dismounting. Nobody lived at the old cottage she and David used to live in, but the pastureland was still good and the fence was intact so the community used it for grazing. She unlatched the gate and swung it wide so the other two could pass through. Then she led Dan through, closed the gate and pulled herself back into the saddle.

"Wanna race, Papin?" John asked. "It's a good quarter mile yet and the land's flat."

"No," she said, gripping the pommel even tighter. "My luck ol' Jackie here will find the one divot in the whole field."

Sarah realized that Papin was more insecure than usual about riding. The two of them had covered nearly fifty miles last year on horses over countryside and never once did she see the girl gripping the pommel instead of the reins. Something had spooked her.

"You okay, Papin?"

The girl turned and grimaced at her. "Why wouldn't I be? Am I not keeping up or something?"

"No, you are. It's just that I noticed you seem a little hesitant."

"Because I won't race around the pasture like a damn *eejit* and risk getting my neck broke? Some mother you are! I'd've thought you'd want us to be careful." Papin dug in her heels on her pony, prompting it into a jerky trot, but Sarah noticed she didn't ungrasp the pommel.

They rode in silence until the small white cross was visible.

Planted by the fence on the very spot he died. Sarah would have preferred to bury him in the little church graveyard near Ballinagh, but she hadn't been around to make that decision.

John had decided where they would bury his father. She watched him as he jumped off his pony and walked to the grave.

"Oy, John," Papin said softly. "It's so sad and lonely way out here for himself."

John knelt by his father's grave and touched the white cross. "He liked it out here," he said, his voice so quiet, Sarah nearly didn't hear him. She slid to the ground and looped Dan's reins over his neck to lead him in closer.

The marker read, *David Woodson, Born 1969 Died 2013, Beloved Husband and Father.* Tears sprang to Sarah's eyes when she read the words again. They were John's words, in the middle of the worst time of his life having lost one parent and fearing the likely loss of another.

My darling David, I would give everything in this world if you were coming home with us, Sarah thought, her throat burning with the urge to weep.

"I wish I coulda met him," Papin said.

"He was a great guy," John said. "The greatest." He looked up at his mother. "Can we pray, Mom?" He stood next to Sarah and they both folded their hands.

"Lord, we know you look over our beloved husband and father," Sarah said. "And we pray he's with you in heaven waiting for us. Please let him know he's always in our hearts and that we'll remember him with love all the rest of our days until we can see him again."

"Amen," John said solemnly.

"Amen," Papin and Sarah said together.

BRIAN WATCHED the big gypsy pick up Donovan's sister and swing her in his arms before planting a lewd, wet kiss on her face. The sight nearly made him want to puke but he forced his face into the same lines of generous acceptance the rest of the community's members seemed determined to adopt. At least publicly. In private, he had plenty assure him the community members were as repulsed by the mixed marriage as he. *Did the woman have no pride? Had she been just desperate to marry?*

It was one more reason why the community had lost respect for Donovan. He should have intervened. He should have ensured the gypsy bastard never put his filthy hands on his sister. It was just one more reason why Brian was sure the community would vote Donovan out.

He turned to stack the last basket of beets on the little pony trap. The rest of the harvest, the all-important wheat for the bread that every family would depend on in the winter, would be gathered and winnowed in two weeks time. The tall sheaths of bound wheat studded the harvested fields all the way to the horizon.

The view was misleading, Brian knew, as the field was actually only about ten acres of wheat. Still, it had been a decent harvest. Next year, under his management, it would be much better, but still, they should survive the winter, if not comfortably, at least survive. He nodded at the driver of the cart, who tapped the pony's rump with a long whip and took off down the lane toward the community.

"Well, that's that, then," he said to Iain Jamison, who stood next to him wiping the sweat from his brow although, from what Brian could tell, he'd done very little that morning. "The harvesting done and the only thing left to do now but the celebrating."

"Without grog," Iain said and spit into the dirt.

"True. Maybe next year." He watched Cooper and his wife walk back to the community behind the pony cart. His stomach lurched when he saw the gypsy reach down and squeeze her buttocks. She squealed and trotted away, prompting Cooper to run after her. He could hear their laughter on the air and perversely felt a moment's longing to have his own darling Katie by his side, although he would never have dreamed to touch her in such a manner. Especially in public.

"Yeah?" Iain looked at him with interest. "You gonna bring back whiskey?"

Brian shook the wanton images out of his mind and began picking up the tools and raglan bags that had been used to haul the kale in from the fields. "That is one of my campaign promises."

"Yeah, well, most of us just hear the word *promises*," Iain said.

"I well understand after the man who's led you this last year. But *my* promises will be kept. We will celebrate next *Lughnasa* with beer and whiskey."

"Well, ya got my vote then."

"Actually, Jamison," Brian said, choosing his words carefully, "I was hoping to have something more from you." He waved to a very pregnant young woman who appeared out of the field, holding the hands of two small children. "Afternoon to you, Moira. Any day, is it?" She blushed and nodded before hurrying on.

"More how?" Iain said.

"I'll be needing a second in command, like."

"I thought that was Declan Cooper. The two of you're thick as thieves, yeah?"

"Cooper has been very helpful, that's true. But there are two reasons why I am not able to utilize him, I'm afraid, in a position of that kind of responsibility."

"I'll bet one of 'em has to do with the fact that he's a bloody wog," Iain said, throwing a pebble across the field.

"Although I would have phrased it differently," Brian said, "I admit, I don't think the people in camp could respect a man of his ethnicity."

"And the second reason?"

"Are you familiar with Shakespeare, Jamison? I'm specifically referencing *Othello*."

"That the one with the black guy?"

"Yes. There's a quote in it where Iago counsels Othello not to trust his beloved Desdemona, who lied to her father in order to be with Othello. Iago says: *Look to her, Moor, if thou hast eyes to see. She has deceived her father and may thee*."

"Okay."

"It means by lying to her father she revealed herself to be a liar."

Iain looked confused.

"Cooper has no difficulty in betraying Donovan."

"Oh, I get it. You don't trust him."

"Exactly."

"So what would the job be?"

"My thinking is that it would entail camp security, as Cooper is presently doing, only of course with the implementation of my new plans. And also camp discipline."

Iain shrugged. "Okay."

"I'll have to ease you into the role, so don't worry if it doesn't happen immediately upon my taking control of the camp. I have a timeline for everything."

"What did you say you did before the lights went out?"

"I worked in an office in Dublin."

"What kind of office?"

"That's not important," Brian said. "So, what do you think? Are you interested?"

"Free whiskey and a license to kick arse? Hell yeah, I'm interested. Sounds like it was fecking made for me."

"That's just what I thought." Brian said, clapped him on the back as they began the long walk back to camp.

TWO DAYS later the camp evolved from a largely muddy refugee tent camp to a bustling county fair, complete with livestock judging and pie baking contests.

Because Sarah hadn't lived there last year and had only heard about it from John, she was astonished to see the trouble and effort the community went to for the harvest celebration. Over the camp's main center fire pit a metal spit had been erected, on which hung the large hog that Mike and Iain had slaughtered the day before. Two men from Declan's clan flanked the slowly rotating pork, painstakingly basting and seasoning it as they would for several hours more until it was golden brown and falling off the spit in tender, juicy slabs.

Tables were set up in concentric arcs from the where the hog cooked in the center of camp, groaning with more food than Sarah had ever remembered seeing. Just to see so much filled her with a feeling of accomplishment at her part in it, and sadness that she was leaving it all behind. One table was lined with no fewer than ten berry pies—most still warm, having been pulled from ovens and cook pits that morning. Each pie would be judged before the day was out, the proud baker to strut about the festivities with a red ribbon of honor for her efforts.

Another of the gypsies—Declan's cousin—had found a beehive, and so all bakers had sweet honey for their pies and cakes, cookies and bannocks, puddings and grilling sauces. Another table was full of platters of roasted potatoes and crocks of fresh creamery butter and chives, squares of honeyed cornbread, and plate after plate of roasted carrots, parsnips, broccoli and cauliflower.

Beyond the food tables, Mike and some of the other men had set up competition sites for horse shoes, scarecrow making, pumpkin carving, sack races, tug-of-war, seed spitting contest, egg tosses, and an archery competition. On the other side of where the hog roasted, a long wooden stage was constructed.

As Sarah wandered through the festival, her mouth open with wonder and delight, six camp children clogged with force and gusto to the tunes played by a gypsy band of musicians, their shoes pummeling the wooden boards in time to the beat and creating their own musical tempo.

Papin and John had instantly melted into the crowd of laughing, happy people and Sarah let them go. This was a day for celebrating what they had done and to come together in fellowship for what they had all worked so hard for.

She, herself, had supplied three dozen cookies, sweetened with the gypsy honey, and even without baking soda or chocolate chips, they melted in your mouth and she was proud to offer them as her contribution. She put a plate together of stuffed eggs, pickled relish and still-warm bannocks dripping with butter and turned to find a seat for the horse race that would be the official beginning of the *Lughnasa*.

She waved to Fiona, who was sitting on a blanket with nearly forty other people on the outskirts of the camp. She knew Declan was one of the jockeys. Fiona was dressed in a toned-down version of her wedding dress. Her cheeks were flushed pink and her eyes sparkled as she strained to catch a glimpse of her husband on one of the horses.

Sarah settled down next to her. "Oh my gosh, this is so much fun," she said, offering her plate to Fiona, who waved it away.

"If you'd've told me at last year's *Lughnasa*," Fiona said, "that I'd be watching my *husband* race in the next festival, I would have thought you were completely crackers." She turned to look at Declan as he patted his horse's neck and prepared for the race. "And yet, here I am."

"Yes, you are," Sarah said. "Is Mike racing?" she asked innocently.

Fi wrinkled her nose. "Mike's too old for this sort of thing. He'd like to kill himself. They all cheat desperately, you know. And half of them try to flog each other or knock the other out of the saddle. It's mad fun."

"Yeah, sounds it."

Sarah hadn't exchanged a word with Mike since the night he turned down the pleasure of her company in his bed. Four days ago. She was sick at the thought that they had wasted the bulk of her remaining time in camp with a misunderstanding and now she was leaving tomorrow and all that was left to say was a stilted, rushed and very public goodbye.

It's true she'd been angry with him and it had taken her some time to unhook from that anger. But she missed him desperately. And the lack of communication after having had it for so long felt like the loss of a limb.

"Oh! There he is!" Fi said, gushing like a young bride. "Isn't he handsome?"

Sarah noticed Fi was totally absorbed in memorizing every inch of her husband as he rode to the starting line and that her hand went to her stomach without thought.

Oh, my, Sarah thought. *She's pregnant. Dearest, darling Fi is going to have a baby. And I'm going to miss it.*

"They're off!" Fi said, clapping her hands with delight. "Bloody hell, Dec's in the lead! I told him to pace himself. Now they'll all be targeting him. Go! Go! Go!"

Sarah got to her feet to see better and saw the cloud of dust and dirt that heralded the start of the horserace. As Fi jumped up and down in excitement, Sarah scanned the crowd of onlookers for Mike. When she spotted him, her stomach gave a delightful lurch as it always did when she saw him. So tall and oblivious to how truly gorgeous he was. She watched him push his long hair from his eyes and respond to someone who had spoken to him. He laughed, and when he did his whole face opened up. She remembered him doing that because of something she had said to him.

She remembered a very special night too...

"Sarah? Can you see them? They're coming around the corner. Can you see who's in the lead? Oh, I can't look!"

The riders were just visible coming from the north pasture.

They must have hooked back at the fork of the largest oak in the pasture to swing back to the finish line. Declan was indeed in the lead. Sarah could see his long legs wrapped around the middle of his big bay—it looked like he was riding Mike's gelding, Petey—and hunched down low to the horse's neck to allow the long galloping strides as little interference as possible.

"He's winning," Sarah said, grabbing Fi's arm. "He's in the lead!"

"Oh, please God he doesn't break his neck," Fi murmured, but her eyes were open as she watched him come thundering past them, just yards from the finish line.

Suddenly, the rider on the horse on Declan's far side swung out a shillelagh that hit Declan full in the face. Fiona screamed and began running toward the finish line, but Sarah could see that Declan stayed in the saddle. Her heart pounding and thinking they might need her testimony against the dirty rotten cheater who'd done such a foul thing, Sarah moved through the crowd toward the finish line.

While it was true she hadn't exactly seen *who* had smashed Dec with the club as he was coming down the stretch, surely it would be simple enough to determine it? The crowd of people blocking the way to the clearing had increased and it seemed as if they were all pressing in to get to the scene at the finish line. Sarah jumped up and down to try to see over shoulders and heads and pounded on backs for people to let her pass.

"I need through!" she yelled. "I saw who did it!"

"Bugger what you saw," one woman said to her. "The fecking gypsy was cheating and got put in his place. That's what we all saw."

Sarah was aghast this woman would speak so openly in such a way, and that nobody seemed to take exception to it. Was there racism in the camp and she wasn't aware of it?

"Fi!" she called. "I'm coming, Fi!"

Ducking down, she aimed for holes between elbows and

bodies and squirmed her way to the scene at the finish line. Mike stood at the rope that marked the finish and held the reins of Declan's horse. He was clearly trying to get people to move back and alternately growled and shouted at people by name. For a moment their eyes met, but she couldn't detect anything in the glance and he soon looked away and continued his attempt to get people to move.

Fiona literally hung on Declan's arm trying to drag him from the man who faced him, his hands up ready to fight. It was Iain. Declan's face was covered in blood, his nose obviously broken.

"You bastard!" Declan snarled at Iain, as he tried to unwrap Fiona from his arm.

Sarah saw Mike give up keeping the crowd at bay as he thrust the reins of his horse into someone's hands and took two steps to come between Iain and Declan.

"Stop it, the both of you," he ordered thunderously. "No fighting today."

"Tell him that," Iain said pointing at Declan with the most ridiculously false attempt at looking innocent Sarah had ever seen. She ran to him and grabbed his sleeve.

"I saw you!" she said.

"Sarah, stay out of this," Mike said. "You'll make it worse."

"What did you see?" Iain said, sneering. "You didn't see me. You saw nothing."

It was true. She had seen the club come swinging out and catch Declan, but she hadn't seen who swung it. She felt so impotent and helpless she wanted to punch him, herself. She felt a strong hand clamp onto her upper arm and haul her out of the center. Mike gave her a push that made her stumble to stay on her feet.

"What part of *stay out of it* is unclear to you?" he said harshly as he turned back to the two men.

She stood behind them, panting in anger and embarrassment as Mike spoke to the two men. When she looked around her, she could see faces in the crowd—faces she knew well as acquaintances if not friends—smiling smugly at her. In amazement, she realized some of these people had been waiting a long time for her to keep her comeuppance.

And they were enjoying it now at her expense.

When she deliberately turned her back on them and their smirks she saw Declan and Iain, if not exactly shaking hands, were walking away from the fight. She wasn't sure what magic words Mike had said to them, but whatever it was it worked. She watched as Fiona tugged her Declan back toward their cottage and when she looked to find Mike, she saw that he'd gone back to his horse and to speak to the person whose hands he'd shoved the reins into.

Aideen's.

Sarah watched as Aideen listened to Mike and nodded her head sympathetically. And then, when Mike turned to leave, Aideen looked up and caught her eye. And smiled.

The rest of the festival had lost much of its charm for Sarah. It was hours before Declan and Fiona returned, and then they were subdued and focused on each other. If it was true that Fi really was pregnant, it stood to reason they'd be even more focused inward than before. Sarah wouldn't intrude. She caught glimpses of Papin and John from time to time, mostly at the food table although a brief conversation with Papin revealed that John and Gavin had been on the sporting fields most of the day and that John had a bashed shinbone that would need to be dealt with eventually.

Sarah could see some of the men had gathered at a new table —one that rumor had it was stocked with a small amount of poteen, the homegrown whiskey from one of two stills in the camp. Up until now, the product from the stills hadn't been drinkable although most of the men had still sampled and served as guinea pigs. Armed with her new knowledge that perhaps she wasn't the most popular person in the community, Sarah sat alone in front of the clogging stage and let the music and the rhythmic pounding of the young people's hard shoes sooth and distract her.

When Papin finally found her and slumped down next to her, as exhausted as if she'd been one of the girls dancing the ages old Irish jigs on the stage, she came with a wee dram of the now-drinkable poteen which Sarah tipped into her tepid tea mug. It looked like Papin had sampled quite a bit of the new product, herself.

"Sleepy, sweetie?" Sarah said, patting her leg.

"Mmm-mm," Papin said, leaning on Sarah's shoulder. "Tell me when it's over."

It's over, Sarah thought as she looked up at the dancing children, her heart heavy. *It's definitely over.*

After the last dance and just before she intended to help Papin to bed and go find her son, Sarah hesitated as she saw Brian Gilhooley come out on stage after the children bounded from it. Everybody clapped wildly and cheered when he came out. Sarah couldn't believe how popular he was. She looked at the happy, flushed faces of the people around her. Everywhere she looked, she saw people whistling and cheering for this man.

There was no way he wasn't going to win tomorrow's election.

"Oy! Thank you everyone," Brian said. "And although not being the one to organize the *Lughnasa* or to take credit for the great harvest this year, I'm grateful for that vote of confidence. And as your candidate for leader of this fine community, I would just like to say, if elected I will do everything in my power to make sure you get everything that's yours—not just because you're a personal mate of the leader—but because you're a valuable member of this community. If elected, I will make sure that life is fair again, that celebrations have something besides barely drinkable swill to celebrate with..."

A cheer rose up and Sarah watched as Gilhooley waited patiently for the crowd to simmer down before continuing.

"...and that you are, each and every one of you, proud to call yourselves Irish in this new and changed world of ours!"

The crowd roared its approval, many people standing in the process, and Sarah could not believe they were being swayed by such bullshit language of jingoistic nonsense.

Gilhooley nodded and smiled and pointed to people in the crowd as if the knew them personally and wanted them to know they were special and then left the stage.

The crowd waited expectedly. Not only was it natural to assume that Mike—the other candidate and incumbent—would speak in rebuttal, but it was at least assumed that he would speak to them as master of ceremonies of the festival and commend them all on their hard work.

Sarah craned her neck to see if she could find Mike in the crowd or the audience.

"Isn't Da going to speak?" Papin asked sleepily

"I don't know."

As the murmuring of the crowd increased, punctuated now by a few titters as if off-color jokes were being passed around, Sarah saw movement to the side of the stage. She was stunned to see Aideen climbing the steps and striding on stage. She had to admit she was beautiful. Her complexion—all roses and cream—especially in the flicker of the campfire and the half moon over them—looked flawless and aglow. The crowd hushed to a complete silence in anticipation.

"Hello," Aideen said, her voice strong and warm and ringing with those cultivated tones that were neither English nor somehow Irish. "I'm here to speak to you on behalf of the other candidate who, frankly, is too modest to toot his own horn."

A few in the crowd laughed at that but Aideen ignored them. "Mike Donovan took care of me and my daughter at personal risk to himself," she said, speaking clearly and looking at each person in the first row of the audience. "He did that for me and I have seen him do that for many others. In talking with some of you since I first came here, I've heard story after story of how Mike Donovan has worked to protect you, feed you, and give you shelter.

"You know him. You know Mike Donovan. He's solid and he cares. I'm not saying anything against Mr. Gilhooley there, I'm sure he's fine, especially in the circles he comes from in Dublin..."

Sarah had to admire that dig. Most people in the community naturally did not trust outsiders and particularly not from Dublin.

"...but Mike Donovan is one of you. And when it comes right down to it, you can't buy that or make it. You might wonder why it is I, a relative newcomer, might know that. I know it because I have the special privilege of being able to announce tonight that I am officially engaged to Mike Donovan to be his wife. And as such, I will do everything in my power to help him be the best leader for you that it is in his power to be. Thank you. And God bless Ireland."

The applause, although not as riotous as when Gilhooley left the stage, was nonetheless warm and authentic. Papin woke up long enough to yawn and applaud.

Sarah sat with her mouth open, hands limp in her lap.

10

Mike *was engaged?*

Sarah worked to control her face as the crowd applauded and then moved on to the next interesting thing at the fair. She heard someone yell out that there was a scuffle going on behind the poteen shed and she watched Declan materialize from nowhere and head in that direction, his best *I will kick some arse if I have to* face firmly in place.

"Blimey, that was a surprise, wasn't it, Mum?" Papin said. "Or did you know about it?"

Sarah forced a smile and gave what she hoped looked like a casual shrug. "Not really. But I knew they were old friends."

"Well, a little more than friends, it looks like. I'm knackered, Mum. Are you ready to head back?" Papin stood up and began walking to the cottage before waiting for Sarah's answer.

"I'll be there in a sec," Sarah said to her retreating back. She stood up from her seat and immediately saw Fiona heading her way. By the look on her face, she hadn't known either. Which was good. Sarah couldn't take one more betrayal tonight.

"Oy, Sarah, you alright, then?" Fiona frowned in concern as

she reached out and touched Sarah's arm. "I swear I had no idea what the silly cow was about to say. None."

"I know. It doesn't matter," Sarah said wearily.

"Well, if you could see your expression, you wouldn't be surprised that I don't believe that. You look like you've been blind-sided."

Sarah glanced around at the people standing near her and realized the community's favorite soap opera, the *will-they-won't-they* saga of the American widow and the camp leader, had taken a decidedly delicious turn.

Fiona noticed too. "It's only because they don't have the telly to distract them any more," she said, glowering at a couple nearest them, who was openly snickering at Sarah. "Are you staring at *us*, Jimmy Dorsey?" she said sharply to the man in the couple. "Because I have a few juicy tidbits I could be sharing with the camp if you have a moment, as you seem to." The couple quickly turned and slipped away.

"It doesn't matter," Sarah said. "It was going to happen sooner or later anyway."

"Later would have been more sensitive, seems to me," Fi said, watching her friend with sad eyes. "I know I was teasing you about it, Sarah, but I didn't know it was this serious, not at all. You have to believe me."

"It doesn't matter," Sarah said again more firmly. "I'm outta here in two days' time. And if Mike wants to take one last swing at me because he's hurt and angry—"

"You know that's not Mike's way."

"Well, I'm sure he had his reasons for speeding things up. And as I am no longer a consideration for him—as I guess I shouldn't be—well, I'm the last person with a right to be upset."

"That's very mature of you, Sarah," Fiona said, tucking Sarah's hand under her arm and turning toward her own cottage. "There's no way I would be so reasonable were it my Dec who'd just announced his engagement to some skivvy."

"She *is* a skivvy, isn't she?" Sarah said, feeling tears close.

"Damn right she is." Abruptly, Fiona turned and corrected course.

"Where are we going?"

"My place for a strong cuppa," Fiona said a little too brightly.

"Then why are we going left? Your place is..." Suddenly Sarah saw why Fiona had tried to maneuver them onto a different course. Aideen and Mike stood thirty yards away, directly in their path. She saw Aideen rise up on her toes to kiss him, and while his hands stayed on his hips and didn't reach for her, the image burned into Sarah's brain as if he'd clasped the woman in a passionate embrace and kissed her deeply.

Her stomach lurched painfully and she felt her face flush hot. Mike turned his head and saw her. He spoke a few words to Aideen and then moved toward Fi and Sarah, his face serious, his eyes on hers.

"He's coming," Sarah said, her voice more of a squeak than she'd like.

"Oh, shite. Don't worry, Sarah, I won't abandon you."

Mike intercepted them quickly and without a word, reached out and plucked his sister's arm from Sarah's and pulled her away. "Off you go, Fi," he said, his eyes still on Sarah. "Sarah and I need a moment."

"No, we don't," Sarah said, reaching out for Fiona again. "I'm done for the night and Fiona was just walking me home." But Fiona was already moving away, giving Sarah a contrite look over Mike's looming shoulder as Mike took Sarah's arm and turned her away from the camp.

"I don't need or want an escort," Sarah said breathlessly. The recent image of Mike and Aideen—so intimate, so much a couple —was working to trigger a riot in her stomach. She needed to be alone so she could cry or scream into a pillow. It wasn't fair. He didn't get to ask for her blessing this soon after she'd been kicked in the gut!

"I want you to know that I had no idea that Aideen was going to say what she did," he said as he led Sarah away from camp and away from the noise and the music and her cottage.

"So, it's not true?" Sarah hated herself for the irrational surge of hope she felt when she said those words. "You aren't engaged to be married?"

A quick intake of breath stabbed to death any further hope along those lines.

He's trying to find a kind way to tell me.

"Aideen and I have an understanding," he said carefully.

Sarah stopped and turned to face him. As in control as he had acted up until this moment, it wasn't until now she realized he wasn't comfortable or at all confident.

"Does this *understanding* involve you and her getting married?"

He hesitated again.

"It's a simple fucking question, Mike. Are you engaged? Yes or no?"

"Yes."

"Great. That wasn't so hard, was it? Congratulations." She jerked her arm out of his grip.

"Sarah..." he said.

She could feel his helplessness, his despair rolling off him in waves. And it was infectious. It was seeing how unhappy he was that ignited the fuse in her brain, unfurling the bud of fury that had been there all along just under the surface.

And being pissed as hell felt a whole lot better than wanting to curl up in a corner and die.

"So let me see if I have things straight. You turned down my invitation for a last night together to spare Aideen's feelings, yet you let her humiliate *me* in front of the whole community?"

"I told you, I didn't know she was going to say anything tonight. Especially not in front of the whole fecking camp."

She watched his discomfort give way to a defensive stance.

His hands were on his hips now. He shifted on his back foot, away from her as if ready to swivel on it and leave. In fact, it occurred to Sarah that if Aideen could see the two of them right now there was no way she would be jealous about anything they might be saying.

If anything, she would be crowing.

Sarah's anger surged. "You have made this so much easier for me, Mike Donovan," she said, trying to keep her voice down but feeling the anger build in her chest like a churning thunderhead. "Showing me this late in the game who you really were all along. I want you to know that I'll be happily remarried within the year to someone who's everything I thought *you* were. Whoever he is, I can wait."

Mike looked like he'd been punched, and for a moment Sarah felt a needle of guilt at hitting her target so accurately.

"Sure, no harm in waiting," he said, recovering, his eyes hooded and unrevealing. "Some of us do it all the time."

"I wish you every joy on your wonderful news and please do not hesitate to clinch the deal on my account. I'll be gone before you have time to hang out the bedclothes."

"Thank you for permission to sleep with my own fiancée. It'll mean so much more to me when I finally get her under me that it was with your blessing."

Before the words were completely out of his mouth, her hand jerked out to slap him across the face, but he caught her hand midair.

"You don't get to be mad at me for finding love when you're leaving," he said, his eyes flashing, his grip tightening on her wrist. "If you wanted me to be yours, you know you only needed to say the word."

Fury pumped through her. "How about if I tell your *intended* that she's second place? How about if I tell her she's only with you because I'm not available?"

"She knows that."

The energy drained out of Sarah and she let her hand go limp where he held her.

"Shit."

"I'm sorry, Sarah."

"Oh, shut up."

"There was no way you leaving was going to be easy for anyone."

"Just leave me alone, Mike."

She turned from him, hoping he wouldn't touch her, praying he would. After a moment, she heard his footsteps as he moved away back to camp.

THE NEXT MORNING, Mike sat on the porch of his hut. Even with the harvest over, there was still plenty to do, but Fi was right. It didn't look good for him to totally ignore the election. For reasons he couldn't fathom most of the members of the community were excited to cast their vote for who would lead the camp. He watched them line up and approach the table that Fiona and Declan had set up in front of the main cook fire at the center of the camp.

Gavin jumped onto the porch next to him and settled down on a step. Mike glanced at him. "So did you vote?"

"Aye. I mean, I know you always say this isn't a democracy, but here we are voting. Pretty cool, huh?"

Mike grunted. He scanned the line of people waiting to cast their ballot and found himself growing angry. Some of these people he had literally carried on his back to get them to this place. And here they were, shrugging him off for the first shiny new face that came along. These were his friends, hell, his *family*. He glanced at Gavin again. He had no doubt his own son had voted for that bogger, Gilhooley.

He watched as Sarah walked up to the table and handed Fiona a cup of tea. She had not been allowed to vote since she was soon to be leaving the community. It hurt just to look at her. To think that this is the way they would end, the way they would say goodbye, after everything that's happened just turned his stomach sour. As he watched her lean over to whisper something in Fiona's ear and then turn and walk back to her cottage, he never took his eyes off her, the way she moved, the lines of her body as she moved away from him. Ever away.

"Oh, hey, Missus," Gavin said, hopping up from the porch, his hands suddenly awkward appendages he clearly didn't know what to do with. Mike turned to see Aideen appear from the narrow alleyway between his hut and the one next to it.

She held out her hand to Gavin to prompt him to pull her up onto the porch with him, which he did, but not before stumbling and nearly landing both of them in the violet patch at the base of the porch. Aideen laughed good-naturedly and Mike found himself grateful for her uncomplicated, good humor. As much as it killed him to give up one single night with Sarah, it still felt like the right thing to do.

"Morning, Aideen," he said, shifting over on the bench to allow room for her. "I suppose you've voted this morning?"

"I did," Aideen said, settling down next to Mike, her hip squeezing into his leg as she did. "But I'm afraid I have bad news along that score."

"Get a peek at the ballot box, did you?"

"I didn't have to. I got a peek at your sister's face. She's doing the counting."

"Right."

"I just didn't want you to be shocked should things not go your way, Mike."

Mike laughed bitterly. "That's not what would shock me. I expect to lose."

"Well, I think it's rotten. After everything you've done for them."

"Dad? I'm heading out to check on the jail. I told Dec I'd feed the prisoners while he's handling the ballot box."

"Be careful, son. They don't look dangerous, I'll grant you, but desperate people can do desperate things."

Mike watched Gavin stride away.

"You're talking about poor Ollie?" Aideen said, slipping her hand under Mike's and entwining her fingers in his.

Mike grunted. He craned his neck as the line to the voting table shortened. "Where is that sod, Gilhooley? I thought he'd be waving flags and getting the band ready to play his victory march."

"He left last night."

Mike turned to look at her. "What the hell are you talking about?"

Aideen squeezed his hand. "I thought you knew. He went to Dublin to bring his family back."

Mike stared at her and then turned to look at the last of the voting crowd. "The cheeky bugger. He didn't even wait around for the fecking votes to be counted. He's that sure." A weight seemed to settle on his shoulders and he sagged where he sat. "Shit. I'm that sure, too."

An hour later, Declan stood in the center of camp and announced that they had a new leader, one Brian Gilhooley. Most of the camp gathered in front of him and applauded politely when he made the announcement.

Mike hadn't moved from his bench on his porch. He watched Fiona as she stood behind her husband. She turned to catch his eye a few times. He did not let that happen.

"As you know," Declan said to the gathered crowd, "Gilhooley's in Dublin collecting his family. Mike Donovan will continue as camp leader until Brian gets back. Brian wanted me to thank everyone for your vote of confidence and announce that, starting immediately, every family will begin receiving an extra pound of flour and sugar."

Mike snorted. "That means they'll run out of bread by Christmas."

"I thought the camp had no sugar," Aideen said.

"We don't. But everyone'll receive an extra pound of the nonexistent sugar. Listen to the idiots cheering. Where do they think he's going to get the damn stuff?" Mike shook his head.

"I'm sorry, Mike."

"Yeah, it doesn't matter."

Declan waved everyone to silence. "Now, the first project of Brian Gilhooley's tenure will be the building of a proper detention hall..."

"What's he talking about?" Aideen whispered.

"A jail."

"...followed soon after by the forming of a defensive army to protect us here. All able bodied men over the age of fourteen are welcome to apply. And one more thing..." Declan waited with his hands raised for the crowd to quiet down.

Mike had to hand it to him. The gypsy knew how to make the most of a dramatic presentation.

"From this day forward, the community will have a new name."

Mike heard the murmuring of the crowd grow louder with anticipation.

"Our new name," Declan said, "will be Daoineville."

The cheers that followed Declan's proclamation were louder and more frenzied than Mike remembered hearing at the last World Cup football playoffs.

SARAH DRAGGED the Pullman out from under the bed. She had bought it at an outlet store in Atlanta a few months before she and David and John had left on vacation. In the meantime, it had only been used once in a transatlantic flight, but it had been pulled out of a fire and dragged by pony cart to three different cottages. She smoothed a hand over the rough canvas. Both David and John's luggage had been destroyed in the fire at Cairn Cottage within months of their arrival in Ireland.

For a moment, she had a flash of the afternoon she bought this bag. She remembered the store, the hours it took for her to select just the right bag, and the excitement she felt in anticipation of the trip. She sighed and zipped up the empty case. She had already decided not to bring any clothes with her. The women in the camp could use whatever she didn't take. They'd put this bag to good use too.

"Mum?"

Sarah turned to see Papin standing in the doorway. There was something about the expression on her face that didn't look right. Sarah frowned and turned away from the bag. "Are you all right, Papin? You look sick." She reached her hand out to touch the girl's forehead but Papin dodged her.

"I'm fine, only Auntie Fi's asked me to tell you John's to bunk in with Da, and me with herself so's Brian's family can have our place when they come. Can they do that? Just bung us out in the street?"

Sarah looked over Papin's shoulder to the bustle of the camp outside. She sighed. "I thought your da was giving this place to Aideen and Taffy?"

Papin shrugged. "I just know what Auntie Fi told me. You're to go to the Widow Murray's. She says it's just for the night. Is that right? Are we leaving in the morning?"

"Two nights," Sarah said. "We'll leave Wednesday morning early. Your da's arranged to have old Jimmy Dorsey take us."

"Why can't he take us, himself?"

Sarah felt very tired. "Well, now that he's no longer camp leader, maybe he can," she said.

"You and him broke up, didn't you?"

"I'm not sure we were ever together."

"That's weird."

"What's weird?"

"Nothing. It's just that it's not like you to out and out lie like that."

Sarah's mouth fell open. She wanted to respond sharply to her. Tell her to watch her tongue, respect her elders...but she knew she couldn't. *Papin was right.*

Papin grimaced and sat down on a wooden chair as if her legs suddenly gave out on her. "When you first told me about him? You know, in Wales?"

Sarah nodded.

"I thought you were in love with him. You talked like you were."

"You're confused, Papin. I'd just lost my husband."

Papin shrugged. "Just saying what it sounded like to me."

Sarah couldn't help notice how pale Papin looked. She was almost positive she could see the girl's hand was shaking.

"And then all year long everyone's asking me when you two were getting married or at least moving in together and I was totally clueless. You could tell you were a couple in every other way, you know?"

Sarah turned to the sink to fill the teakettle and set it on the stove although it was cold. "I guess that's what it looked like," she said.

"Only now, he's snogging old Aideen and we're pissing off to America like nothing ever happened."

Sarah forced herself not to react to the image of Mike *snogging old Aideen.* "Things don't always turn out the way we think they will."

"Only this time it's not *things turning out* a certain way, but *you* making them *be* a certain way."

"I thought you wanted to go to the States."

"I do."

"But?"

"But I thought you loved Da."

Sarah looked at Papin and heard what the girl was really asking: *What about the next time you tell me someone is important to you?*

"Go tell John to get his things, will you? Unless you'd rather lie down. You look all in, sweetie."

Papin stood up slowly. "I wouldn't mind a wee kip," she said, her voice soft and heavy with disappointment.

Bugger, Sarah thought as she heard Papin's bedroom door close.

Bugger, bugger, bugger.

AFTER MIKE SETTLED young John in on a bedroll in the front room of his small hut, he stood out on his porch, smoking and surveying the camp. The gypsies alternated between monopolizing the main cook fire—to sleep, play music, cook—or they kept to themselves for weeks at a time at the south end of the camp. It bemused Mike that there was no real set pattern to their schedules or behavior. Sometimes they were there, and sometimes they weren't.

Tonight, a few of the gypsy men had dropped their bedrolls in front of the fire. One of them had a guitar and the soft strumming melody caught on the summer evening breeze and crept into every cottage and tent in the camp.

He and John had eaten at Aideen's tonight. It had been a quiet meal, with Aideen clearly afraid to put a foot wrong in front of her main rival's son. Mike knew she needn't have worried. John had many things on his mind tonight but Aideen Malone wasn't one of them. Before they'd left for dinner, John had revealed to Mike that he'd done everything but beg his mother to reconsider leaving.

"Surely, that's a bit of an exaggeration," Mike had said to the boy, grinning. John was very different from his son, Gavin, but

Mike always surprised himself to realize that he loved John Woodson every bit as much. The lad was smart. And whereas it was true Gavin could easily find his way out of a woolen jumper given some advance notice, brains were not what one first thought of when describing him.

The singular intelligence in John's eyes always belied the fact of his years. *Speak to him longer than ten minutes and you'll forget he's a kid.* How many times had he told Sarah that? He smiled ruefully and stepped off the porch, his heart aching in his chest. God, he was going to miss that boy.

Declan waved to him from the porch of his own cottage and jumped off the deck, heading toward him. They hadn't spoken since the news of the election. As far as Mike was concerned, it had always been clear who Declan wanted to lead the camp.

And that hurt.

"Mr. Cooper," Mike said, nodding to Dec as the two met by the fire. "May I interest you in a post-election tot?"

"You got booze?" Declan asked.

"No, but there's always the swill from the still."

Declan made a face. "I get a bigger high from me cuppa. And it tastes like petrol."

"That it does."

The silence bloomed between them and Mike let it stay. He had something to say to his brother-in-law and he didn't consider having him comfortable as the most ideal condition to hear what he had to say. Just before he was about to speak, he noticed Sarah slip out of the shadows. The flickering firelight played shadows against her face as she moved toward Mike's hut.

Mike waited until she was in earshot and then called to her. "Sarah, love. If you're going to stay goodnight to yer boy, he's already asleep." He watched her stop and then hesitate as if she might just go on anyway or turn and leave the way she'd come. He held a welcoming arm out to her, and after the briefest of pauses, she joined them at the fire.

"You all tucked in at the Widow Murray's?" he said.

"The woman doesn't speak English," Sarah said.

"She speaks Gaelic."

"If you say so."

"I'm glad you wandered by, Sarah," Mike said, keeping his voice light and casual. This was the first time the two had spoken since she'd berated him for his engagement.

He turned to Declan. "Dec, you remember what happened when we executed Caitlin's bloke, Aidan?"

Declan looked up in surprise. Mike could tell he hadn't expected a discussion on the upcoming execution—although it was clear to Mike by the way the man trudged through the motions of his day lately that he'd been thinking of little else.

Aidan Walsh was the boyfriend of Mike's sister-in-law, Caitlin. Late last year he'd been found guilty in the murder of Sarah's husband, David. Caitlin was exiled from the community for her involvement.

But Aidan had been hung.

"Do you not remember the shadow that came over the whole camp for *months* afterward?" Mike put a hand on Sarah's shoulder and was surprised to feel she was trembling. "Was it healing, Sarah? Did it help your grief at all?"

"No."

Mike turned back to Declan. "The killing of another human being...when you *have* to do it, in a fight for your life, that's one thing, but to take a life in the name of justice, well, I'm not sure any of us is qualified for that, eh?"

"You were there, too, Declan," Sarah said. "You have to remember what it was like after Aidan...died. And for me and John, it was worse. I didn't feel like David was avenged or anything like that. I just felt sick. Like I was no better than his killers."

"Maybe it was the way we did it," Declan said. "We hung Aidan with him screaming and kicking and shitting all the while." He shook his head. "Maybe if we did it more gentle like."

"What Ollie did is what they call a crime of passion." Mike waved down the start of an argument from Declan. "Now before you go taking that wrong, I'm not letting him off the hook for what he did. It was murder and he should pay for the taking of a life."

"But not with his own life."

"I just don't see how that helps."

"Maybe you should ask Eeny's folks if it helps. Maybe *they* should be the ones to decide."

Mike was tired. He looked to Sarah but saw she'd already given up on the outcome of the discussion. And why wouldn't she? After tomorrow, she was no longer a member of the camp.

"Besides," Dec said, "it's not up to us. Or you, anymore."

"Aren't I a part of this community? You're so determined to be democratic and making sure everyone gets a say, so why are you just going along with what Gilhooley says? Seems like that's no difference than when I was in charge."

"I still think what he says makes sense."

"Ollie's just a boy."

"And Eeny was just a girl. A girl who'll never get a chance to grow into a woman now thanks to him."

"Banish him, Dec. Turn him out on his own, but don't kill the poor sod."

"Not up to me, Mike. I'm thinking now I'm kind of glad about that."

"Except it'll be you who puts the rope around his neck. The rest of us can go back to our huts and pretend it never happened. It'll be you who looks into his eyes then snuffs the light out of those eyes."

"Brian says he wants everyone gathered for the hanging. Kiddies too."

Man turned and spat in the dirt. "Man's a monster."

"Mind you don't let Muffin out when you use the bog at night."
The older woman sat rigidly on the old sofa stroking a large
orange tomcat that had one ear chewed off.

"I'll be careful, Mrs. Murray," Sarah said, lighting a lantern
and adjusting the wick. The camp was low on kerosene and she
was surprised to see the old woman had any at all. *Must usually be
in bed before it's dark*, she mused as she turned to survey the small
cottage interior. It wouldn't be wonderful but for two nights, it
beat sleeping in a bag by the fire, which she assumed was her
only other option.

Sarah had grumbled about clearing out before Brian and his
family arrived. But Fiona insisted she needed the extra time to
make it fit for him.

*She's lucky I'm not the sensitive sort when it comes to my house-
keeping*, she thought, feeling another in a long endless line of
stabs to the heart when thinking about her friend and all that she
would soon miss about being here. She set the lantern down on
the table next to the sofa where Siobhan Murray was squinting at
a crossword puzzle over the cat's purring body. Sarah could see
the puzzle had already been filled in—probably months ago.

"I'm just going to step outside for a little air."

"You don't have to tell me when or where you go," Mrs.
Murray sniffed without looking up. "I'm sure it's none of my
business."

Sarah didn't know how to respond to that so she let herself
out of the cottage and stood on the rickety front porch. The old
widow's cottage was situated at the back of the camp, nearly a city
block from the center where the main cook fire was. It was darker
this far back, too, for that reason. On the other hand, it was
quieter.

The only thing behind the row of shacks, tents and falling
down cottages was a small pasture and a line of fir trees that

stood at attention guarding the back of the little community. It surprised Sarah that Mrs. Murray felt comfortable back here. With nothing but field behind them, it felt very exposed to her.

Sarah settled down on the top step and strained to catch the sounds of the gypsies' music as it lofted gently in the night air. *One more night after tonight*, she thought, *and then we're gone.*

She hadn't been sure what to expect when Mike called her over to him this evening. The truth was she wasn't sure how she would react to him either. To have him behave as if nothing had happened, as if she weren't about to leave for good, or that he wasn't engaged to marry someone else, had been almost as bad as if he'd made a scene. She knew him well enough to know he felt it. Unlike the gushy, demonstrative American, he just didn't show it.

A sound caught her attention on the narrow gravel path that led to the interior of camp and, because she'd been thinking of him, she irrationally jumped to the hope that it was Mike. A moment later, she could pick out the distinctive business-like lope of Fiona hurrying up the dark path toward the Widow Murray's cottage.

"Evening, Sarah! I hoped I might catch you still awake."

As Fiona reached the porch steps, Sarah saw that she carried two mugs of tea.

"This is a nice surprise," Sarah said, reaching for one of the mugs. "I guess Declan lets you out this late when you have company?"

Fiona laughed. "Trust me, he doesn't care *who's* in the house when he's in the mood." She sat down next to Sarah. "No, I just wanted to have a quiet word with you before things got crazy tomorrow."

"Things are going to get crazy tomorrow?"

Fiona shrugged. "Well, I guess it's more like we haven't really had much time together since the harvest and now you leaving so soon."

Sarah sipped her tea. If Fiona had something to say, she'd do it in her own time.

"I wanted to be the one to tell you that Declan and I have some very special news to announce."

Sarah put her mug down and put her arms around Fiona. "I think I already know," she said. "It is just the best news ever. How far along are you?"

Fiona patted Sarah's back and when she pulled away, Sarah could see the elation in her face. Her eyes sparkled and her cheeks were flushed with color "I don't know exactly, mind, but he or she'll be born in January, which isn't the best time but can't be helped."

"I am so happy for you, Fi. Both you and Dec. Mike doesn't know yet?"

Fiona shook her head. "I wanted to tell you first."

Impulsively Sarah reached over and touched Fiona lightly on her stomach. "I hate that I'm going to miss meeting her. Or him."

"I know."

There was a comfortable silence between the two as they resumed drinking their tea.

"I have to say, though," Fiona said quietly, "that it's given me some new perspective on you leaving."

"How so?"

"I can see why you'd do anything to make sure John had the most he can have. I get it."

"A mother's sacrifice," Sarah said wryly with no humor in her voice.

"I get it," Fiona repeated. "And I also wanted to take the time to tell you..." She took a long breath as if for courage and for a moment, Sarah braced herself for what she might say.

"I wanted to say, in case time got away from us, how much I have enjoyed your friendship these past eighteen months." She reached out and took Sarah's hand. "You are the closest thing to a sister that I'll ever have."

"And you, me," Sarah said, her eyes filling with tears.

"I'll never forget you," Fiona said, her voice shaking now, "and if you write, I'll write back until...until things get sorted out again."

"And one day I'll come back," Sarah said.

"I know. Come back with John to show us what a fine young man he's grown into. Probably a Don or Professor or some such thing. He's so smart, we'd none of us expect anything less from him."

"I will. You know I will."

Fiona leaned over and patted Sarah's hand, both their tea mugs empty now. "There's just one more thing I need to tell you and this one's a tough one."

"Tougher than saying goodbye for almost forever?" Sarah frowned.

"It's about Papin."

Sarah moved her hand from Fiona as if she might need it to grip something in order to hear what Fi would say. "Did the two of you talk? Did she tell you why she's been acting like a little shit for the last while? What's going on?"

Fi took another breath and then retrieved Sarah's hand holding it in both her own. "Well, there's no easy way to say it. She's up the pole, petal, and that's pretty much the long and short of it."

11

D eclan stood with his hand on the latch to the jailhouse door. He took a breath, straightened his shoulders, and jerked open the door. It wasn't a pleasant place. It wasn't designed to be.

His cousin stood up from a crouching position over by the far wall. Declan wasn't worried. He had heard the poor bastard's sobs from halfway down the path leading to the jail. Up until today he'd let Gavin feed and tend to Ollie. But he knew he was just putting off the inevitable. Sooner or later he had to deal with him.

"Pull yourself together, man," he said to Ollie as he entered the room. Originally a two-stall stable, the room was divided in half by thin wood planking that had had a hole kicked into it by some horse. The straw bedding had long been stamped to incorporate into the hard, dirt floor.

He'd let Padraig out within hours of detaining him for beating his Missus. There wasn't any point in keeping him. *It sure as shite wasn't going to make him stop.* And hanging onto him would only ensure poor Annie got it even worse when he finally got home.

Still, Padraig wasn't a bad sort and Declan was sure his company in the little jail had given some comfort to poor Ollie.

"I was afraid you wouldn't come, Dec," Ollie said, wiping his snotty nose with a sleeve. He wasn't even out of his teens, Declan knew.

"You'll likely be sorry I did," Declan said going over to him and starting to unknot the restraints.

"Is today the day, then?" Ollie's voice seemed full of hope.

"The day?" *Did the daft bugger think they were letting him go?*

"The day you hang me."

Declan's fingers stilled for a moment and he looked in his cousin's face. "Jazus, Ollie,.Why the hell did ya have to kill her?"

"I didn't know! I wasn't thinkin' right!" Ollie's face screwed up into a terrible visage of agony and Declan jerked the boy's hands free of his bonds to distract him.

"All right," he said. "Although it smells like you've been happy to piss right where you sleep."

"I loved her, Dec," Ollie said, hiccoughing with renewed tears as he stumbled after Declan through the open door. "I loved her like my life. To think I coulda hurt her, that I killed her..."

"Well, you did kill her, right enough. Here then, go piss against that tree."

Declan stepped away from the boy and got a flash of what it would feel like the day he put the noose around his neck. He flinched and wiped a heavy hand across this face as if to erase the vision.

"What happened, exactly?" he asked tiredly. The details didn't matter. Nothing could save him. The boy would die in two days' time no matter what. Gilhooley had made that clear.

"Eeny was mad at me," Ollie said, turning back toward Declan. His arms hung limply at his side as if he didn't have the strength or the will to lift them.

"Why?"

"I did something stupid and fecked."

"You cheat on her?"

"Is it cheating when it's just a blow job? Or not much more?"

Declan almost wanted to smile. He was so young. "I'm sure it counts as cheating," he said, motioning the boy back toward the hut.

"She just went mental, saying I was a feckin' cheater and had betrayed her and on like that. I felt guilty, you know? I just wanted her to shut up, only she was right to say the things she did. I just wanted them not to be true so I tried to get her to stop saying them."

"I'm sorry, lad. Has your mother been over to see you?"

Ollie nodded miserably. "She says I've disgraced the family."

"Is that all?"

Ollie looked at Declan, his face a mask of shame and pain. "She says she still loves me."

This just sucks every way that it can suck, Declan thought as he motioned him back inside.

"I'm sure she does. And I know you're sorry it happened."

"I *want* to die. I *want* them to hang me."

"Go on, now, boyo. In you go. Nothing's happening today."

"Tomorrow then? Only it would help to know."

"Not tomorrow either," Declan said. He took a shallow breath in defense against the rank smell of the interior of the hut and picked up the rope.

"Soon, though, right? You'll do it soon?"

Declan fastened the rope around Ollie's wrists, already rubbed raw, and looped the end through a metal ring fastened to the stall wall.

"Don't worry about when, Ollie. If you've got a mind to do it, though you might pray. It can't hurt."

"Not for my life. I won't pray for my life."

"Maybe just for peace or forgiveness. I don't know. Mind you don't piss in here again, yeah? Or I'll make you clean it up."

"Okay, Declan. Thanks, mate."

For what? Declan wanted to say. *For washing me hands before I put the rope around your neck?* He shook the image out of his mind and exited the stall before Ollie could say anything more. He threw the bolt and locked the door and found himself jogging to get away from the place.

THE THREE WOLF puppies—two males and a female—bit and pawed at the basket that contained them. They had rough dark brown fur and big dark eyes. Their tongues lolled around in their mouths in between the playful snapping they launched at each other. Mike still couldn't believe they were real. Had there been any wolves in Ireland in the last seven hundred years?

"Where in the name of God did you find them?"

John grabbed one of the wolves before it escaped from the basket and shoved it back inside. "Whoa! That one nearly got me! You see those teeth? We're talking sharp."

Gavin dragged the wooden cage over to where Mike and John sat with the puppies. When John had come to get him to see something outside the camp, for some reason Mike thought it was an edible plant or maybe a broken snare. He should have known when John wouldn't tell him what it was that Gavin had to be involved.

And it had to be something daft.

"Did you just find them in the woods? Is that possible?" Mike stretched a hand out to the basket and all three puppies attacked it with their tongues.

"Is that what John told you?" Gavin said, grinning. "Yeah, that'd be the luck, wouldn't it? No, Da. We got 'em for trade when a bloke came by the came this morning."

"What bloke? When did somebody come by the camp?"

The rules were clear about strangers approaching the community. If any did they were to be immediately brought to Mike.

Obviously the rules of the old regime had been quickly scuttled.

"He was just a trader, like, Da," Gavin said in his best scoffing tone. "He said he'd run into Brian on the way to Dublin and that he was to bring this lot straightaway to us."

"*Brian* told him to give you fecking wolves?"

"It's for the camp's defense, Uncle Mike," John said, scooping up one of the puppies and cuddling it in his arms. "Mr. Gilhooley says we can train them. Other places are doing it. People have been bringing 'em over from the UK to train as guard dogs."

"He is totally off his nut. That is the craziest idea I ever heard of."

"Brian said you'd say something like that."

"Watch your mouth, boy." Mike stood up from the crouch he'd assumed to examine the dogs and straightened his back. With dinnertime almost upon them, the temperature had dropped and so had the light. "Who knows anything about training wolves? It's insane."

"Well, if other places are doing it, we can learn to do it too."

"What did you trade for the puppies if I may be so bold as to ask?"

Gavin looked at John as if to warn him to keep his mouth shut. He shrugged. "Brian had already given the bloke whatever he needed for 'em," he said.

"They're not living with us," Mike said. "And they're not getting any of my meat ration, either."

"It's for the good of the camp!" Gavin said.

"Bullshite."

"John!"

Mike turned in the direction of the camp entrance one hundred yards away. "Is that your mum, John? Sounds like she's looking for you."

John stood up, still holding the little female he'd picked up. "But who'll take care of the puppies?"

"They're all going back to our place for the night any way," Gavin said reaching for John's dog. "Go see what she wants."

"They are not coming back to our place," Mike said. "I'll not have whining and crapping and peeing all night long—at least not any more than I have to put up with living with the two of you."

"Da, please! John and I'll take all the care of them."

"We will, Uncle Mike. You won't have to do a thing."

"John! Are you outside the camp? Answer me!"

Mike gave John a gentle push toward the camp. "Go on now before she sends out the militia. The dogs'll be back at our place when she's finished with you."

John grinned and handed the dog to Mike before dashing off in the direction of Sarah's voice. Mike looked down at the little wolf, who promptly licked him in the face and whimpered.

"Jaysus, Joseph and Mary," he muttered, wiping off his cheek. "Whatever the hell next?"

"Da, can you carry the cage back to our place? Now that John's buggered off, I can't do both."

"I reckon that's what you'll say when he climbs on that helicopter day after tomorrow, too, Gavin. How are you going to handle these three on your own?"

"I can do it, Da. Brian has a book on training 'em."

"Right. Because you are so good with rubbish you learn out of books." But he handed the puppy to Gavin and bent down to pick up the cage. When they turned back to the camp entrance, Mike was surprised to see the new addition of a large white sign that was nailed to the gateposts. He stopped to stare at it.

"It's Mary Collins painted it," Gavin said, seeing where he was looking. "She used to do computer graphics before the bomb but she has a fair hand at drawing letters."

The letters were stark black against the white background of the back of a placard. It had once been a sign in Ballinagh, Mike knew. In another life, it had hung over the hardware store entrance.

It read, *Welcome to Daoineville*

"It just made sense to change the name, you know?" Gavin said. He kicked at the dirt with the toe of his trainer and hoisted the basket of puppies higher into his arms.

Mike grunted.

"*Daoine* is Gaelic for people," Gavin said.

"Mebbe. But adding ville to the end is just barking."

"Well, at least it sounds less like a dictatorship."

"I never named the place Donovan's Lot! That was a joke!"

"Still. Better not to have a joke name, don't you think?"

"Bugger it."

"Did you hear Brian's thinking of requiring Gaelic be taught in the school? And only Irish is to be spoken in the home? And any newcomers wishing to be considered for entrance have to be fluent in Irish?"

"Hey, it's what the buggers wanted. *He* is what you all wanted."

"He's doing some real good, Da."

"Aye, and Hitler always had the trains run on time."

"Well, it must be change everyone wanted," Gavin said. Mike could tell the boy didn't know how to comfortably speak to him about the election.

"I hear you're already working on a new jail?"

Gavin nodded, not looking at Mike. "Declan set me to it," he said. "Me and Iain."

"And you're fine with them executing poor Ollie tomorrow?" He watched his son closely. "The two of you were mates, weren't you?"

"We never were. We played football in the field sometimes is all."

"So, you're okay with them hanging him?"

"Da, he killed Eeny."

"It's not that simple, Gavin."

"Brian says it is," Gavin said as he pushed past his father to enter into the camp. "Brian says sometimes the clearest most rightest things are the simplest."

"Does he," Mike muttered. "I think that's the same thing some serial killers say."

"After the jail, we're gonna build a school. Did you know that? We've got enough kiddies now. And Brian's wife is a school teacher *and* a nurse."

"She's *both*?"

"Brian says she's an angel. You should see him, Da. He gets tears in his eyes just talking about her."

"Very touching."

"Who do you think the father of Papin's baby is?" Gavin nodded to his girlfriend, Jenna McGurthy, as they walked past the camp center cook fire, a bubbling rabbit stew in the large black pot. "The gypsies have odds on it."

"That's disgusting."

"They tell me I'm the leading suspect."

"*You*?" Mike stopped walking. "In the name of all that is holy, boy, tell me there's no truth to that...that..."

"Blimey, Da, you're gonna have a stroke. Of course not. Papin's like me sister...or a really cute second cousin."

"Gavin..."

"I'm having you on, Da."

"And you have no idea of who it might be? What about that shifty little bastard, Bobby McClure?"

"Nah, he hasn't got the stones. It can't be anyone in camp. Are we even sure she's really up the flue? Mebbe she's lying?"

"Aunt Fi says she's puking pretty steady mornings."

"Oh, well."

"If you hear of anything, you'll pass it on to me, ya hear?"

"Sure, Da."

Mike shook his head as Gavin quickened his pace heading

toward their hut, the wolf pups whining rising higher and higher on the escalating night breeze.

THERE WAS A TIME, *she would've told me,* Sarah thought as she hurried to Fiona's cottage the next morning. Her mind was a jumble of questions that had kept her awake most of the night. When she went to Mike's to see if John was up yet, she found the place empty. She called out his name as she walked over to Fiona's place.

Where could the boy be? Wherever he was, he must have gone there even before the camp was awake.

Was she losing total control of both her children?

As she drew closer to Fiona's cottage, she saw Papin sitting on the front porch. Papin startled when she saw Sarah and jumped up.

"Oh, no you don't, Papin," Sarah called. "I will just track you down wherever you go."

She watched the girl slowly turn back and slump down into her chair. Sarah stood facing her. "Who is the father?"

"That's all you care about, isn't it, Sarah?"

"Who is it? Is it that little rodent, Jimmy Dorsey?"

Papin made a face. "Don't be insulting. I wouldn't let Jimmy Dorsey touch me tits for a dollar."

Sarah knew Papin was trying to shock her. "Wow. Good to know you have boundaries."

Papin pointed to her stomach and smiled smugly. "Well, clearly not."

"This isn't a joke, Papin!" Sarah ran her fingers through her hair. "You're going to have a baby!"

"Did it ever occur to you that maybe I *want* this baby? That maybe this *isn't* an accident?"

"In that case, you're more confused than I gave you credit for. Who did this, Papin?"

"No."

"Why are you protecting him? Is he married?"

Papin stood up and Sarah could see her bottom lip was trembling.

Had she hit a nerve? Was the baby's father married?

"I'm done talking with you about this," Papin said, her voice shaky. "Auntie Fi says I should rest a lot so I'm going in."

"We're not done, Papin," Sarah said. But Papin fled into the house and slammed the door. Sarah sat down on the wooden bench on the porch. The confrontation had left her shaky, too.

Why wouldn't she say who the father was?

Papin hadn't left Donovan's Lot even for fifteen minutes, except for last week when they rode to David's grave, not since the moment Mike brought her here from Wales. As she sat on Fiona's porch watching the clouds gather in the sky again for another morning downpour, it suddenly occurred to Sarah that Papin had been nearly terrified to go as far as David's gravesite.

Maybe it hadn't been a fit of nerves with the horse but more about leaving the camp that had her so nervous? And if Papin had developed into a king-size agoraphobe during the last seven months, just what exactly would the thought of flying to the States and starting a new life there do to her, I wonder?

She glanced in the living room window to see Fiona talking to Papin. Sarah watched her hand Papin a mug of tea and put a shawl around the girl's shoulders.

Me, she runs from and keeps secrets but for Auntie Fi, she's a purring kitten. Maybe I should let Fi raise her.

"Mom? You wanted me?"

Sarah was startled by John's sudden appearance in front of her and took in a quick intake of air. "Lord, John, I nearly jumped out of my skin. Yes. Where were you? I couldn't find you anywhere in camp."

"I was right outside the entrance with Gavin and Uncle Mike."

"Whatever for?"

"It was just something we found we wanted to show him. Did you need me for something? I'm still staying at Gavin's tonight, right?"

"Something interesting happening at Gavin's tonight?"

"Not really. Whose house am I eating at?" He wrinkled his nose and looked up at Fiona's cottage. "Don't tell me the Widow Murrays. I heard she once cooked her cat."

"No, she's going to Aideen and Taffy's place tonight. I supposed you can either go wherever Mike goes or you can come to Fi's. Your choice."

"Where are you eating tonight?"

"Fi's."

"Then I will, too."

Before he could leave, Sarah moved down the steps toward him. "John?"

"Yeah?"

"I just wanted to...thank you for being okay about our leaving tomorrow."

"I'm *not* okay with it."

"No, I know. I meant, in spite of the fact that you don't want to go, you're not giving me a hard time. Thank you."

"Okay. Is that all?"

She nodded. "Sure. See you at dinner in an hour."

But he had already trotted away in the direction of Mike's place. She watched him go and envied the fact that he was welcome there.

Dinner was a disaster right from the start.

Sarah had not expected Mike to be there. When her bunkmate, the acerbic Widow Murray had received the dinner invitation for dinner at Aideen's, Sarah assumed Mike would be in attendance there. After all, Aideen was his effing fiancée now. Sarah had been invited too, but Sarah sent her roommate off with her regrets.

Actually, the exchange had involved a healthy dose of the old widow's opinion that turning down friendly dinner invitations was part and parcel of the main reason "why no one likes you, Miss America, because you're always thinking you're better than everyone," although what prompted the outburst or the opinion was beyond Sara's ability to understand.

But still, she had assumed Mike would be *there*.

Unless *he* had assumed *she* would be there? And so *he* was trying to be *elsewhere*?

In any case, the table at Fiona and Declan's held the two love-birds, a chatty and oblivious John, two people who were careful not to look at, speak to or, God forbid, touch each other all during dinner, and a sullen, pregnant gypsy teenager.

The numbers rounded out to a classic family table: two parents, two kids, and a loving aunt and uncle. It made the reality all the more painful to bear. The minute Mike walked into Fi's house, Sarah's stomach did its usual flip-flop just to see him. His hair blown thick and wild around his face and his eyes, so blue, so piercing, it was all she could do not to fan herself.

There was nothing comfortable about the feeling.

Except for John and Declan, Sarah had a bone to pick with just about everybody at that table. She thumped down a steaming bowl of buttered squash.

"Sorry about the election," she said to Mike without looking at him.

He ignored her and sat next to Papin at the table. Sarah watched him pull Papin's chair over to his where he leaned over and looked into her eyes and spoke in a low voice. A part of Sarah was relieved that Mike was there to back her up, to talk to Papin, to possibly get something out of the girl besides sass and mono-syllables. One look at the exchange between them quickly dashed her hopes.

Papin had never openly defied Mike and so to see her cross

her arms now and resolutely refuse to even look at him or speak was shocking to Sarah. She watched frustration war with outright anger in Mike's face as he continued to talk to Papin, but it was clear from her expression that no naming of the father would be forthcoming tonight.

"I don't understand why you won't tell us," Sarah said, sitting next to Papin. "Why the big secret?" she said with exasperation.

"I'm handling it, Sarah," Mike said quietly.

"Well, no you're not. She's sitting there rolling her eyes and you're talking to a wall. Is it a boy we all know? Is he afraid he'll be banished from the community?" She looked at Mike. "Is that the punishment for this sort of thing?"

"How the feck would I know?" he said, finally looking at her. "I'm not in charge anymore. For all I know, they'll want to tar and feather him."

"Michael Donovan!" Fiona said as she came to the table with a large tureen of rabbit stew. "You'll not say such things at my dinner table!"

"Yeah, sorry, Fi," Mike said, leaning back in his chair. He looked behind her. "Dec not here tonight?"

"He's late. Obviously," Fi said, putting the tureen down but keeping her voice hard. Fiona didn't forgive easily, Sarah knew. *It had been a pretty terrible thing to say.*

But Papin appeared oblivious to everything happening around. Sarah couldn't understand it. It was like Papin had morphed into a different person. And while Sarah had heard of such things happening—especially with girl teens—the speed of the transformation was staggering.

"Besides," Fiona said, picking up Papin's bowl and ladling stew into it. "It doesn't matter anyway. Papin's going to the States tomorrow so it doesn't matter who the father is."

John looked at Papin for the first time. "So will it be born an American even if its parents are both Irish?"

"I'll know who the feck it is before anybody leaves for anywhere," Mike said pushing back in his chair.

"Well, I don't know how you will if she won't say," Sarah said.

"Then you'll not be taking her."

"What? You can't do that," Sarah said hotly. "She's coming with me and that's final." She turned to Papin. "You still want to go, don't you?"

Papin just shrugged and picked up her spoon.

"Of course she wants to go," Fiona said. "And it's the best thing for her, too," she said to Mike. "There'll be all sorts of... resources for her there. A lot more than we can do for her here, living in the equivalent of the eighteenth century."

Sarah glanced at Fiona and wondered for the first time if she felt insecure about having her baby without a doctor or the blessings of modern medicine. Of course she must. It stood to reason. There had been several babies born in the camp in the last two years, but it hadn't been an easy time.

Not a bit of it.

"I'll have the name of the bastard who did this or nobody goes anywhere," Mike said, but Sarah could see the heat had gone from his voice. He wouldn't stop them. He just didn't know what else to do.

"I'm not hungry," Papin said, standing up. "Auntie Fi, can I retire for the night?"

"It's not even six o'clock," Sarah said.

"Auntie Fi?"

"Yes, of course, darlin'," Fi said. "Go on now and lie down. I'll be in to see you in a bit."

Papin smiled thinly at Fiona and, not giving a glance to either Sarah or Mike, excused herself and left the table.

Sarah looked at Mike. "She's mad at us."

"American pop psychology?" he said pulling the stew tureen toward his plate.

"It's obvious. I can't believe you can't see it. It's classic. We're splitting up and she's behaving like every other child of a divorce behaves when that happens. She's angry at both of us."

"Well, it's not *my* fault, is it? And she knows that. Hell, the whole camp knows that."

Then she's mad at you because you're not stopping me.

Suddenly John jumped up and ran to the door. He had it open and was leaping off the porch before Sarah realized he wasn't trying to compete with Papin for throwing the biggest tantrum of his life.

There was a gas-powered vehicle roaring up to the front of the cottage right through the center of camp.

SARAH WASN'T the last person to reach the porch to see for herself what all the excitement was about, but she was the first to realize it wasn't good.

A young man dressed in the uniform of a first lieutenant in the United States Marines sat astride a military-issue motorcycle with the insignia of the United States decaled on the side. Sarah watched him remove his goggles, his machine idling loudly between his legs as he waited for everyone to gather around.

Were all young American service personnel this confident of their place in the world? she thought with wonder as she watched the young man grin lazily at two gypsy girls tittering from the front row of the growing crowd.

Mike walked up and the young officer, his smile never leaving his face, and nodded pleasantly at him.

"Good evening, sir," he said. "I'm sorry if I interrupted your dinner."

Sarah could see that Mike, like everyone else in camp, was mesmerized by the sight of the motorbike. It had been so long since anyone had heard the sound of an engine running that it sounded as unnatural now as if it were the call of an African baboon.

"No problem," Mike said, still looking more at the man's bike than at him. "Can we help you with something? I assume you have GPS and aren't here accidentally."

The young man laughed, and even from the distance of the front porch where she still stood Sarah could feel the charisma pinging off him in waves. He was a man used to having people listen to him, like him, and envy him.

Especially here, especially now.

He unbuttoned the top button of his shirt pocket and pulled out an envelope. Even before he spoke, Sarah knew it was for her.

"I have a message from the consulate in Limerick for an American national by the name of Sarah Woodson."

Mike turned to look at Sarah, who descended the porch steps. John fell in with her as she approached the officer. She knew the whole camp was watching and she felt a blanket of mortification that this handsome, well-fed and downright cocky young was a representative of her country. He and his careless charm were a billboard exclamation to the whole camp that soon Sarah would be riding in gas-powered cars again, sleeping in the comfort of central heat and air conditioning, living the easy life back in the US.

After she had struggled to put on a decent meal tonight of stew and corn bread—as she knew every other family in the camp had, too—it embarrassed her to have to blatantly admit that, unlike them, soon she wouldn't have to. It said to them all: not everyone is suffering in this new world of ours. Some people haven't even missed a beat

"Mrs. Woodson. Ma'am," the officer said, handing her the message and then grinning at John. "And I'll bet this is, John. How ya doing, sport? You ready to go home? Looks like you'll make it back just in time for the start of the school year. Sorry about that."

Sarah watched John smile politely, but his eyes—like everyone else's in camp—were on the motorcycle. She stuffed the envelope into her jeans pocket and nodded to him. "Thank you, Lieutenant." She just wanted him gone, although the damage was well and completely done by now. "Is a reply from me needed?"

"No, ma'am. You don't need to do anything but show up in Limerick tomorrow. This is just a formality." He revved up his machine and Sarah watched Mike take an involuntary step back. The rest of the men in the camp, John included, moaned with pleasure at the sound as the man resettled his goggles on his face, gave an airy salute to Mike and a thumbs up to John, and turned around to drive slowly out of camp.

Before anyone had a chance to move, the sound came to them of the squeal of the bike's motor as the officer shifted into a higher speed for his ride back to Limerick.

"Holy shite," one of the gypsies said. "Looks like it really is business as usual for the Yanks. In-feckin'-credible. Did you see that beauty? What I wouldn't give."

Declan pushed his way through the throng to where Mike, Sarah and John were standing. "What did he want?" he asked, looking at Sarah.

She pulled the envelope out of her pocket and moved to the camp center cook fire to read its contents by its flickering light.

With the bike gone, John went back to Fiona's for the rest of his supper. Sarah watched the rest of the crowd disperse as she drew a single sheet of paper out of the folded envelope.

Declan and Mike flanked her as she read it.

"I don't believe this," she said, reading and re-reading the short missive. "This can't be right."

"What is it? Is it about the trip tomorrow?" Mike said.

Sarah turned to look at him but she didn't see his face. What she saw were the first crumbling pieces of her dream as they began to shatter at her feet.

"It's about Papin," she said. "Because she's a British subject, they won't let me bring her with me."

12

The gypsies slept so soundly out in the open by the long-spent campfires that it made a person wonder how they lasted this long not falling prey to every highwayman, wild animal or natural disaster that could creep up on them in the night. Mike walked as silently as his size would allow, slowly picking his way past the recumbent forms of snoring men sprawled across the gravel path that led to the stables.

If he hadn't known for a fact there was no real alcohol to be had in the whole camp, nor had there been for months, he could have easily believed they were all stone drunk. Certainly didn't do much to fight the prejudice that the buggers were as lazy as sin, he thought as he stepped over the last somnolent body in his path.

The early morning was as dark as the inside of his hat. It was probably closer to midnight than to morning, if he had to guess. He was glad it was summer time. He wore a thin tee shirt and jeans. He didn't need to be loaded down with a thing more than he already was.

And that didn't even cover the hefty dose of shame he'd

pulled on before his feet had even stepped out onto his porch this morning.

But even the guilt and the creeping sense of wrong doing was better than remembering the look on Sarah's face last night when she realized she wasn't going to be able to bring little Papin back to the States with her. For a moment, for one mad, crazy moment, Mike thought it might be enough to make her stay.

But no. It was just one more crippling heartbreak to add to all the rest of them.

There was no moon tonight, luckily for him. And of course, also going in his favor he knew was the fact that even if he was caught skulking about the camp at two in the morning, or whatever the hell time it was, no one would dream to think he was up to something he shouldn't. Across his shoulders he carried a saddlebag crammed with corn bread, a water canteen and dried meat. He thought about slipping in a few apples but those were easy enough to come by on the road. A meal's worth of jerky to fill an empty stomach wasn't. And protein would give him strength.

By the time he reached the stables, Mike had broken out into a light sweat. Whether from nerves or the exertion of the walk loaded down as he was, he wasn't sure. He paused at the stable door and listened to the silence of the early morning before sliding the door open and slipping inside. His first idea had been to saddle his own horse, Petey, but as he wasn't absolutely sure what that wanker Gilhooley would do if the deed were successfully laid at Mike's feet, he thought he wouldn't do him any favors by making it so easy on him. Stealing a horse was a serious crime —a hanging crime, just like back in the days of the old Wild West in America—but at least it wasn't a giant erected billboard pointing the way to the guilty party.

Mike grabbed his saddle and tacked up one of the young geldings.

In for a penny...

He wasn't sure exactly when he'd gotten the idea that he needed to do this. Probably it had been building and festering ever since Gilhooley won the election. In any case, once he got the idea in his head, there was no way around it.

The young horse nickered softly and Mike patted him on the neck. How he would explain this if he were caught, he had no idea. He hadn't gone far enough down that road to imagine it and now was probably not the time to start. He tied on the saddlebags and pulled the horse by his bridle out of the stall and into the dark morning air. Again, he was assailed by the perfect quiet of the camp. In a week's time he'd never be able to do this. Nobody would. Gilhooley would have armed patrols combing the camp twenty-four seven.

He walked to the back of the camp, being careful to keep the horse off the gravel path. He wasn't shod but the noise would be enough to wake everybody sleeping in the camp, and the Balli-nagh graveyard twenty miles away, too. Now that he was moving and out in the open, Mike's blood began to race in his veins at the thought of being caught in the act. Aside from swearing he was just running away from home or something near as daft, there was nothing else he could say.

And once he had Ollie mounted up and headed toward the camp exit, he wouldn't be able to say even that.

At one point in his endless musings before he finally realized what he had to do, it occurred to Mike he could argue that, being the de facto community leader, he wasn't actually breaking any rules taking an early morning ramble down by the jailhouse.

That was good for, if not a chuckle, at least a half smile.

There was nothing forgivable about what he was about to do. And there was no way he couldn't *not* do it.

As he approached the ramshackle hut that served as the camp jail until the new one could be finished, he muttered a prayer of thanksgiving that Declan hadn't bothered to post a watch. Mike knew Ollie was compliant—even ready to assist the hangman in any way he could—so it didn't surprise him that Declan wouldn't feel a need to stand guard over him.

Dec was going to be royal pissed off.

Mike dropped the reins and reached for the door latch. The smell of the interior of the place nearly pushed him back outside. The door creaked open wide and he saw young Ollie, on his feet and staring at the open door with eyes as wide as a child on Christmas morning.

I guess I made more noise than I thought.

Without speaking, Mike moved to where Ollie was tethered. He knew a knife cut on the ropes would reveal without a doubt that Ollie had an accomplice to his escape, but it couldn't be helped. Mike didn't have the patience to work out the knot. He drew his knife and cut the bonds. Ollie's arms fell to his side. Mike saw the boy look past him to the outside, which gave Mike a little reassurance.

He wasn't totally sure the stupid bugger would even agree to being sprung.

"Is it just yourself, then, Mr. Donovan?" Ollie said, breathlessly.

"Keep your voice down." Mike grabbed him by the arm and pulled him out of the foul-smelling cell and led him to the horse.

Ollie looked at the saddled horse and then at Mike. Although most gypsies were good riders, it wasn't common for one of them to actually own one. Ollie would have little to no expectation that he might some day.

"Is he...is it mine?" he asked as he touched the horse's flank.

"Mind you don't kill him along the way," Mike said gruffly. As Ollie stood staring at the horse, clearly astonished, Mike took him by the arm and shook him to get his attention.

"You'll lead him out on foot through the south entrance, you hear me?"

Ollie turned his stunned expression to Mike and didn't answer.

"Once you're clear of the camp, take the roads at a canter. Don't go into the fields until it's light, ya ken?"

Finally, Ollie nodded.

"If he hits a pothole in the dark that'll be the end of both of you. Take the fields and head east if you've a mind to go to Wales, which I'd suggest. There are plenty of your kind living there. Or west if you think you can live off what you can pull out of the ocean."

Ollie looked back at the horse, and this time his fingers wrapped around a stirrup as if to convince himself it was real.

"But whatever you do, boy," Mike said, looking over his shoulder toward the center of camp, "don't ever come back here again. Go away and start over fresh."

"Why...why are you doing this?" Ollie said, his voice shaking.

Mike placed a hand on the boy's shoulder. "Consider it my last official act as camp leader." Mike reached for the reins and handed them to Ollie.

"Can...can you tell me mum I'm sorry?" Ollie took the reins.

"She knows that, son. Now, go."

Mike watched as Ollie walked away, slowly at first and then at a trot beside the horse. When he disappeared into the gloom, Mike waited until all sound of him was completely gone. And then he turned and made his way back to his own cottage, his heart lighter than it had felt in weeks.

"ALL I'M SAYING IS MAYBE it's better this way." Fiona whispered as she closed the door behind her to Papin's room. "She's still asleep."

"How can this be better?" Sarah spent the night sleeping on Fiona's front parlor couch. She sat now with the ubiquitous cup of tea in her hands, and life not looking one bit better now that it was the morning. "You said yourself her problems would be best handled in the US."

"I really just said that to make you feel better." Fiona sat down on the couch and reached for her own teacup. "Papin's problems have to do with the fact that you and Mike are imploding in front of her very eyes *and* she's being taken from the only home she's ever known."

Sarah stared at her. She wanted to argue with her. She wanted to utter the one statement that would wipe that all-knowing look off Fiona's face. But she couldn't.

Fiona was right.

"She's going to feel abandoned," Sarah said, tears gathering in her eyes.

"We will do everything in our power to make sure she doesn't." Fi put her arm around Sarah's shoulders. "Mike and Declan and I will love her and care for her—and her baby—and she will always know that you love her, too."

Sarah shook her head. "How am I going to tell her?" she whispered.

"You'll tell her there's a wee snag on this end and that you'll sort it out from the States and send for her."

"That's true. I can send for her." Sarah looked at Fiona, her heart leaping with hope.

"Sure, Sarah. Only you have to know that isn't likely. In the middle of an international crisis? What made you think in the first place the Americans would ever let her come?"

Sarah shook her head. "I just...wanted it so much, it didn't occur to me. She's my daughter."

"Except she isn't."

"How am I going to tell her?" Sarah covered her face with her hands and slumped back into the sofa.

Suddenly the front door of the cottage burst open and Declan charged in. He looked at the two women sitting there and then went into the kitchen before coming back.

"Declan!" Fiona shouted. "Whatever is the matter with you? What's happened?"

"He's gone," Declan said. "Ollie. He's been let out."

Sarah saw Declan's face creased with anger and...relief. She had never seen this side of him, and she wondered if Fi ever had either.

"So you think he's hiding in *here*?" Fiona said incredulously. "Does that even make sense?"

"It's not Ollie he was looking to find here," Sarah said calmly, her eyes on Declan's face. Before he could speak, Gavin and John pushed into the cottage.

"It's all over the camp, Dec," Gavin said. "Jamie says his green colt, Bumper, is missing, too."

Sarah was very aware that Declan had not taken his eyes off her. She stood up and straightened out the blouse she'd slept in. "Thanks for the tea and talk, Fi," she said. "I ...I should go check on the Widow Murray."

"Okay," Fiona said, frowning, still confused.

Sarah hurried past Declan and squeezed out of the door. From the porch she could see that the camp was aroused and active this morning. At least ten people were waiting outside Mike's hut. A sick feeling slid down her throat. It was not like Mike not to be up yet. As she jogged down the porch steps, she saw Aideen striding across the camp center toward Fiona and Declan's cabin. She looked bewildered.

"Sarah!" Declan's voice was harsh, and for a moment Sarah couldn't believe he was directing it at her. She slowed her steps but didn't stop.

"Mind if I ask you where Mike is this fine morning?" He called to her, his voice sarcastic and commanding.

Well, there it was. If Ollie was sprung then who the hell else could it have been? Mike had spent more time arguing against hanging him than he had campaigning for himself.

"Well, how would I know?" Sarah said without turning.

Aideen moved swiftly in front of her and put a hand against her chest to stop her forward moving. "I, for one," she hissed, "do mind very much you asking *Sarah* where my fiancé is."

"Get out of my way."

"I don't think so, Yank," Aideen said. "Is there a reason why anyone would think *you* know where Mike is before *me*?"

"If you don't move your hand, you're going to be pulling it out of your butt in about two seconds," Sarah said, her eyes hard as flints.

Aideen gasped and dropped her hand but didn't move out of the way. "Why are you still here? You're living on the couch of an old addled widow woman! How much bigger a picture do we need to draw for you? It's time to go!"

"I'll go when I'm ready, Aideen." Although several inches shorter than Aideen, Sarah pushed past her, nearly knocking her off balance. Sarah continued walking until she felt a hard hand grab at her shoulder and twist her around. Before Sarah could say another word, Aideen backhanded her across the mouth, knocking her on her butt in the dirt.

"Fight! Fight!"

Sarah heard some of the gypsy men yelling and she was aware of a small crowd beginning to hem her in as she scrambled to her feet. Aideen stood facing her, her expression contorted into an ugly mask, her hands held up in front of her like claws about to slice pieces off Sarah if she dared to come at her.

Before Sarah could take a step toward her, Fiona was between them, her arms outstretched.

"Ladies, ladies!" she said breathlessly. "This is not the sort of camp entertainment we like to encourage. Both of you take a breath. Now Dec has gone off in search of Mike and he—"

"The bitch slapped me!" Sarah said hotly, her face stinging

and the feeling of blood seeping into her mouth where a tooth had cut into her lip.

"I know and I'll be needing you to say sorry, Aideen," Fiona said, looking at Aideen and trying to smile encouragingly. "If you please."

"Bugger that!" Aideen said. "She's dragged this goodbye out so everyone in camp can't wait to see the back of her! I'm not a bit sorry."

Fiona turned to Sarah. "Now Sarah, you'll not want to be carrying on like this in front of John, am I right?"

Sarah glanced away from Aideen for a moment to see if John was near. She glared at the gawking bystanders, most of them men.

"Why is she still here?" Aideen said to Fiona, clearly not ready to let it go. "Can I hitch up the team for you?" she shouted at Sarah. "Or do you need Mike to do that for you? Piss off, you!"

"I'll leave when I'm ready, or not at all," Sarah said. "How about them apples, sister? How about if I just stay right here? You know, the more I think of it, the better I like that idea." Sarah knew she'd hit pay dirt. The light in Aideen's eyes turned into something wild and chaotic.

"You're leaving!"

"No. I don't think I am!"

The urge to pound this creature with her fists, to rip the smug, self-satisfied smile from her face was overwhelming. For over a month now, Sarah's world had been a festering pile of ugly glances, harsh words, and disappointment. She'd hurt every single person who loved her and been thoroughly trounced in return. And now she was going to hit this woman who Mike had chosen over her, hit her until—

Aideen held her hands up with her jagged talons poised to rake Sarah's face, her eyes when Sarah pushed Fiona out of the way and hit the taller woman around the midsection bringing her crashing down under her in the dirt. She could feel Fiona slapping her on the back to get her off of Aideen but she ignored her, clutching at Aideen's deadly nails to keep them from reaching her throat. She felt the anger and the frustration pump through her arms, as if she had every person in camp who'd ever turned on her beneath her. Her arms shook with the exertion and the need to hit something.

Somewhere in her head she heard Fiona screaming and the gypsy men howling with delight, but all she saw was Aideen—the face of every broken promise and good thing that had turned sour in her whole life represented in one snotty Irish woman who had pushed every one of her last buttons. She was milliliters from smashing that nasty, gloating face. And then she was being jerked up and away. Her hands windmilled in the air for purchase, grabbing at Aideen's jacket or hair, but Aideen's reach was longer. She lashed out with a fist that caught Sarah on the ear before Sarah was wrenched away.

When Mike set her down, her ear stinging and seeming to vibrate such that all the noise seemed to make no coherent sense, she lurched back at Aideen but was caught by Mike again. He grabbed her by the middle and this time carried her several steps away from the fight. When they stopped, she could see Fiona helping Aideen up from the ground.

Sarah turned on Mike. He was breathing hard and clearly trying to get himself under control. She knew she had never seen him so furious. Not even when Gavin knocked over the milk shed the day he tried to get all the goats in one harness. Her eyes flicked back to Fiona leading Aideen away. Aideen was watching her over her shoulder.

"I assume that was all bullshit just then to get a rise out of Aideen?" Mike bit off every word as he spoke, his hands on his hips and towering over her.

For a moment Sarah couldn't imagine what he was talking about and was seconds from reminding him that *she* was the wounded party in all this when her words came back to her. She licked her lips and looked away.

"That's what I thought," he said.

"The bitch is crazy," Sarah said, her ear stinging like mad but the frustration at not having gotten off a single punch slowly receding. "But if that's the kind of woman you want—"

"She is exactly the kind of woman I want," Mike said, narrowing his eyes. "Or I wouldn't be engaged to marry her. See, that's how that works."

"Fuck you, Mike."

"Well, we tried that now, didn't we, Sarah? And I can see you've a mind to haul off and slap me and I'll remind you of how *that* turned out last time too."

"You are the absolute lowest of the low."

"And you will stay in the Widow Murray's cottage until it's time for you to leave."

"You're not the boss anymore, Herr Commandant. You can't order me."

He leaned over until his face was close to her. "You're not in the US of A, now, darlin.' I'll carry your ass over there and throw you in her cottage myself."

His eyes glittered with fury and it occurred to Sarah that she wasn't the only one looking for an excuse to vent a little pent-up frustration.

"I'll...I'll just leave again," she said, trying to sound more sure than she felt.

"You can try."

Sarah blinked at him and then looked across the camp where Aideen sat with Fiona. She looked down at her hands. "Fine," she said and then looked up at him. Her anger was still there but checked, finally. "Fine," she repeated before twisting on her heel and marching off in the direction of the Widow Murray's.

. . .

Aideen watched Mike and Sarah part company like two toddlers stomping off to separate corners. Sarah marched away, obviously heading back in the direction of the Widow Murray's cottage, and Mike just lumbered... away.

Fiona was doing her best to soothe the situation and for that Aideen was grateful, but she noticed she also followed Sarah with her eyes until the American disappeared from view. Likely she'd run over to the Widow Murray's the first chance she got to see how Sarah was, too.

"I know it's a difficult situation," Fiona was saying. "They have a history and you have unfortunately overlapped that by a bit."

"That's one way to put it," Aideen said. "I don't think I've ever felt so angry in my whole life. I honestly don't know what came over me."

"Well, love makes you do crazy things."

"Then how do you explain Mike coming here and taking off with her and not saying word one to me?"

Fiona gaped in surprise. "But, he broke up the fight. He *rescued* you."

"Then why doesn't it feel like a rescue? Why does it feel like he didn't even see me?"

"That's ridiculous," Fiona said, but Aideen didn't think she argued the point very forcefully.

"I'm serious, Fiona. Did you see them over there? The way they looked at each other? I thought he was going to...I don't know, turn her across his knee or throw her down and *do* her right there in the center of camp."

"I can honestly say I didn't see any of that. He was just really angry—"

"They act like they're still lovers."

"Now that's an exaggeration. They've barely exchanged a word in a month—ever since Sarah announced she was leaving."

"Let me ask you—do you know what the opposite of love is?"

Aideen continued to look in the direction where Mike had disappeared.

Fiona frowned and then shrugged. "Hate?"

"You'd think so, wouldn't you? But it's indifference. Trust me, Fi. Mike is not *indifferent* to Sarah Woodson. Not at all. Not even a little bit. Did you see how she got him so riled up? People who don't matter to you can't do that to you." She shook her head sadly. "I'd love to have that kind of effect on him."

"Well, Sarah is a strong woman, and she's brutally stubborn," Fiona admitted. "I personally have wanted to whack her with a crop between the eyes on more than one occasion."

"Except that is not what it looked like Mike wanted to do to her."

"Best not to let your imagination get carried away. She'll be gone soon."

"Will she?" Aideen glanced again in the direction that Mike had gone. "Seeing them fight was worse than seeing them kiss. It was just so...intimate."

"Well, Mike has a temper on him and you're best knowing that going in." Fiona put her arm around her. "Come on, Aideen. You and I are going to be sisters, and what with Papin staying and both of us expecting at the same time, I'm going to need all the help I can get from my new sister."

Aideen took a deep breath and shook off the emotions as best she could. Fiona was Sarah's best friend in camp. For her to take Aideen under her wing was just about the best thing short of Mike getting short-term amnesia that Aideen could hope for. She leaned in and gave Fiona a quick kiss on the cheek.

"Thanks, Fi," she said. "I couldn't ask for a better sister or a better friend."

MIKE NEEDED TO HIT SOMETHING.

Hard.

He removed himself from the cluster of people—and particularly Sarah—before he did something he knew he'd regret. He literally felt his hands tingle with the need to put his hands on her.

Damn the woman! When the feck was she leaving? I'm not sure how much more of this I can take.

He took a long breath, knowing Aideen was watching him, knowing how upset she was after her tussle with Sarah—especially after witnessing his own set-to with Sarah. *Thank God for Fi.* He knew he didn't have the stomach for reassuring Aideen at the moment.

The way he was feeling—the way his body was feeling—he didn't think he could stand near her and pretend he wasn't furious and aroused and fit to be tied all at the same time.

Not believably anyway.

"Da!"

Mike heard Gavin yelling his name from through the cloud of anger and frustration that enveloped him and turned toward its source. There, past where Aideen and Fiona sat huddled on the center bench near the cook fire, he could see his son cantering his pony into the clearing. Riding at any speed more than a walk inside the camp was strictly forbidden. Mike felt his insides clench at what could possibly have made Gavin break the rules.

Within seconds, he saw what.

Pulling into the center of camp was a large work wagon hauled by two older draft horses. Gilhooley rode the horse he'd borrowed from camp for the trip back to Dublin. Mike saw the man looked positively buoyant, as if he were a part of some kind of ridiculous cavalcade.

Flanking the horse-drawn wagon were two riders on nearly identical bay geldings. Their matching red hair prompted a sudden twisting sensation in Mike's gut.

He knew them.

He walked slowly toward the advancing wagon as he searched

the driver seat for the man he now knew—incredibly—would be there: his father-in-law, Archibald Kelly.

And next to Archie, dressed in a long woolen suit buttoned to her neck and tucked under her prim, severe mouth, sat his daughter, Gilhooley's bride, and Mike's own ex-sister-in-law...

Caitlin.

13

Sarah made it as far as Siobhan Murray's front porch when she saw the gypsies streaming toward the center of camp. Siobhan came out of her front door squinting into the daylight like a mole.

"What's going on? Where are they going?"

"Go back inside," Sarah said over her shoulder as she turned back toward the camp's center. *Mike be damned.* If something was going on, she needed to make sure Papin and John were safe. She caught up with one of the heavier-set gypsy women struggling up the gravel path.

"What is it?" Sarah asked. "What's happening?"

"Gilhooley's back," she said, without looking at her. "He's brung his whole family and a wagon full of supplies, maybe even booze."

When she entered the camp, Sarah saw Brian in conference with Declan, his head bowed and nodding seriously. The wagon was indeed groaning with bags of rice, flour, sugar and building supplies. Two men in their mid-thirties—looking alike enough to be twins—sat silently on matching bay geldings, their faces severe and closed. An older man sat stiffly in the driver's seat, the reins to the two draft horses looped over his knees.

Next to him was none other than Caitlin Kelly.

Sarah ran up to Fiona and Mike where they stood on the perimeter of the camp center.

"How can this be? How can she be here?" She glanced at Mike to see if he was leaning toward manhandling her back to the Widow Murray's but he just shook his head as if trying to wake up from a bad dream.

"Not just *here*," Fiona said with disgust, watching Caitlin. "But First Lady of here."

Aideen slipped under Mike's arm, claiming him, and patted him on the chest. "Who is she?" she asked.

"My dead wife's sister. Caitlin Kelly."

Aideen looked at Fiona and then back at Mike. "How in the world can that be? She's married to Brian?"

"It appears so."

"I thought his wife's name was Katie?"

"Close enough."

"So do you know the old man? The other men?"

"My father-in-law and brothers-in-law."

"*Ex*-in-laws," Fiona muttered. "Ellen's gone. The tie to them is broken."

"Grandda!"

Sarah watched Mike close his eyes in resignation and defeat.

"Not entirely," he said as Gavin leapt onto the wagon and threw his arms around the old man.

"The shite's in the pan, Mike," Fiona said in a low warning voice. "Dec is filling Brian in on the jailbreak. Don't suppose you know anything about that?"

Mike didn't answer but Sarah saw him shift his attention from the wagon to where Declan and Brian stood together. He noticed that Iain Jamison was near enough to hear the two of them in conference. Suddenly, Brian threw up his hands and twisted on his heel away from Declan. He marched back to the wagon where Gavin sat with the old man and Caitlin and turned to face the gathering crowd by the camp center.

"Greetings, good people of Daoineville," he said loudly. "As you can see, I have returned with my family."

Sarah was annoyed and surprised to hear a spattering of applause from the gathered people.

"While I hope you will take the time to get to know each of them individually, I would like to introduce you to my wonderful wife, Katie, before we go—"

"Only we know her by a different name!" someone yelled out.

Sarah watched Brian's back stiffen as he stopped in his turn toward Caitlin. He turned back to face the crowd. "Who said that?"

No one answered.

"Because if you mean she is also known as Caitlin and known to you good people as well, I assure you, I am aware of that."

"Bloody hell," Mike muttered. "What is that feckin' Caitlin up to?"

"I am aware that my lovely bride has once lived among you and I want you to know that I am completely prepared to forget and forgive any injustices she may have suffered at your hands."

Sarah saw Brian turn and look at Mike.

"So long as there is not a hint of disrespect or ill will demonstrated in her direction. I hope I make myself clear." He paused and then turned to Caitlin. "Stand up, my dear," he said. "Let them see the mayor's wife."

Mayor? Sarah shared a look with Fiona. *This wasn't good.*

Caitlin stood up on the wagon, placing a hand on Gavin's shoulder to steady herself. Sarah saw that she was wearing a very conservative dress. The hem when past her knees and the neck was buttoned to her chin.

She must be miserable in all this heat. Quite a change from the micro-mini skirt and halter-top Sarah had last seen her in running from camp and screaming like a demented woman.

When Caitlin leaned down to blow Brian a kiss, Mike made a noise of disgust in his throat. Brian turned back to the crowd. "So we'll be getting settled in and there's just one or two things I need to attend to before I can address the camp again tonight right here by the camp fire after dinner." His eyes strayed to Mike as he spoke and Sarah felt a clutch of fear.

Declan strode up to the four of them and touched Fiona on the arm. "He needs you to bring his wife to their new cottage and get her settled in."

Fiona looked at her husband, appalled. "You know who she is, Dec?"

"Yes, of course. I was here, wasn't I?'

"I'll not escort her to the feckin' bog were she exploding with the runs and putting out all the cook fires with her piss!"

"You'll do it, please, as I'm asking you to do it," Dec said, his eyes glittering with meaning.

"She is a loathsome skank who nearly destroyed this community the last time she was here," Fiona hissed. "*And* she has vowed revenge on every one of us standing here, including yourself."

Declan glanced at Mike and then took Fiona by the arm and led her away from the group. "*We are holding our friends close,*" he whispered meaningfully to her. "Ya ken, darlin'?"

Sarah heard what he said and then saw Fiona look at Caitlin who was watching the interaction with interest. Fiona nodded solemnly, then turned and walked toward the wagon.

And our enemies closer.

"A word, Donovan?"

Mike turned to see Iain Jamison approach the group. While the man spoke to Mike his eyes were on Declan, as if he didn't trust how the gypsy would react.

"Mr. Gilhooley would like to speak with you at the jailhouse, if you have a moment."

"And if I don't?"

"I'm assured that you have plenty of time to spare."

Mike watched Iain's face contort into a facsimile of a smile. A very false one.

"May I ask what this discussion is in reference to?"

Declan made a snort of impatience. "Can we quit fecking around, please? Come on, Mike, let's just get this over with." He pushed out of the group and began walking in the direction Brian had gone with a few well-wishers moments earlier. Mike shrugged and moved to follow him. He saw Fiona struggle with a large suitcase as she trailed behind Caitlin in the direction of Sarah's old cottage. Before he passed them, Caitlin turned and looked at him, her eyes full of malice and intent.

"Donovan!"

Mike turned to see the old man—Ellen's da, Archibald—standing up in the driver's seat of the horse drawn wagon. The last time Mike had seen him was seven years ago at Ellen's funeral. He looked like he'd aged twenty years since then.

"Archie," Mike said solemnly, nodding to the old man.

"Caitlin told us what you done to her," Archie said, his face a mask of hatred and impotent violence. "What you did to Ellen." Mike saw his ex-father-in-law's arms flex by his side as if imagining the weapon in them that would take Mike down. Long ropy veins crawled up his arms, a fisherman's arms, used to dragging in hundred pound nets from the ocean.

Mike turned away as the two men on horseback, Caitlin and Ellen's twin brothers Cedric and Colin yelled to him, jeering.

"We ain't done with you, Donovan! Not by a long shot!"

Mike left the crowd ogling the newcomers and focused on Declan's back in front of him. He was aware that Jamison followed close behind so that he was being escorted to Brian as one might a prisoner.

14

Fiona sat by the main camp cook stove, snapping a bowl of green beans in her lap. She liked sitting out here. It gave her an opportunity to see the camp moving around her. It made her feel a part of its inner workings. Besides, the cottage was too depressing to be inside on such a beautiful late summer day. Already she had felt the coolness in the mornings that heralded the fact autumn would soon be upon them.

Out of the corner of her eye, she caught the motion of John Woodson coming out of Mike's cottage with one of the little wolf puppies on a leather leash.

Now that really had been one of more daft suggestions of Brian's— if it was true it really had come from him and not just John and Gavin wanting to have dogs. Fiona remembered that John had had two dogs last year. One was killed in the attack that also killed Seamus and Deirdre. She wasn't sure exactly what had happened to the other. She seemed to remember Sarah saying there'd been an accident last fall.

"Morning, Auntie Fi," John called to her. "Lot of excitement today, huh?"

She smiled at him. She would miss this lad when he left. "You could say that," she said. *If you call having the one person in the world who'd like nothing better than to set a match to the whole camp with everyone in it actually be in control of the camp excitement.*

"How you doing with the wee wolves?"

"They're a little resistant at the moment," John admitted, tugging on the leash to try to pull the scampering bundle of black fur back into line by his heels.

"That's one way to put it," Fiona said laughing. A few of Declan's cousins came to stand next to where she was sitting by the cook fire to stir the embers and reignite the blaze. She saw one of them had a large black cook pot he was obviously thinking of putting onto the smoldering fire. She nodded politely to them.

It wasn't like they shunned her or anything. It's just that she wasn't one of them. And marrying Declan—the favored gypsy son—made no difference in her status as far as they were concerned. Declan shrugged off their coolness toward her as being unimportant and encouraged her to do the same.

Behind them she saw something that made her fingers stop their constant activity on the green beans. It was all she could do to stifle the involuntary gasp that came to her lips.

Caitlin was coming out of Sarah's old cottage, her arm around the thin shoulders of Papin.

Fiona watched the two descend the steps of the cottage together and she saw Caitlin put her hand into Papin's long hair as if she might be talking about hairstyles. Fiona watched the two as they walked, their backs to her, into the interior of the camp.

Now what do you suppose that was about?

If there was anything Fiona knew about Caitlin Kelly, whatever was going on, it wasn't innocent.

DECLAN RODE his roan mare to the edge of the pasture where Gilhooly and Jamison stood talking. He still hadn't forgotten it was that bastard Jamison who bashed him with the bat at the Harvest Festival. As much as Declan was careful to let Mike and Fi believe he'd put it behind him, the truth was he couldn't. And he wouldn't until he'd had his moment alone with the bastard.

He slowed his horse as he approached the two and noticed they both stopped talking immediately.

So that's the way of it, eh?

"Afternoon, Coop," Gilhooley said, pleasantly enough. Declan noticed that Jamison turned, pretending to look at something of interest in the pasture. "Iain and I were just discussing the progress that's been made on the jail in my absence. I have to say, I thought we'd be further along."

"Well, up to now we've had to do it on the sly," Declan reminded him.

"You should know, Coop," Gilhooley responded coldly, "that I can't abide excuses for poor performance. Speaking of which, there's the matter of your cousin's escape happening on your watch."

Declan's eyes flickered to Jamison, now not bothering to pretend he wasn't interested in the conversation. Was Gilhooley going to flay him over that in front of that bastard?

"While it's clear Donovan did the physical deed, I have to admit to a lack of confidence for your part in the crime."

"*My* part? You think I helped Ollie escape?"

"What would *you* think if you were me? You weren't keen on performing the execution and he's your kinsman."

"Am I to be tried?" Declan bit the words out, the fury and loathing he was directing at Jamison was so palpable, he was surprised the man didn't physically recoil from it.

"I don't think we need to go that far," Gilhooley said. "Unless you've a mind to confess, we have no evidence."

"Not for Mike either," Declan reminded him.

"Perhaps not. At least not yet. Along those lines, I have a way in which you might be able to unblot the old copybook, Coop. You interested?"

Declan grunted and forced himself not to look at Jamison. He could see out of the corner of his eye the lying berk was grinning in anticipation.

"You bring me the evidence to convict Donovan of the crime and we'll call it even between you and me."

I deserve this, Declan thought. *He's seen me go behind Mike's back and betray confidences. He naturally thinks I'm capable of doing this.*

"Sure," Declan said, realizing it was all over now. Gilhooley had made his choice—probably had made it weeks ago—and Declan was back to being the head Pikey, whose only distinction was that he'd had the nerve to marry the camp leader's sister. "I'll get right on it. Am I still camp sheriff?" He hated to ask it in front of Jamison but he needed to know.

"For now."

~

SARAH STOOD on the porch of the Widow Murray's and checked off the final basket of produce that was the widow's by right of her membership in the community. The old lady hadn't picked a strawberry in the whole time she'd lived there, but the generally accepted feeling was this was her time to have people do for her.

Siobhan Murray stood next to Sarah. "Make sure they don't cheat me, now," she muttered.

"How can you be cheated when it's free food?" Sarah said. She smiled at the young man who was climbing back up into his pony trap, focused on his next delivery.

"They think because I'm an old lady they can stint me on the meat," she grumbled. "They give excuses like the young ones need it more or some such rot."

"Those damn *young ones,*" Sarah said, tossing down the sheet listing the baskets of kale, carrots and potatoes that were Siobhan's. "When they collect the wheat and bring it to the mill, will you get an allotment of flour? Because I hadn't heard that you were to get any. Is that a mistake?"

Siobhan made a rude noise and turned to go back inside. "My days of making me own feckin bread are over," she said. "Let the young ones have all the flour they want. Just bring me the baked loaves."

"How old did you say you were?" Sarah asked.

"I'm not dying anytime soon if that's what you're asking. And what's it to you? You'll be gone this time tomorrow. At least I hope and I pray." She disappeared into the cottage.

Sarah sat down on the porch steps. Later today she'd drag all this produce to the small root cellar the widow had in the back of the house. It felt somehow dismissing to have worked so hard on the harvest, only to be left out of the distribution. She thought ruefully, *if I'm feeling ambivalent about leaving, I can only imagine how Papin and John must be feeling.*

No, correct that. John, at least, wasn't the least bit ambivalent about leaving.

"Ahoy, the Widow Woodson!"

Sarah looked up to see Fiona and Declan approaching from around the last line of huts before the pasture and the camp's exterior perimeter. She was surprised to see them, assuming Brian would have them both busy all day getting his family moved in.

"Hey, you, two," she said, standing up. "Everything okay?"

"Right as rain," Declan said.

"As long as we're talking acid rain," Fiona added. Sarah saw Declan carried a large picnic basket. "I threw together a few things and thought you might could use the company."

Sarah nodded, "Well, sure. Always." But this wasn't a typical visit—both of them in the middle of the day—and she'd feel better when she knew what was going on. "Shall I go fetch the old broad? She's such a sweetheart and I know she'll add so much to any party."

"Okay, no," Fiona said. "We are well acquainted with your roommate and just this time we'll enjoy only yourself for lunch. And Mike. And Aideen. If that's all right."

Sarah sighed. It hadn't been two hours since her throw-down with Aideen and she was in no mood to see Mike—especially not with Aideen hanging on his arm.

"Must we?"

"We must," Fiona said, as Declan thumped the picnic basket down onto the porch. "But as we'll need a little more privacy than the good Widow Murray generally allows, Dec and I are really here more to collect you."

"Suits me. Just let me drag some of these baskets into the living room where the old dear won't trip over them."

"Allow me," Dec said, walking over to the porch and hefting a big crate of corn to his shoulder. As he trotted up the stairs to the cottage, Sarah turned to Fiona.

"What's going on?"

"Can you not wait until we're all together, then?"

"Why is Aideen coming?"

"Like it or not, Sarah, she's a part of this camp *and* our inner circle."

"She's not a part of *my* inner circle."

"Be that as it may—"

"She hit me this very morning, *twice*! How do I know she's got control of herself? And don't say *Mike* will make her behave because he acted like *I* was the problem!"

Declan came back out to the porch and lifted two more crates into his arms.

"Now, Sarah," Fiona said soothingly. "I'll be needing you to act like the grown up I know you to be because we all have bigger problems to deal with and it would help if we're not trying to kill each other first."

"Tell *Aideen* that."

"I have it from Mike that he's telling her exactly that in no uncertain terms so does that make you feel better?"

It didn't, actually. In fact Sarah hated the idea of Mike sitting Aideen down and laying the law down to her. "Does this mean that Mike's one-man house arrest of me at the Widow Murray's is no longer in effect? Am I allowed to walk as far as the outhouse if I'm in the mood?"

"Okay, Sarah, I'll be grateful if you get all this out of your system before we meet up with them. Which, as it happens, is sooner rather than later because here they come."

Sarah looked over Fiona's shoulder to see Mike and Aideen walking toward them. Declan came back out on the porch and picked up the picnic basket. He trotted down the porch steps and Fiona hurried after him.

Allowing one scowl to the approaching couple, Sarah and followed too.

MIKE LED the group to a small clearing just on the outside of camp. A picnic table would have been preferable, but because he and Declan wanted privacy over comfort the ladies would just have to adjust to spreading their cloth out on the hard ground. He watched Aideen as she plucked the creases out of the cloth and settled herself on it. He'd already gotten eye contact with Sarah once and the experience didn't encourage a second time. Besides, Aideen didn't need to see him looking at Sarah.

Fiona unloaded the picnic basket and laid out cold chicken sandwiches, corn on the cob in congealed butter, and a plate of fruit and goat cheese. Mike couldn't help but think if they had a bottle of good wine—and a few less people—it might be a nice little afternoon. At the thought, his eyes went again unbidden to Sarah.

Damn! How much does it take to keep your thoughts on your own damn woman?

Declan leaned back against a rock and started peeling an apple with his pocketknife. The fruit was green. It would be at least two months before the rest of the camp would be picking apples for pies and fritters, but that didn't seem to stop the big gypsy.

"Dec and I have a few things we want to say," Fiona said, handing Mike a sandwich. "And we wanted just to tell our nearest and our dearest first."

"You're pregnant," Mike said, nodding his thanks for the sandwich.

Fiona looked at him with her mouth open. "How...how did you know that?"

"It's true, right?" Mike grinned and held out his arms as she slipped into them and gave him a tight hug.

"I already knew," Aideen said, patting Fiona as she went back to her place on the blanket.

When he looked at Sarah, he saw she was smiling at Fiona, making it pretty clear she had already known too.

"Good job, Dec," he said wryly and lifted his sandwich up as if in a toast.

"Thanks, Mate."

"The second bit of news isn't so great," Fiona said passing out the rest of the sandwiches. "But it needs saying."

"And *saying* is definitely me wife's specialty," Declan said, his eyes smiling. For the wonderful news they'd just shared, Mike couldn't help but think Declan seemed a little deflated today, which wasn't at all like him. Declan's mood was usually up for no good reason just about all the time.

"The fact is," Fiona said, taking a long breath and looking at Mike. "Dec and I didn't vote for you in the election—"

"Aw, you didn't need to tell 'im that!"

"It's not like I didn't know, Dec," Mike said. "Is there mustard?"

"Well, we did because we felt like we wanted a new community, like, to match our new life together."

"Sounds like you rehearsed that line," Sarah said. She held up her hands when Fiona turned on her. "Hey, I'm just saying…"

Fiona turned back to Mike, her eyes snapping with annoyance and guilt. "And we were wrong," she said. "Gilhooley was a mistake even without Caitlin as his wife. And I'm sorry, Mike. We were wrong."

Mike shrugged. "That's okay."

"Well, it isn't," Declan said, not looking at anyone. "It's fecked. And I hate feeling fecked."

"Has something happened?" Mike narrowed his eyes at Declan, then Fiona. He glanced at Sarah to see if she knew what they were talking about but she looked just as puzzled.

"I'm sheriff for now," Declan said, "until Gilhooley can get Jamison into the slot."

"I'm sorry about that," Mike said. *But not surprised.*

"Anyway, that's the row I hoed for myself," Declan said. "But I wanted to say there may be some good to come out of the fact I haven't been booted just yet."

Fiona spoke hurriedly. "Dec still has their ear for now. They want your hide, Mike. Brian as much as told Dec that."

"I know," Mike said. "When they brought me in for questioning on Ollie's escape, he said Archie blames me for Ellen's death. It's a toss up which one they go after me for. Ollie or Ellen."

"I thought she died from a fall from a horse," Sarah said.

"They're saying somehow Mike must have orchestrated it," Declan said. "And that he was Caitlin's lover."

"Jaysus, Joseph and Mary."

"And Caitlin says she had to flee for her life when he met you, Sarah because he was going to murder her like poor Ellen."

"I see."

"But at the end of the day, Brian wants you held responsible for Ollie's escape."

"Held responsible, how?"

No one spoke. There wasn't a single person sitting on the blanket that didn't know springing Ollie was a hanging offense.

"What can we do?" Aideen asked, her voice frantic and high.

Mike leaned over and took her hand, mindful Sarah was watching every move he made. "I guess that's why we're here?" He looked at Declan who nodded solemnly.

"Should we try to talk to Caitlin?" Sarah asked. "Is there any use in that?"

Mike grimaced. "You think she's going to listen? She's in the catbird seat now and everyone she ever wanted to get back at she's now in a position to do it."

"Well, maybe Brian then?"

"Brian thinks the sun shines out her arse," Declan said.

"How in the world did the two of them even meet?"

Fiona cleaned the cheese knife on a dry cloth. "When I was showing her about the cottage, she mentioned one of the twins introduced them."

"She moved things along pretty quickly."

"She probably took one look at how easy Brian was to manipulate and went charging ahead to get him to marry her."

Declan laughed rudely. "In a moment of early camaraderie before I turned back into a slimy Pikey before his very eyes, Gilhooley mentioned his sainted wife miscarried before they were wed."

"Bingo."

"Yeah," Mike said. "That would do it."

"She's playing him until she gets what she wants," Fiona said.

"I wonder what that is."

"To see the camp torched, I'll wager."

"Yes, but how? Or do you mean literally?"

"I don't know how this fits into her plans," Fiona said looking at Sarah and then Mike. "But I saw her this morning with Papin looking very cozy."

"Papin?" Sarah looked at Mike, and for the first time since they'd sat down there didn't seem to be a hidden meaning in her look. She raised a shaking hand to her mouth, her eyes wide. "What would Papin be doing with her?"

"I don't know."

Declan frowned. "Can't you just tell her to stay away from Caitlin?"

Mike and Sarah locked eyes again. "Not really," Sarah said.

Fiona put a hand on Declan's knee. "Telling teenagers not to do something just makes 'em want to do it all the more."

"Blimey."

"But since Papin's *leaving* tomorrow, it's not really a problem," Aideen said.

Mike cleared his throat. "Does she know she's not going to the States yet?"

Aideen snapped her head around to face him. "Papin's not going?"

Sarah ignored Aideen and answered Mike. "I haven't told her," she admitted.

Fiona said, "So Papin taking up with Caitlin is *not* something that'll be resolved tomorrow when Sarah leaves since Papin is not leaving. In fact, it'll be *my* problem, then."

Mike saw a look come over Sarah's face that he couldn't decipher. She looked away and stared into the woods and no one spoke for a beat.

Aideen looked from Fiona to Mike and then to Declan. "So?" she said. "What can we do?"

Mike got to his feet and held out a hand to Aideen to help her up. "Nothing," he said. "Until she makes a move, we just need to sit tight and wait for it."

"Well, that's a crappy plan," Sarah blurted out, and for a

moment Mike remembered the Sarah who tried to bulldoze him into marching into a camp of fifty murdering bandits with just herself and two others. He nearly grinned.

"Well, crappy or not," Declan said, "until we know what's coming at us, we wait."

AFTER THE PICNIC BROKE UP, Sarah walked back to Fiona and Declan's cottage with the two of them to have a word with Papin. She knew she couldn't tell her not to hang out with Caitlin, but she could at least try to see if she was more amenable to talking about the identity of the baby's father. And Mike was right. Somehow she needed to tell Papin she wasn't coming to the States right away.

When they reached the cottage, Iain Jamison was sitting on the front stoop waiting for them. As Sarah pushed past him he snaked a hand up her leg and pinched her bottom through her jeans. She whirled away from him and fell, tumbling down the steps. Before she could get to her feet, she saw Declan had Iain on the ground, and was pushing his face in the dirt, and smashing his fist into his kidneys. Within seconds a crowd began to gather to cheer Declan on.

Sarah scrambled to her feet. Her ankle felt weak and she staggered to the steps trying to avoid the two men now rolling in the dust. Fiona charged from her front door but Sarah grabbed her and held on. "Fi, don't!" she said. "Let Declan sort it out."

It became quickly clear to anyone watching that Declan's idea of *sorting it out* looked like it might require a body bag for Iain before he was done.

Why did that cretin Iain touch me like that?

"Dec, stop!" Fiona cried. "You're killing him!"

The sound of the gunshot felt like it went off by Sarah's ear. She screamed and jumped forward, not entirely sure they weren't being fired upon, when she saw Brian push through the crowd holding the blocky, black form of a semi-automatic handgun.

When she turned back to the two men on the ground, she saw Declan rising to his feet, his eyes blazing with anger. Iain, although moving and groaning, stayed down.

"What the hell is the meaning of this, Cooper?" Brian said. "Answer me!"

"The maggot attacked Mrs. Woodson," Declan said, brushing off the dirt from his jeans.

"He assaulted you?" Brian turned to look at Sarah. Brian crunched his face into an expression of obvious disbelief.

"Yes," Sarah said.

Sarah saw Caitlin appear by her husband's side, her eyes going first to Sarah and then to Iain. "Katie, darling, stand back. I won't have you hurt."

Caitlin moved to where Iain lay struggling to sit up and knelt by him. His face was bloodied and it looked as if Declan had rearranged his nose.

"I told you the Pikey was unpredictable, didn't I?" she said over her shoulder to Brian. "Now just look what he's done. He's an animal."

Brian held the gun, now pointed in the general direction of Declan.

"What the feck is going on?" Mike's voice boomed out from behind the crowd of gathered community members and they quickly moved to let him through. "Jaysus, Gilhooley, did you shoot your own man? Already?"

"Shut up, Donovan," Brian said, not taking his eyes off his wife's careful and tender ministrations to Iain. "Jamison, did you lay hands on Mrs. Woodson?"

Sarah watched the toad shake his head in denial. He spat out a loose tooth. "I never," he croaked.

"That is a lie," Sarah said, forcing herself not to look at Mike. She could feel the anger roiling off him even from this distance.

"Well, as it's your word against his, the way I see it the only crime that's been committed is the brutal beating of an innocent man. Cooper, you are relieved of your position as sheriff of Daoineville. I'll ask you to stay confined to your cottage until Sheriff Jamison and I come to a decision as what's to be done. Come along, my dear. I'm sure *Mrs.* Jamison will want to attend to her husband."

Caitlin stood up and glanced Sarah as she turned to her husband. Sarah was astounded to see her smile coldly at her. "Dearest?" Caitlin said to Brian as the group began to break up. "Perhaps this would be a good time for me to make our little announcement?"

Sarah looked at Brian, who had tucked his handgun back in the belt of his pants. He held a hand out for Caitlin but she ignored it. Instead, she walked up the stairs of Fiona's porch and turned to face the growing crowd.

"Good people of Daoineville," she said, holding her hands out to them. "Thank you all for your warm welcome. My father and brothers thank you, too." Sarah turned to see that Archie Kelly and the twins had joined the crowd. Mike stood with his arms crossed. She could tell he was working to keep control of his temper. Declan and Fiona stood just inside the door of their cottage, his arms wrapped protectively around her.

Caitlin walked to the edge of the porch and beckoned to someone in the crowd to come forward. Sarah craned her neck to see who it was and failed to prevent an escaped gasp when she saw Papin reaching a hand up to Caitlin to be helped up to the porch.

"Papin!" Sarah took a step toward her but Iain was still sitting in the dirt and, because of the gathered crowd, blocking her way around him. She turned to see Mike's surprise, then his face contorted into a thunderhead when he saw whom it was.

Papin stepped up to stand next to Caitlin. She was wearing a new dress, obviously one of Caitlin's since Sarah had never seen it

before, and unless she'd become about four months more pregnant since the last time Sarah had seen her, she was wearing a
pillow under her dress, too.

What was going on?

Caitlin addressed the crowd. "Some of you don't know me,
but for the ones who do, as my husband has already said, I hope
that our time together here will erase old hurts and put us on a
path to a more united community. I'm sure everyone would agree
we can't truly be healed if we don't address the wrongs that have
hurt us. And nowhere is that more true than in the damage that
was done to our own Papin, who came to us as a hurt and
wounded soul only to find treachery and betrayal."

Sarah was on the porch, pushing past Caitlin when her
fingers wrapped around Papin's thin arm. "Papin, I don't know
what you think you're doing—"

"Ow! Mum! You're hurting me!" Papin whimpered, trying to
pry Sarah's fingers from her arm.

"Unhand her!" Brian roared. He pulled his gun back out as
Mike and Declan both made movements to step forward.
"Nobody is to go near my wife or her...or Papin."

Sarah took her hand away. "Papin, what is going on?"

"What is going on, Mrs. Woodson," Caitlin said, firmly
pushing Sarah away from Papin. "Is that Papin has finally gotten
the courage to name the father of her baby."

A murmured wave of whispers swept the people standing,
watching. Sarah saw that the crowd had grown now. It wasn't just
the gypsy men gathered and listening with rapt attention but
almost every single person in camp. Caitlin had timed her exhibi-
tion well. It was the hour before dinner when most people were
in camp.

Caitlin turned back to her audience. "And why wouldn't she
be afraid to name him? He, the vile sod who took her—a child,
herself—by forcing his perverse lusts upon her?"

What was she saying? That Papin was raped? Sarah twisted

around to see Papin's face but it was implacable. Neither guilt nor shame nor fear showed there. If anything, she looked like she was beaming.

"Aye, who is it among us who could have done this horrific deed? Papin? Will you, name him, lass? Will you name the animal what done this to you?"

Sarah could hear the far off whine of one of John's wolf puppies. She was grateful he wasn't here to see this. She watched as Papin nodded sweetly to Caitlin and then stepped forward to address the crowd. The quiet was absolute.

"The man what done this to me," she said, her voice breathless and small as her hand came to light on the swelling beneath her dress, "is me own *da*, Mike Donovan."

15

S arah's mouth fell open as Papin addressed the crowd. Caitlin stood next to her with her hand on Papin as if in support. In the crowd, she saw the look of confusion on Mike's face as if he was sure he hadn't heard correctly. Two young men—both from the gypsy group—appeared on either side of him, flanking him. They hadn't touched him yet. Their eyes were on Gilhooley as if awaiting orders.

The crowd gasped in surprise and turned as one to look at Mike. Some craned their necks to see Sarah's reaction.

"Only, I did want to clear up one thing," Papin said meekly. "It *weren't* rape. I was happy to do it to please him."

The roar that came next could only have come from one source. Sarah recovered her senses in time to see Mike being restrained now by the two gypsy men. His face was purple with fury as he struggled to free himself.

"Papin! What are you saying, girl? Have you gone mental?"

"I know it were a secret, Da," Papin said, shrugging. "Sorry for telling."

"Papin, me girl, if I get my hands on you, I swear –"

"Perhaps you've done enough damage with you having your

hands on her," Gilhooley said, stepping in front of him, his hand once more on his pistol.

Mike lunged at him. "You disgusting pervert, I consider her my daughter."

"Which makes this situation all the more revolting. Laying with your own adoptive daughter—and a child, at that!"

"Papin!" he shouted. "Tell them the truth or so help me God—"

"Maybe you could stop threatening the poor child," a voice yelled out from the crowd.

Gilhooley turned to the girl on the porch and addressed her kindly. "Papin, lass, if you're afraid to tell us the truth, you needn't worry that Donovan will lay another finger on you."

"No, I'm not. Only he didn't force me."

"Papin, tell them the truth!" Mike shouted.

"I am, Da," Papin said, her eyes round and wide. "I mean, I told Caitlin it were only the one time and you and me know it was lots more." She smiled shyly at him.

"I will *throttle* you, Papin!"

"Now, now, that's enough of that," Gilhooley said. "Since she's obviously afraid to stick by her original report of rape, it looks like we'll not have the pleasure of you in our new jail facility, Donovan. But neither can we abide having a child molester in our community. Remove him from the camp at once."

"It *was* rape!" Caitlin said, who seemed to be as stunned as the crowd at Papin's words. "She told me he took her against her will! Didn't you?"

"I'm sorry if you was to misunderstand me, Missus Gilhooley," Papin said. "But it were never rape."

Caitlin was red-faced and sputtering, looking very much like she needed to be restrained herself. If it weren't for the large crowd, Sarah had little doubt Caitlin would have physically launched into Papin.

"This is fucking barking. I never touched her and she knows it."

Sarah watched as the two gypsy men began to try to haul Mike out of the crowd. She had an irrational image of King Kong flipping a swarm of natives off him, only in this case, the natives were winning.

"Let him go!" she shouted as she watched Mike grapple with the men. She turned to Gilhooley. "You can't accuse people without evidence. It's insane to think he touched her."

"I'd say the *evidence* is prominently displayed for all to see, Missus," Gilhooley said primly.

Declan leapt off the porch in a sudden movement that made Sarah jump and stumble backward onto the decking, but Iain stopped him with a hard fist to the stomach. Declan crumpled to his knees as Sarah watched in horror as Iain lifted a large cricket bat over his head and brought it crashing down on his head.

Fiona screamed and ran to her husband, immobile in the dirt and the gravel.

"Motherfucker tried to interfere with camp regulations," Iain said, tossing down the bat and wiping blood from his mouth from his earlier beating. "Looks like we'll have at least one person in the new jail. Get him outta here." Two more men—friends and neighbors—materialized from the crowd to grab the unconscious Declan under the arms and begin to drag him off.

Sarah ran to where Fiona was pounding on the backs of the men hauling Declan off and pulled her away. "You can't stop it, Fi," Sarah said. "You'll just end up getting hurt."

"Wise words, Mrs. Woodson," Gilhooley said as he watched the proceedings with grim satisfaction. "You'll need to heed them yourself if you have any ideas about interfering with camp justice. As you are no longer a member of this camp, I'll ask you to remove yourself to your quarters."

"Have you lost your mind?" Sarah said. "You can't assault

people or throw Mike out of his own camp! I don't know why Papin is saying what she's saying but—"

"I have the power to do exactly that and more, Mrs. Woodson," Gilhooley said. He turned to the crowd, most of whom were following Mike as he was forcibly escorted to the camp entrance. "I'll ask everyone to clear this area for a time," he said to their retreating backs.

Sarah helped a sobbing Fiona to her feet in time to see Caitlin lead Papin away.

"Papin!" Sarah shouted, but Papin never turned around. "Papin!"

"Sarah, what is happening?" Fiona said, her face streaked with tears as she looked in the direction Declan was taken. "What will they do with him?"

"Come on, Fi," Sarah said. "Let's get you inside. Who knows what that lunatic is capable of next." As she climbed the stairs, she saw Gavin standing alone in the crowd looking bewildered. "Gavin! Go find John and bring him to your Auntie Fi's. Do you understand me?" She watched him nod as if in a trance and then turn away.

As she stood on the porch watching the last of the crowd disperse, Sarah thought she saw a flash of Mike's blue shirt at the far side of the camp at the north entrance.

Well, she thought. *I guess Caitlin made her first move.*

THE OLD CABIN had been open to the weather in the months since Sarah and David had lived in it. Mike stood on the rickety porch and got a flash of memory of the many times he'd visited Deirdre and old Seamus here. Hard to believe the couple was dead and gone these past many months. He pushed open the front door with his foot and was rewarded with the sound of rustling in the interior. Something had obviously taken up residence over the summer.

The two-mile walk from camp had helped work off his anger, so that by the time he reached the old cottage he felt relatively calm. Although at first he was aghast and furious with Papin, it didn't take long to work out that the real culprit in this piece was Caitlin. Although how she got Papin to mouth the words she needed saying was anybody's guess.

He shook his head and sat down on the wooden chair on the porch.

*What a mess. Me, exiled from me own camp. Everyone thinking I took advantage of a young girl, for cripe's sake. And Sarah...*the walk to the cabin had given him some time to think of Sarah's reaction, too—what he'd had a chance to see.

No, she'd not doubt him, he knew that. But still, she had to be sick about it.

"Hello! Mike!"

He jerked his head up to see Aideen riding down the winding drive from the high road in a small pony trap. Taffy sat next to her, clutching the seat, her eyes wide. He stood up and dropped to the ground from the porch to put his hand on the pony's caves-son. "Whoa, there," he said. "Jaysus, Aideen, what are you doing here?"

He had to admit, she looked beautiful. Her fair skin was pink in the late afternoon breeze and her eyes were lively and intent.

"What do you mean?" she said handing the reins to Taffy and jumping down to the ground. "Where you go, I go. If they don't want you, they don't want me either."

"I'm sure it'll all be resolved shortly," Mike said. "Did you bring your clothes and belongings?" He moved to the back of the cart. There were only a few boxes. Taffy's toys—most of which required batteries and didn't work any more—and two suitcases full of clothes.

"I told Jimmy I'd return the cart in the morning," Aideen said, reaching in the back to drag out a suitcase.

Mike put a hand on her arm to stop her. "Aideen, no," he said. "You'll go back tonight."

"But Mike, why? Not only do I not want to be any where near those hypocrites and back stabbers you call friends, but I prefer to send the message of where my loyalties lie."

"You don't have to send any message to me," he said, shoving her bag back into the cart. "Hello, darling," he said to Taffy who stared at him with big frightened eyes. He had to hand it to Aideen, by bringing her own daughter to him she was broadcasting to the world her complete faith in Mike.

He put his hand on her shoulder and felt a rush of relief and gratitude toward her. She really did love him. "Come in and let's put together a cup of tea," he said, dropping his hand to her waist and guiding her around the back of the cart toward the cottage. "And then I'll drive ye both back to camp."

"Mike, no," Aideen said. "We're here to move in with you."

"I know that, lass," Mike said, reaching up to help Taffy to the ground. The child looked terrified. "But it's not a good idea."

"I don't care what they think."

Mike watched Taffy grab at her mother's pant legs and look up at him with wide eyes. He sighed. "It's what I think, too."

Aideen watched him silently for a moment as she combed her fingers through Taffy's hair. Finally, she leaned down to the child and whispered to her. Taffy turned and climbed into the back of the cart, digging out a doll wearing a wedding dress.

"All right, Mike," Aideen said quietly. "Are you breaking it off with me?"

"I'd rather not have this conversation in the road."

"I don't really feel like I can wait until we have optimal conditions. Why, may I ask?"

Mike ran a hand through his hair. The truth was he hadn't known what he was going to say anything until the words were out of his mouth. But there was something about standing here looking at this cottage—with the community he built barred to him—and then seeing her, that made him realize once and for all that it was a lie.

"I don't know why. And I know that's no answer. And I'm sorry as I can be about it."

"Even with Sarah leaving?"

"This has nothing to do with Sarah."

"Oh, I believe you. Millions wouldn't."

"I just can't..." He shook his head. "I am so sorry, Aideen. You are a great woman. You're gorgeous and smart and sexy as all hell—"

"Stop it, Mike."

Mike could see she was fighting to keep the tears in and it made him feel about two inches tall to know he'd led her so far down this rosy path.

"I just know it wouldn't work," he said, looking away.

"So you're just going to live in this cottage by yourself and become the Irish hermit?"

"I told you. I have every reason to believe this Papin thing will get sorted out."

"Well, if you think that, then you haven't been listening. This is the first wave of the attack. They wanted to get you for *rape*. If you could've seen Caitlin's face when Papin wouldn't stick to the script, you'd realize that *banishment* will not satisfy her."

Mike frowned and glanced in the direction of the community.

"Plus," she said, "you do know they beat up Declan and hauled him off to the jail?"

"What?!" Mike took two steps toward the community and then turned back to her, his eyes flashing, his fists clenching. "When? Why?"

"I think mainly because Brian's an asshole being led around by his psychopath wife."

"What's the charge against him?"

"I don't know that there *is* one except for Iain hating him. Still think Taffy and I are better off there?"

Mike looked into her eyes and saw the utter defeat reflected in them. "No. The two of you'll stay here with me."

THE PUPPIES WERE a welcome distraction to a somber house Sarah thought as she poured the fourth pot of tea in two hours. It wasn't like Fiona to go all weepy and distracted. Sarah figured it was probably pregnancy hormones kicking in. The two boys alternately played with the dogs and whined about not being able to leave the cottage.

"John," Sarah said, putting her hand on him, "I might need you to run an errand for me, but until then I appreciate you sitting tight, okay?"

He turned his face to hers as if to determine whether she were serious or merely placating him. "Sure," he said. "But the dogs need to go out. I mean, unless Auntie Fi doesn't care if they wee all over her living room rug."

"Fine. You and Gavin take them out, but don't dally and don't wander over to the cook fire. You don't need to hear what people are saying right now."

Sarah watched them as they herded the wolves out the front door and then she turned to Fiona curled up on the couch and wrapped in a wool afghan in spite of the summer weather. "You okay?"

Fiona looked at the closed front door as if seeing an apparition standing there.

"Fi?"

"I'm fine," she croaked. "It's just...it looked like they'd killed him, Sarah."

"I know, Fi, but I saw him moving when they took him." That

wasn't true, but Sarah couldn't imagine it would be helpful at the moment for Fiona to believe Declan was dead.

Fiona looked at her suddenly. "Isn't today the day you're supposed to go to Limerick?"

Sarah shrugged. "I'm not going."

Fiona nodded. "Well, obviously. But I imagine they'll have a flight out tomorrow."

"I'm not going at all, Fi."

Fiona stared at her in silence. If Sarah had been hoping for a look of uncontrolled delight on her friend's face, she was disappointed.

I guess we're a long way away from happy dances.

"When did you decide this?"

"Somewhere between learning that Papin couldn't come to the US and watching her become BFFs with a pit viper."

Fiona sighed heavily and nodded. "That would do it. Well, I'm glad. We've got to fix this shite, Sarah. I don't know how, but we have to fix it."

"We will." Sarah poured another cup of tea for herself and sat down on the couch with Fiona. "I'll talk to Papin. She'll recant. Mike will return. Dec will be released."

There was a moment of silence.

"Mike won't return. They'd never let him."

"You're probably right."

"I tried to think of what possible reason Papin would have for accusing Mike of being the father of her baby."

"Well, obviously Caitlin put her up to it."

"Sure, but why would Papin do it? She *loves* Mike."

"I know. I don't know. She's so sweet and dear and cheerful most of the time, we tend to forget she's basically pretty fucked up."

"Poor lass," Fiona murmured.

The front door banged open and Sarah dropped her teacup on the floor with a clang. John stood in the opening with all three squirming dogs in his arms. They appeared to be trying to bite his fingers.

"Ouch, bastards! Stop that!" John said, yelping.

"For the love of God, John," Sarah said, leaning over to pick up the broken china. "What's the matter?"

"Winky and Dez said they saw Aideen and Taffy leaving in a pony cart a couple hours ago."

"Who in the world are Winky and Dez?"

"The two gypsies who play the guitar by the fire. Anyway, people are saying they went to stay with Uncle Mike at our old place, Mom."

"Mike went to our old cottage?"

"That's what people are saying."

"Where's Gavin? I told you boys to come right back."

"Sorry, Mom. Gavin didn't think you meant him." He nodded at Fiona. "He went to see Uncle Dec."

Fiona gasped and dropped the afghan on the rug. Sarah grabbed for her cup in case there were more broken pieces of china to deal with.

"Is he okay? Is he badly hurt?" Fiona asked.

"I dunno. Gavin's still down there. But Mr. Jamison came by when I was out with the dogs and he told me the camp's in lockdown and if anybody leaves, they won't be allowed back in."

Fiona turned to Sarah, her face a mask of determination and fear. "What are we going to do, Sarah?"

CAITLIN TOOK a long breath and tried to at least muffle her fury. It wouldn't do any good for the idiot wog to get the wrong idea about her intentions. She straightened the jacket on her ridiculous pantsuit—*what idiot wore these things?*—and went to the back bedroom to sit next to Papin where she lay in bed.

"You feeling better?" Caitlin asked her as she smoothed out the top coverlet of the bed.

Papin smiled sweetly at her. "I'm good," she said. "Thank you, Caitlin. And I'm sorry about today. I know you wanted me to say it were rape."

"That's all right, dearest," Caitlin said. *Gypsy bitch!* "It was hard enough to say what you did say, I know."

Papin didn't answer.

"Did it help at all, seeing the expression on Mike's face? I told you there would be some healing as soon as the words were out of your mouth. Was that true?"

Papin hesitated. "Oh, sure. It helped a lot seeing him all..." Papin swallowed and Caitlin could see she was wrestling with herself about something. "Seeing him all upset and buggered. It was real good."

"See? I told you." Caitlin patted her hand. "And now we just have to do one more thing and we'll put it all to rest and won't that feel good?"

Papin nodded, her eyes watching Caitlin's. Was the girl afraid of her? Perhaps she was just tired. "It will," Papin said.

"You do want to stay here in camp, don't you?"

Papin nodded. "More than anything."

"Well, once we do this one little thing, you can count on being here for always."

"And Sarah, too."

"Yes, dearest, of course. And Sarah, too. Now let's go over it, then you can sleep."

Papin struggled to sit up. She didn't look pregnant yet, Caitlin observed. But she did look filled out in all the right places, as Caitlin knew her husband, Brian, had also observed.

"I'm supposed to go to Auntie Fi's first thing in the morning," Papin said, as if reciting, "and slip the ground-up mushrooms you give me into her tea or whatever's to hand."

"That's right."

"And you promise they'll just make her sick and no more?"

"They're not poisonous, just mildly toxic. What next, Papin?"

Papin looked at the ceiling as if trying to remember the next steps. "You'll make sure me mum comes to the house with the thermos of poisoned soup. What if she drinks the soup before she gets there?"

"She won't. I'll tell her it's for Fiona on account of her being sick. Don't worry. Nobody is going to eat the soup."

Papin nodded. "And when me mum comes in, I run out and fetch Mr. Jamison saying I think me mum's trying to kill me auntie."

"Very good."

"You're positive she won't get in real trouble?"

"Of course, dearest. She'll be briefly detained in her cottage— just long enough for you to miss your flight to the States."

"Won't she just try again?"

"We'll think of something for the next time. And the next time. You do trust me, don't you, Papin?"

Papin nodded sleepily and scooted back under her covers, her eyes closing. "I do," she murmured.

"Good night, dearest," Caitlin said, leaning over to make a kissing sound by Papin's cheek but stopping short of actually touching her. She stood, then blew out the candle and went to the interior of the cottage. Out the front window the riff-raff gypsies had gathered to play their music and tell stories. *Even without grog*, she thought with amazement. She'd have to get Brian to put an end to all that.

She sat in a chair by the window to await Brian's return from camp patrol, and gave herself a few moments of pleasure re-living the expression on Mike Donovan's face when he realized he'd been fingered as the father of the gypsy skank's unborn child. She smiled and felt the tingling sensation of pure joy as she re-envisioned his eyes, shocked and uncomprehending, his shouts of disbelief and shame.

Yes, it would have been so much better to have been able to drag him to jail and hung for rape. That little turn of events had been supremely disappointing. But it just meant that a greater pleasure waited.

The death of his dear sister Fiona and the execution of his lover for the crime would do in the meantime to make up for the annoyance of his escape today.

I wonder, Mike, when you hear of their deaths, if you'll feel anything like what I felt when you put that rope around Aidan's neck —the only man who ever truly loved me— all because of the lies of that American bitch.

She watched Brian climb the porch stairs to their cottage.

And best of all? It's only the beginning.

16

apin was wearing a purple sweater and sitting on the ground by the main cook fire playing with the gypsy babies when Sarah came out of Fiona's cottage the next morning.

She acts like nothing's happened, Sarah thought with amazement as she trotted down the steps and walked purposefully toward her adopted daughter. One of the gypsy women saw her from over Papin's shoulder and scooped up her toddler and ran toward the interior part of the camp where the gypsies had set up their main settlement.

Papin twisted around to see what had startled the woman and, seeing Sarah, her eyes widened in alarm. Before Sarah could reach her, Papin was on her feet, but Sarah lunged for her and grabbed her by the arm before she could move away.

"Just one minute, young lady," Sarah said, cursing how ridiculously maternal she sounded. "I need a word with you."

"Caitie says nothing good can come from you and me talking, Sarah," Papin said, her face contorted into a grimace as she attempted to unhook Sarah's fingers from her arm.

"Oh, does she?" Sarah forced herself not to shake Papin until her eyes rattled. While she didn't let go of her, she did force her voice to remain calm. "Whatever you think you're doing, Papin, it will *not* work. Whatever mad idea you've got for saying Mike is the father of that baby, will not work, do you hear me?"

"Well, I'm sorry, Mum," Papin said. Sarah could see a few people had stopped their chores and were listening to them with evident fascination. She watched Papin's eyes and it was clear she noticed them too. "I knew you were hurt about me not telling ya about the baby, but how could I tell you?" Papin said, raising her voice now. "I knew how you burned to be in Da's bed. How could I tell you it was *me* he chose over you?"

"I think you've got your pigtails screwed in too tight, Papin, if you think for one moment that anyone believes you and Mike were lovers."

"They all believe it!" She waved her free hand toward the camp. "Just like Caitie knew they would."

"*Why* are you spending time with that woman? You've heard the stories we told about Caitlin before you came—"

Papin finally pulled her arm away. "Yes, I heard them and now I know they were not true."

"*Not true*? You've known her all of twenty-four hours and you believe her lies over the people who love you?"

"Is this love? Really? Doesn't feel that way to me. You don't care who you hurt to get what you want. Not me or Da or John. I saw it in Wales...I saw it the first time I met you. You let Evvie die because she was too slow!"

Sarah gasped and put a hand to her mouth. "That is not true," she whispered, the pain and grief of the dear woman's death still not muted enough to bear hearing her name.

"It's what I believe," Papin said, tears streaming down her face. "I believe every thing bad that's happened to us is because you needed to do things your way no matter who got hurt. Ask Da if it's not true!"

"Papin..." Sarah reached out for her again.

"Don't touch me!" Papin said, jerking her arm and taking two steps away. "I'm sick of people saying they love me only for what they can get out of me. Fact is I hate you, Sarah!"

"Papin!"

The girl turned and ran from the camp center, pushing past the group of people who had gathered to hear the argument. Sarah stood helplessly, watching Papin go, then turned her back on the gawkers and walked back to Fiona's cottage.

It wasn't until she was back inside Fiona's living room Sarah realized she hadn't told Papin they were staying.

GAVIN SAW her coming down the path from the corner of his eye. It was hard not to see her, wearing that outlandish purple jumper —*in all this heat?* He gave his fishing pole a shake hoping the bait would look a little more alive to whatever fish was eyeing it below the surface of the pasture pond. Da said he was crazy to think he'd pull anything out of it and he was determined to prove him wrong.

Da. Gavin hadn't been there yesterday when the whole ruckus went down but he'd seen the aftermath, with Brian's blokes dragging Da out the front gate. At first he thought they were just playing around. It didn't seem possible—not in any universe he could imagine—that they were actually throwing him out.

How could that be? The fecking place was called Donovan's Lot!

Or at least it used to be.

Gavin watched Papin pick her way gingerly down the path to where he stood at the pond's edge. "Oy, Papin," he said. "I can't have a lot of chatter, mind, or I'll never catch anything."

"I'll be quiet," she said, sitting in slump at his feet and knocking over his canteen.

"Something the matter?"

She looked up at him and he could see she'd been crying. *Aw,*

I don't want to deal with crying. He jerked his pole and tried to concentrate on how the line pierced the placid surface of the water.

"Are you serious, Gavin?" she asked. "Were you not there yesterday? Did you really not hear?"

"Oh. You mean yesterday."

"Aye, where I announced to the world that Da was the father of me baby?" She looked out over the water.

There was a moment and then Gavin spoke. "So, that's not the truth of it, then?"

She snorted and looked down at her hands. "What do you think?" she said quietly.

"Then who?"

Papin acted as if she hadn't heard him and Gavin watched her straighten out her legs and pull at the grass to sprinkle it onto her legs. Just when he gave up and turned his attention back to the fishing line in the water, she cleared her throat.

"You remember Ollie?"

Holy shite. "It was Ollie who got you up the spout?"

She nodded.

"And that was the reason he was fighting with Eeny."

"Just say it, Gav," Papin said jumping to her feet. "It was me that got Eeny killed. I know it! You don't think I don't know it?"

He stumbled back a step, surprised at her outburst. "Hey, settle down, Papin. You're scaring the fish."

She hugged herself and turned her back on him.

"So why'd you say it was Da?" Gavin asked. "So people wouldn't know you were the reason Ollie killed Eeny?"

She turned to look at him like she would burst into tears any moment. He didn't know why she was so upset but he knew it was probably something he said.

"I'm sorry, Papin," he said. "I always say the wrong thing. You should talk to Auntie Fi or someone. I'm a right berk when it comes to talking to girls."

She shook her head and sank back to the ground. "No," she said. "No, you're not a berk, Gav. You tell the truth and there's few girls don't like to be dealt with straight."

"So *was* it because of Eeny you blamed it on Da?" He frowned because he was working hard on trying to figure out how blaming Da for it would help anything.

"No. It was because I was mad at Da. And Mum." She ripped more grass with her hand and flung it back to the ground. "And someone told me it would help."

"Mad because of you having to leave and go to America?"

"Yes. *And* for the two of them breaking up in the first place. But now that I've slept on it, I don't think it was such a good idea." She looked up at him and he thought her face looked like that of a little girl. "Can you forgive me, Gavin?"

"Forgive you? Cor, I'm just glad you didn't pin it on me!"

She smiled ruefully and that made him glad. He seemed to be cheering her up some. She had such pretty brown eyes. Almond-shaped, like most gypsies.

"And I'll miss you, Papin," he said, reeling in his line to cast again. "You and John both. Heaps."

"Well that's one good thing out of all this anyway," she said with a sigh. "We'll not be leaving after all."

"You won't?"

She stood up and shook the grass from her clothes. "No. And it's Caitie who helped me see how to do that." She put a hand on her still-flat stomach. "Now that I'm going to be a mother meself, I need to start figuring out solutions to my problems. That's what Caitie says."

"Well, she's probably right about that at least."

"Have you seen Da since...you know, yesterday?"

Gavin shook his head. "Camp's in lockdown. Nobody allowed to leave right now. I'm sure he's fine. Besides," he laughed, "he'll need time to work off that temper you put him in!"

He watched her face crinkle up into a smile and she laughed, too. "Oy, you shoulda seen how mad he was! If he coulda reached me, I know he'd a killed me!"

"You're likely right about that."

"You think he'll forgive me?"

"You know Da."

"Yeah. I do." She stood on tiptoes and gave Gavin a quick kiss on the cheek. "Sorry if I buggered the fishing," she said. "And thanks for the talk, Gav. You're the best big brother a girl could ask for. I feel tons better."

"Glad I could help. You heading back?"

She turned and started back up the footpath to the main camp and he noticed she walked with more energy than when she'd come.

"Aye," she said, patting the pockets of her pants as if trying to confirm she still had something. "But first I have to pay a little visit to Auntie Fi."

CAITLIN THUMPED the bowl of soup down in front of her father. The old git must imagine she was Ellen to be thinking she'd wait on him hand and foot like this. Brian leaned over the table to give her a chaste kiss before leaving to patrol the camp with his men. She smiled and waved him off, knowing how important it was to act all sweetness and light in front of Brian—and that included the nauseatingly painful chore of acting the dutiful daughter to this old redheaded windbag. The only thing that made it bearable was the fact she also knew she wouldn't need to do it much longer.

When she first met Brian, she could see he wanted something pure and untouched, and because all he ever did was talk about the need to find a rural community he could run, she made sure she was all that for him. She also made sure they did it at least once, and it wasn't easy—he was that determined to keep her pure. But she needed the fake pregnancy and miscarriage to clench the deal. And stupid though he was, he wasn't so stupid as to think she could get pregnant without doing the deed at least once.

Before they married she would sneak out of her father's house to have it off with any wally in the local pubs who wasn't too drunk to get it up. After they tied the knot it had become a little trickier. On top of that, it had become quickly clear that, as far as Brian and sex were concerned, a little went a long way.

"You need to move out, old man," Caitlin said to her father as she sat down at the table with him. "Go sleep with Cedric and Colon."

Archie Kelly looked at her with surprise. "The boys are sleeping on mats out in the fields," he said.

"Yeah, so?"

"I can't sleep out of doors, ya selfish hoor! Do you want me to tell that idiot husband of yours who you really are? Ya can't be throwing your own da out into the street."

"I heard Brian tell you to take Donovan's old place."

"Pshaw! It's a dump. The bed is more like a wooden crate with rags thrown on it. I can't believe the bastard actually lived there."

"Well you can't live here. I'm a fucking newlywed. We need our privacy."

"Why don't you pull the other one, Caitie? It's got bells on it."

"Look, you can go easy or you can go hard, old man," she said pulling his soup bowl from him.

"Hey! That's mine!"

"God. You're like a two year old. Totally fecking useless."

"Aye? Well it wasn't me went arse over tit with yon Donovan, now was it?"

"You don't know what you're talking about."

"I know he had the both of you, Ellen and yourself. Makes me want to puke to think of it."

"Did I ever tell you about the time he had us both together?"

She watched his hand start to shake, the spoon banging onto the table as it did.

"You're just trying to take the piss out of me. Why you're so cruel to your own da—"

"Oh, sod off with that *your own da* shite," she said with disgust, pushing his soup bowl back to him and spilling most of it on the table.

"What with me and your brothers come all this way to make right what that sod did to you and Ellen, you'd think you'd be a little more grateful."

"You came all this way because you had no place else to go," Caitlin said. "And trust me, the only *right* you'll be making is whatever you produce later in the loo."

"You've a disgusting tongue on you, Caitlin. If your poor mother could hear you..."

Caitlin stood abruptly and went to the sink. It was her fault. She shouldn't let the old tosser get to her like that. Brian had insisted he and the twins come with them, and after everything that was happening in Dublin it had seemed a good idea at the time.

She reached into the pocket of her jeans and pulled out a handful of the dark mushrooms she had found earlier, the dirt still clinging to them.

"Cedric says he followed Donovan out to a cabin a couple miles from here so we know where he is."

"*Everybody* knows where he is," Caitlin said. She picked up a large cleaver and roughly chopped the mushrooms into a small pile on the kitchen counter. It was important they still be recognizable as mushrooms even after several hours sitting in hot liquid.

"We aim to see him pay for Ellen's murder," Archie said, slurping loudly as he picked up his soup bowl and held it to his mouth.

Caitlin clenched her teeth at the sound. She glanced at the

pot of soup on the stove and pulled it to her. The thermos was a wide-mouth container. She sniffed it and could still smell the coffee that it once held. She dumped the pile of mushroom into the bottom of it, then carefully ladled soup on top.

"Is there more soup?" Archie called from the table.

Caitlin glanced at the tainted thermos and for a moment, she hesitated but got control quickly. *No sense in jeopardizing the plan for a moment's annoyance*, she thought.

"Sure, Da," she said sweetly, carrying a ladle of hot soup from the stove across the kitchen to where he sat with his back to her at the table. She filled his bowl, dropping a couple of drops on the back of his hand.

"Ow!" he yelped. "Watch what you're doing, girl!"

"Sorry about that." She tossed the ladle back in the soup pot and screwed on the lid to the thermos. She heard dogs barking and glanced out the window to see Sarah's boy playing with a bunch of mangy animals in the camp square. Her eyes narrowed.

Fiona and Sarah today. Mike tomorrow. And eventually every goddam one of them who watched while I was dragged out the camp entrance and thrown into the bushes.

Before they murdered my Aidan.

"Caitlin? Did you hear me?"

Caitlin shook herself out of her reverie, surprised at the flush of lust that had rushed between her legs.

"No, I didn't," she said. "Quit making so much noise. You sound like a pig rooting for corncobs." She picked up the thermos and went to the door. On the other porch, she stood and checked to see who was around, who might see her talking to him, and then descended the steps.

"Oy! John!" she said, holding the thermos carefully as she walked to where he stood with the dogs and smiling broadly. "A word, please."

⁓

"SO WHAT WILL YOU DO?" Aideen sat across from Mike the next morning. There was no tea, no food except the small hamper Aideen had brought with her. "You have no crops, no meat, not even a gun to shoot something."

"I'm sure Gav will be along shortly," Mike said. "He'll bring me a few things."

"Will you leave?"

"The area?" He frowned. "I can't leave Fi and Gavin."

"But you can't stay with them either. Perhaps they'll come with you?"

"I'm not ready to give up just yet."

"With Declan imprisoned and you gone, I think giving up needs to be a serious option."

"Maybe. But I'm not there yet."

"You're stubborn, Michael Donovan. But wishing won't take the place of facts." Aideen looked over at Taffy playing at their feet. Mike had eaten very little this morning so the child could have a full stomach. "You can't make it right for everyone all the time. You're not infallible."

He grunted and she reached across and touched his hand. They had slept the night at opposite ends of the house and, for once, she knew that neither of them felt tempted to crawl into bed with the other.

And not just because Taffy was there. Something had changed. She felt it too.

"Can you tell me how you feel?" she asked.

"How do you think I feel? It was because of what I told you about the community in the first place that made you come all the way here and now it's not safe to be there."

She shook the hand she was holding and leaned earnestly across the table to whisper so that Taffy couldn't hear. "The place isn't why I came, Mike."

He closed his eyes. "That just makes it worse," he said, his voice soft and sad.

· · ·

How could a day start out so shitty and evolve into something so right? Sarah stood in the front room of Siobhan's cottage and folded the few pieces of clothing she still owned. Some of them were hers, but most of her clothing had been lost in the fire that destroyed Cairn Cottage. Since then she had resorted to wearing whatever she could find or was given to her.

She knew Papin was upset with her, but now that they were all staying she would be able to take the necessary time to sort things out with her. Plus, it wasn't out of the question that she and Mike might work something out, too. Sarah wasn't sure what that would look like since she still hoped to go back to the States in due course, but she wouldn't worry about that now.

It worked for Scarlett O'Hara, she thought and then realized: *not really.*

"It's people like you making other people jump through hoops is why we're in this mess," Siobhan said as she sat watching Sarah pack up.

"As usual," Sarah said, "I have no earthly idea of what you're talking about." She smiled at the woman to temper her words.

"Just when I was getting used to you being here and crowding me, making a mess of the place..."

Sarah knew what Siobhan had gotten used to was Sarah doing the laundry and making dinner most nights. But now with her decision to stay, Sarah wanted to move into Mike's place with Gavin and John. Somebody needed to be with the boys. She brightened at the thought of being around when Fi's baby was born, then frowned when she thought of Declan being held by Brian and his lot.

"It's what I've come to expect from you," Siobhan said, the whine in her voice finally hitting a rare nerve in Sarah. "The Americans are always pushing their way into things and then leaving everyone worse off than how they found them."

"Do you want me to come by now and then and do your laundry, Siobhan? Because it would be no trouble. Or, better yet, how about if the boys come over here to live? You've got plenty of room."

Fully expecting the widow to recoil in horror at the suggestion, Sarah was surprised when Siobhan sighed and said, "Well, I wondered when you'd get around to suggesting it. As much of a hardship as it would be for me, I suppose there's nothing for it. The lads need us after all."

Sarah stopped folding and stared at her. *Oh my God. She's lonely.*

She went and sat down next to her, ignoring the old woman's flinch when she did. "You'd be up for that, Siobhan? They're boys and can get pretty rowdy. Plus, they come with three puppies."

Siobhan crossed her arms and looked away. "Pshaw. I raised four sons."

Sarah did not know that. "Where are they?" she asked gently.

"One died when he was two. Fell off a wall and broke his neck."

Sarah nodded sympathetically. *Remind me not to let you babysit Fi or Papin's babies when they're born.*

"The other three grew up and left home. Left Ireland."

Sarah chose her words carefully. "I suppose you're pretty worried about what must be happening to them."

Siobhan made a noise of disgust. "As it happens, since two went to America I'm not at all worried. They probably read about our troubles on their iPads or whatnot and went back to their big houses and their Episcopalian wives without a second thought."

"And the other son?"

"In prison in the UK, if you must know. I suppose you'll be spreading that everywhere around the camp now."

Sarah stood up and went back to her packing. She buckled up the battered suitcase and shoved it under the table. "Where would the boys sleep?" she asked.

A voice shouting from outside interrupted the moment and Sarah crossed to the front door to see who it was.

"Hey, Mom," John said, dragging three of the wolf puppies along behind him on a leather strap. "Can you come check on Auntie Fi?"

Sarah was out of the house and down the steps in a flash. "What's the matter? Is everything okay? I thought she was down at the jail trying to get Declan out."

"I don't know, Mom. Missus Gilhooley just told me to tell you that she's real sick and needs you."

"Missus Gilhooley?"

"Uh huh. You coming?"

Sarah hesitated and then ran back to shut the door behind her. Before leaving for Fiona's, she had a thought. "John? Why don't you bring the puppies into the Widow Murray's place for a few minutes."

"Are you kidding? She hates kids."

"I think it will distract her. If she's not enjoying it, you can leave."

"Aw, Mom, do I have to?"

"No, but I wish you would. Did Missus Gilhooley say what was the matter with Fi?"

John shook his head and trudged up the steps of the cottage. "She just said to hurry," he said.

Sarah jogged out of the forecourt of the little cottage for the gravel path that led to the main camp. *Was it related to her pregnancy? She had looked fine this morning. Perhaps she'd gotten emotionally overwrought as a result of her visit with Declan? Perhaps she learned that Declan was dead?*

"Missus?"

The little girl was so small and so quiet that Sarah almost didn't see her when she turned the last corner before reaching the path that led to the camp center.

"Oh, goodness, child! I nearly stepped on you." Sarah smiled briskly and was about to continue on when the girl thrust out a hand holding a coffee thermos.

"Missus Aideen says she can't come right now, but if you're going to see Missus Cooper I'm to give you this here soup for her."

Sarah paused. She thought Aideen was outside the camp at Mike's. Obviously she must be back. She took the thermos from the child and smiled. "Thank you, sweetie. And tell Missus Aideen thank you, too, okay?"

The child nodded and then fled down the path.

Boy, it looks like Aideen is doing everything possible to worm her way into Fi's good graces. Sarah hefted the thermos, which felt like it was only half full. *Oh, well. A half gesture is better than none at all.*

She hurried down the path to Fiona's.

"DID you give it to her like I said?"

"Yes, Missus."

"And said it was from Missus Aideen?"

"Yes, Missus."

"Very good, darling. Here's your cookie. Made with real sugar. Mind you don't tell anyone or they'll want one, too."

"Yes, Missus."

Caitlin watched the little girl scamper off clutching her cookie. It wouldn't matter if she did tell someone, she mused.

Who would believe a little gypsy girl over the camp leader's wife?

17

The minute Sarah stepped into Fiona's cottage she knew something was wrong.

There was a feeling of quiet and finality that Sarah had never felt before. It literally made the hairs on the back of her neck stand up—almost as if someone were lying in wait for her.

"Fi?" She shut the door behind her. She was about to look in Fiona's bedroom when she noticed someone lying on the couch in the front room. If Fiona were sick, Sarah knew she would be in her room. "Fi?"

A muffled response from the couch and a glimpse of purple ignited Sarah's instincts to maximum anxiety. In two steps she was at the couch and on her knees, her hands reaching to push the hair out of the eyes of the face she loved so well.

"Papin? What is it? Are you sick?"

Papin gave her a weak smile and her eyes fluttered open and then shut. She licked her lips and gave every appearance of being drugged.

How was that possible? We don't even have aspirin in camp any more.

"Papin, what's the matter with you?"

"I was supposed to give the mushrooms to Auntie Fi to make her sick so that you were blamed for it," Papin said, speaking slowly as if the words were hard to form. "But when she wasn't here I got a tons better idea." She opened her eyes to look at Sarah. "I figured if it was *me* that got sick you for sure wouldn't make us go." She laughed weakly. "I'm right, aren't I, Mum? We're staying now, right?"

"You...you ate poisoned mushrooms?" Sarah said, not believing the words as they came out of her mouth. "You deliberately ate poison?"

"It's not real poison, Mum," Papin said sleepily. "Just enough to make a person sick. Caitlin said they wouldn't hurt but they do a little."

Maybe if she could get her to throw up she could get the stuff out of her system. But first she needed to keep her awake.

"Why did you want to give them to Fi?" Sarah sat on the couch and pulled Papin onto her lap. Her eyes filled with tears. *They had no antidote. It would take a modern hospital and a very fast ambulance to even think about trying to possibly.*

"To make it look like you tried to hurt her. It's not as bad as it sounds. Caitlin promised they'd just make you stay in your cottage for a little bit. But then you and Da would get back together." Papin grimaced and clutched at Sarah's arm in agony. When the moment passed, she relaxed again against the pillows on the couch.

"Papin, dearest girl, we've got to get those mushrooms out of your stomach. You need to sit up now."

"No, Mum. I just want to sleep now."

A pounding on the front door jerked Sarah's attention away from the pale and sweating from trembling in her arms. The door flung open and John stood there.

"Mom? You okay? I saw Auntie Fi down at the jail so I wanted to make sure you...is that Papin?"

"John," Sarah said, her throat closing up to try to keep the tears, the hysteria from pouring out of her. "You've got to go get Mike. Grab your pony. Don't bother saddling him—"

"But Mom, if I leave they won't let me back in."

"It doesn't matter, sweetie. Just go and hurry."

"What'll I do with the puppies?"

"John! Just go!"

Sarah saw the fear on his face as he looked from her to Papin's silent form in her lap. He pulled the puppies out of the room with his leash and she heard his steps pound down the front porch steps. She looked back at Papin. She had a light sheen of perspiration on her brow and Sarah wiped it away with her hand.

"When you see Da," Papin said, her eyes closing, "tell him I'm sorry. I know he knows I am. He always knows. I was just so mad at you for breaking up the family." She froze for a moment and her eyes flew open as if a terrible thought had just come to her but then she relaxed and again, her rigid muscles softening in Sarah's arms.

"Stay calm, darling," Sarah said, hating the fear she could hear in her own voice.

"Caitlin said it would feel good to get back at you but it didn't. It sucked to see the look on Da's face. You never should have sent him looking for me in Wales, Sarah. I was just too messed up from the start."

"Don't you talk like that, young lady," Sarah said, the tears streaking down her face. "And I'm *Mum* to you."

"Don't worry, Mum. It doesn't hurt. I just feel real sleepy."

"My darling girl."

"I see now how you could give it all up—even Da, as much as you love him—for me and John. Aideen told me a good mum would lie down in front of a bus to save her child. I want to be that kind of mum."

"You're going to be a wonderful mother, Papin. I know you are," Sarah said, the sobs wracking in her throat.

"I'm going to sleep a bit now," Papin said, her eyes heavy. "I love you, Mum."

"I love you, too, darling girl." A lump formed in Sarah's throat and she couldn't swallow.

"Remember Evvie?" Papin said in a faint whisper. "I've been thinking of her a lot lately. I miss her."

Sarah held Papin tightly to her chest, Papin's cold hands clasped in her own. She knew Mike would never make it in time. She had brought his poor broken waif through hell and every evil imaginable to this sanctuary. She had given her love and a family, a father, brothers, and an auntie who doted on her. For seven short months, only two hundred days, she had known love and protection and rest. She had belonged to a loving unit, been cherished and allowed to be a child again.

And it had always been too late.

Sarah bent her head to Papin's face and kissed her cheek. She stayed there and listened to the child's shallow breathing until Papin took in one long rasping breath...and didn't let it out again.

This time when the door flung open, Sarah didn't jump. There was no hurry any more. She looked up to see Mike standing there, big and blocking out all light from the outside. He was at her side in two strides and dropped to his knees, his eyes on Papin's face, his own frozen in anguish. Slowly, he put his arms around the both of them. When Sarah felt his arms, warm and strong around her, she let the tears come, the pain, the grief, the guilt. All of it, shared and absorbed by the father who loved her, too.

THE NEXT MORNING, Mike stood between Aideen and Sarah and watched the casket as it was lowered into the ground. This time of year, bodies couldn't remain unburied even for a few hours. Because Papin was buried in the kirkyard at Ballinagh, and not in the camp graveyard, no one accosted him for his presence, although Archie and the twins, Cedric and Colin, watched him intently throughout the brief service.

The priest still lived near Ballinagh, practically the only person who still did. When Mike was head of the community, he had seen to it that the man was supplied with as much food as they could spare. He had no idea if Gilhooley intended to keep that up.

Declan stood next to Fiona, his hand on her waist but his face battered and bruised to testify to the conditions he'd been subjected to while incarcerated. Mike knew it had been Fiona's begging to Brian that had allowed Declan to be released. Mike had yet to tell Fi what Sarah had told him—that it had been *her* who was supposed to have eaten the poisoned mushrooms.

Mike's eyes narrowed as he watched Caitlin stand by the open grave. She tossed flowers onto the casket and brought a white handkerchief to her eye to dab at nonexistent tears.

How could this have happened? Of all the people Caitlin wanted to hurt, how did it end up being poor defenseless little Papin? Mike's anger swelled inside him to combat the growing grief he didn't want to give in to.

His frantic gallop to camp yesterday after John delivered the news that Papin was sick had been filled with every horror Mike could imagine—including the reality when he stepped into Fi's cottage and saw Sarah holding the body of the poor dead girl.

He squeezed his eyes shut and his arm reached down without his mind giving permission to touch Sarah's hand. Instantly, her fingers laced with his. He didn't care what it looked like to anyone else. But it made him sick to know that the one thing Papin wanted so badly, *the one thing she died for*, was the one thing he and Sarah were now doing: standing together, united.

Mike watched as Caitlin looked impatiently around at the mourners and then nodded to Jamison who promptly turned toward where Mike was standing with Sarah and Aideen. Sarah must have felt him tense because she looked up to see what he was looking at.

Jamison stood before them. "Missus Woodson," he said, "I'll be needing you to come back to camp with me for questioning in the death of Papin Woodson."

Sarah just stared at him.

Mike took a step toward him, conscious of the Glock jammed into the back waistband of his jeans. Gavin had brought Mike his guns and his tools before the service.

"Back off, Jamison," he snarled. "She had nothing to do with Papin's death and everybody here knows it."

Within moments, Brian and Caitlin joined Jamison. Mike felt Aideen grab his arm and he knew she was entreating him not to pull the gun, to stay calm.

Caitlin's eyes raked him with revulsion. "She was with Papin when she died and she admitted that Papin was killed with poisoned mushrooms. There was a thermos of poisoned mushrooms in the cottage. A thermos she was seen carrying into the house."

"You got a forensic lab up your arse, Caitlin?" Mike said. "Because unless you do, and can test the body or the thermos, you're fucked and it's a suicide."

Gilhooley sucked in a harsh breath at Mike's language and Mike knew he wanted to chastise him in some way. But they were outside the camp. *He wasn't leader of shite out here.*

"Come, my dear," Gilhooley said, taking her arm. "As much as it pains me to say it, he's right. Everyone believes it to be suicide and there's no way to prove it's anything else. Besides, she was the girl's adopted mother. She had no motive to harm the poor creature." Gilhooley nodded at Sarah. "I am sorry for your loss, Mrs. Woodson."

Mike stepped away from the group and, because he was still holding hands with Sarah, pulled her back with him. He didn't know if she would speak or react, but he was pretty sure it would be better for everyone if she didn't. He realized too late when he moved, that Aideen could see his physical connection with Sarah.

When Brian dragged his wife away toward their waiting pony cart, Jamison turned to Mike. "I know you think you're off the hook, Donovan, what with your boy giving testimony the little gypsy said you didn't shag 'er after all, but nobody believes it. You're still not welcome in Daoineville."

When Mike didn't respond, Jamison gave Sarah a nasty look, then followed to where the Gilhooleys were waiting for him by the pony cart. Mike noticed Aideen had moved a step away from him. He was sorry to have upset her, there just wasn't anything for it.

Fiona and Declan walked over to them and Fi instantly put her arms around Sarah. Mike thought Declan looked to be in pretty bad shape. His face was battered and he limped. He held his arm against his chest at a funny angle too. John and Gavin came from where they had been standing and John slipped his hand into his mother's.

Sarah kissed him and stroked his face. "I can't help but think if I'd have just told her that we were staying after all...none of this would have happened."

"Don't think like that, Sarah," Fiona said. "Therein lies madness."

"You were staying?" Mike was thunderstruck.

Sarah nodded. "I was going to make a formal announcement at dinner last night and tell everyone we were staying. If only I'd told Papin first..."

"Was it because of Papin?" John asked. "The reason we were going to stay?"

Sarah hesitated, glancing briefly at Mike and Aideen, and then nodded.

"So now there's no more reason to," he said.

"No," she said softly, staring at the grave that the men were filling. The priest still stood by the rim, supervising. "No reason at all."

"I'll take you," Mike said gruffly. "Today, if you like."

He had dropped her hand when Fiona hugged her. Now he watched her rub her hand against her slacks. The breeze had picked up.

Already he could feel the coming autumn in his bones. It was going to be a hard winter.

That much he knew.

THE GOODBYE WAS WORSE than Sarah could ever have imagined. She literally clung to Fiona until John had to remind her by patting her on the back that Mike was waiting at the entrance to the camp. Declan had moved back into the cabin but his injuries kept him on the front sofa most of the day.

Whatever fight he'd had in him was gone.

Leaving the two of them like this was nearly worse than burying Papin, Sarah thought.

Nearly.

Her farewell to Siobhan had been brisk and efficient but the old woman actually broken down and wept.

Nobody else came out to say goodbye. Sarah thought that was a pretty fair illustration of how the community had become divided since Brian Gilhooly came. While she hadn't been close to many of the camp women, she had been friendly with them, easily sharing a laugh or lightening the workload of some chore made easier with more hands.

John climbed into the driver's seat of the pony cart to wait for her. Gavin leaned over John's knee and the two spoke in low voices. Sarah realized she was ripping John away from the only brother he'd ever known.

"Mom, come on, Uncle Mike will be waiting," John said, not looking at her. She gave Fiona one more last hug.

"This isn't the end, Fi," she said. "I promise you that. I'll be back to see that little one. This isn't the end."

Although they both knew it was.

"I love you, Sarah Woodson," Fiona said, smiling past her tears. "I've never met a female MacGyver before, eh? And I'll never forget you."

"Nor me you, Fi. I love you, too."

Sarah ran around the front end of the cart and threw her arms around Gavin. "Take care of yourself, Gavin," she said, tears pouring down her face. "And take care of your da, please."

"I will," Gavin said solemnly.

She gave him one last squeeze then pulled herself up onto the cart to sit next to John. She gave a limp half wave to Fiona, standing alone on her porch, her hand on her stomach, her broken husband inside. John drove the trap down the main walkway of the camp. Several gypsies stood and waved to John, a few called to him. Nobody else showed themselves.

John drove through the front gate and brought the little pony to a halt when he saw Mike standing by the first clutch of elm trees. Seeing him standing there, so familiar to her, his hair blowing lightly in the cool breeze, Sarah had to force herself to look at John and remind herself why she was doing all this.

After handing over the reins to Sarah, John settled himself in the back of the cart. When Mike took his place, he leaned back and ruffled John's hair briefly.

"Morning," he said to Sarah.

Not trusting her voice, she merely nodded. Her hands were in her lap, but they were shaking. As Mike drove the little pony cart away from the camp, she shut her eyes against the temptation of turning around to look.

Nothing good could come from that.

After a moment, she let the sounds of the pony's hooves on the hard packed dirt road and the jangle of his harness lull and relax her.

"How long do you think it will take us by cart?" she asked softly.

Mike scanned the clouds as if looking for the answer in the heavens. "Not much longer than on horseback," he said. "Last time you and I went, we stayed mostly on the road anyway."

"Eight hours?"

"Something like that. Did you bring a lunch?"

She nodded. "In the back with John. Are you hungry?"

He shook his head.

She cleared her throat. "Aideen and little Taffy staying with you at our old place, I guess?"

Mike clucked to the pony to increase his trot. "We called it off," he said. "The engagement."

Sarah felt her hands tingle at his words. Now there was nothing standing between her and Mike...but her.

"Mom? Can I have one of these sandwiches back here? I'm starving."

"Sure, sweetie," she said. She turned to Mike and looked at him for the first time since he'd climbed into the driver's seat. His face was implacable, giving away nothing. He kept his eyes on the road between the pony's ears.

What was there to say? That this changes everything? Stop the cart?

Sarah looked out over the Irish countryside. The road they were on was bordered by a long and low stonewall on both sides. It was broken in several sections but that could easily have happened before The Crisis.

How in the world was she going to ride like this for eight hours without sobbing her heart out?

She took a long breath and tightened her fists to give her strength. "It might mean nothing," she said, slowly, "but I was thinking about the thing that started the whole disaster with Declan getting thrown in jail and Papin's little speech."

Mike frowned. "You mean Jamison pawing you?"

"It was so out of the blue. Like he was waiting for me."

"You think he and Caitlin are having it on."

"I don't know, but my read is that Brian is clueless about Caitlin's real agenda."

"So she's taken an accomplice."

"However much knowing it helps."

"All knowledge helps."

"Will you stay in the area?"

"That's just what Aideen asked me. You mean, like start a new community?"

"No, but with Gavin living in the camp…"

"He'll move in with me and Aideen tomorrow."

"So you and Aideen will still live together?"

"Until I can find another place for her."

Sarah nodded and let the information sink in. "What about Fi?"

"Fi has to decide what she and Declan want," Mike said. "If they decide to leave, they're welcome to come to my place, too."

"Seamus and Deirdre's cabin is a little small for seven people."

"Seven?"

"Well, there's the baby soon."

Mike sighed. "Right. Funny how something we were all celebrating just last week now seems like such a complication."

Sarah didn't answer.

"I'll probably leave," he said. "Head back to the coast."

Sarah didn't know why she found that information upsetting. "For the fishing?"

He shrugged. "It's what I know. Makes a hell of a lot more sense than running an inland agricultural community."

"You did a great job running that community."

"Yeah, I believe you," he said dryly. "Millions wouldn't."

"I'm sure everyone is having second thoughts now that

Caitlin's there. Did you hear that she's having stocks erected next to the camp center? For public humiliation?"

Mike grimaced. "She'll probably just rotate all the poor gypsy bastards through it on a weekly basis."

"Plus, there's a rumor that one of her grotty twin brothers raped a gypsy girl over the weekend. But the gypsies are too afraid to report it now that Declan's out of the picture."

"Welcome to Daoineville."

"It's a nightmare."

"That it is."

They were silent for several minutes before Sarah spoke again. "I can't help but think Papin was all my fault." Her voice cracked and she struggled not to cry.

Mike put a hand on her knee. "I know you do. But isn't it enough to mourn her without feeling responsible for her death, too?"

"That makes sense but I can't help it."

"Try harder."

"I really wanted us to be the family she never had."

"And we were. Why not think of it this way: she died because she loved us so much she didn't want to lose us. And *that's* because we showed her what love is."

"Do you think she was doomed from the start?"

"Sarah, we loved her, we did our best by her. It ending like this doesn't alter those facts."

"I just can't believe she's gone." She buried her face in her hands and felt Mike's arm go around her shoulders. From behind her, she felt John's hand on her back.

"We all miss her, Mom," John said. "It's nobody's fault she's gone except maybe Caitlin's."

"And the minute Caitlin came into camp," Mike said, patting Sarah's shoulder, "we, none of us, had any control over what was going to happen next. You said yourself, it was supposed to be *Fiona* dead this morning, and you in handcuffs for murder."

"Is that true?" John said. "Caitlin wanted to frame you for killing Auntie Fi?"

Sarah gave Mike a worried look. "Did you ever tell Fi the truth? She needs to know she's not safe there."

"I told her and Dec both," he said, his eyes on the road, his voice grim. "As I said, they'll make their decision soon enough."

"Well, maybe *not* soon enough."

"In any case," Mike said, glancing meaningfully at her, "it's out of *your* hands whatever they do."

"I just can't believe it's all over," she said, her eyes reverting again to the vibrant green of the Irish countryside. "Donovan's Lot, Papin, our lives, our friends...just a little over month ago we were all so happy."

The memory of the man coming into their camp on the night of Fiona's wedding came unbidden to Sarah as she remembered hearing his news, not imagining then how it would change all of their lives forever.

Mike removed his arm from her shoulders and they drove in silence for the next several hours.

Limerick was very much the same bustling metropolis as the last time Sarah had seen it. Mike drove the cart straight to the forecourt of the American consulate. It was still early afternoon. Sarah knew they had missed the flight they were originally scheduled for but had to assume there would be others.

Although they had stopped several times for everyone to stretch their legs, Sarah still descended the cart with difficulty, her muscles sore and resistant to movement. She left Mike and John with the pony cart and went inside to announce their arrival. Within thirty minutes she was back.

"Well?" Mike asked. "Everything okay?"

She nodded. "They have another transport flight first thing in the morning. We're scheduled to be on it."

She looked at Mike, but in the half shadows of the waning afternoon was unable to decipher his expression. He went to the back of the cart and took out the single small suitcase that held their belongings. He set it down on the pavement next to Sarah.

"Mike, surely you're not going back today? You won't be half way home when it gets dark."

He turned to John and opened his arms to him. Sarah watched her son go to him. She heard Mike's low murmured voice to him and saw John, looking down, nod. Her heart caught in her throat and she turned away from the sight. It had been Mike, without having to be asked, who had made the detour to stop by David's grave at the beginning of their journey. For one last goodbye.

When she felt John rush past her toward the consulate where they would spend the night, she knew the time for the very last goodbye had finally come.

Mike stood by the pony cart watching her, his head cocked to one side as if trying to understand her or read her, his face a mask of such deep sadness, she wanted to look away.

Instead, she steadied her shoulders and walked straight into it. Before she even knew what she was doing, she was in his arms, her hands wrapped around his waist, her face pressed to his chest. She felt him envelop her and for just a moment all pain seemed to seep away.

When she lifted her face to him, he touched her jaw with his fingers and tilted her face towards him. The kiss was urgent and fierce and complete. It was the one to make up for all the others they hadn't had, and for all nights they would never have. Sarah abandoned herself in the feel of his full lips, the roughness of his beard against her cheek. His scent was of leather and the outdoors and she was lost in it.

When he pulled a way, she was breathless.

"Because that'll have to last us awhile," he said, his eyes glittering meaningfully at her.

"I love you, Mike."

"I love you, too, Sarah."

"Meet me in Dublin in five years at the *Grand Cafe*," she said, not knowing she was going to say it before the words were tumbling out of her mouth. "Unless...you know, you're married with kiddies by then. Then don't worry about it. But I'll be there."

She watched his slow grin reach his eyes and rejoiced that either of them could still feel pleasure on such a day.

"I have no idea what to make of you. And *why* would we meet in five years?"

"So that this isn't really goodbye."

"Ahhhh." His smile faltered then, but he brushed a lock of hair from her face and kissed her again, this time gently. "That's fine. So long then, sweet Sarah. Until Dublin."

When he released her, she was smart enough not to hesitate but to turn, pick up her bag and walk away.

And not look back.

18

The Florida coast looked like a painting at this height, Sarah thought. They had stopped briefly in Washington and then flown down the coast before turning inland toward the Jacksonville International Airport. Sarah looked at John, who was still young enough to want the window seat.

The last time they had been at that airport, David had been with them.

A slicing stab of sadness burst into her stomach and began to spread its way to her throat. She'd been enduring and tolerating them all the way from Limerick nineteen hours earlier. Everything about this trip felt wrong.

Even the guilt she felt about that.

"Will Nana and Granddad be waiting for us at the airport?" John asked, not turning his head from the view.

Sarah had called them as soon as they landed in Reagan National. It was difficult to understand her mother through the excitement and inevitable tears.

"Yes," she said.

The flight attendant came down the aisle and smiled at them both. "We'll be landing soon," she said. "Are you ready for this?"

She meant it in a nice way, Sarah knew. The crew had been informed of their special circumstances.

Sarah forgot how intensely people smiled back home. She tried to remember two times the whole time she had known Fiona where her friend had smiled this broadly.

"As we'll ever be," she said. She turned to pat John's knee but he was focused on the upcoming landing and the ground rushing ever closer as they descended.

Her parents looked like they had aged ten years. When her mother saw her and John coming down the jet-way, she mother collapsed and had to be supported by her father, who looked like he wasn't far behind her. Sarah watched John sprint ahead to take his grandfather's arm. She saw her dad look at him with surprise.

It's true, she thought. *He's not the same boy who climbed on that plane two years ago. Now, if he sees a situation he acts on it without asking permission first.*

Maybe that worked fine in post-apocalyptic Ireland.

Probably not so much back here.

She hurried to her parents and smiled, her arms outstretched to them.

"AND THERE'S nobody at all you can contact about poor David?" her mother muted the television set and set down two steaming mugs of coffee. Sarah noticed that they had a new cappuccino machine in the kitchen.

"Not really."

"You'll get his 401K? And the house?"

Sarah frowned at her mother. "I suppose so," she said. "Everything he had, he left to me."

"You might not have to work," her mother said. She was wearing a silk blouse tucked into a pair of pleated linen slacks. Sarah knew her mother loved clothes—and at seventy, she still looked good in them. She also knew her mother had never worked a day in her life.

"Except for getting John enrolled in the Brampton Middle School as soon as possible," Sarah said, "I haven't thought too far ahead."

Her father came into the room and leaned down to kiss his wife. A tall, tan man who had always golfed more than he'd worked, Sarah realized with a pang that there didn't seem to be much to her father.

Funny how living in an environment where wit and courage trump wealth or status—especially status you inherited—can really change your perspective. She blushed at her uncharitable thoughts and forced her face into a smile for her father. She loved him dearly, she reminded herself. Just because I can't imagine him chopping wood or riding a horse down to find a goat trapped into a gully doesn't mean he's not amazing in his own right.

"I can put a word in for you, if you like," he said, smiling. "Brampton is extremely difficult to get into."

"That'd be good, Dad. Thanks."

"And it's expensive."

"I know," Sarah said. "The government is awarding me a settlement sum. I don't know why. I guess they're afraid I'd blame them for what happened with David and try to sue them."

"Many people are doing exactly that."

"Well, I'm happy to take the money," Sarah said. "Without David, I could use it."

"Where's John?" he asked, looking around the large living room. The window opened up to a view of a private lake lined with weeping willows.

Sarah had expected it would feel like a dream—being here after having lived there. She knew she would have to fight to keep her equilibrium after everything she'd experienced. She hadn't expected it to dissolve in her hands like sand in water the moment she stepped back into her old world.

It hadn't taken an hour to realize the pleasures and luxuries she thought she could never in her life take for granted again had clicked back into place as if she'd never left. The first few moments of smelling the aroma wafting out of the airport Starbucks quickly gave way to the assumption that it would be there.

"The jet lag got him," she said. "He'll be up later."

"Is...is there anything you want to talk about, sweetheart?" her mother asked, delicately sipping from her coffee mug.

What in the world could she say to them? That she'd seen David get his head blown off. That she'd nearly been raped by a monster she then killed by slitting his throat. That she'd eaten a rabbit raw to survive and slept in a ditch with three corpses writhing with maggots.

Dear God, did any of that make sense? In light of where she was now?

"Not really, Mom," she said, standing. "But I'd love to take advantage of the guest bath if you don't mind. It's been awhile since I have seen a bar of soap and I'm really looking forward to it."

"Of course, darling. And then maybe later a trip to the mall for some shopping?"

"Maybe. Oh, where's Gunner? I'm surprised John hasn't asked about him yet."

She watched her mother look up at her father as if a previous discussion had placed this ball firmly in his court.

Her father cleared his throat. "We couldn't take care of him ourselves, obviously," he said. "And after it became clear you weren't coming home any time soon, well, the holding facility wouldn't keep him indefinitely."

"You put him in a...you boarded him somewhere?"

"Well, darling, you know we're not dog people. We certainly couldn't keep him."

"So you killed him? Is that the long and short of it?"

"Well, we didn't personally kill him, no," her father said, looking at her as if she were misbehaving in some way.

No, because that would take some backbone. You paid someone to do it for you.

Sarah knew she was going to overreact, and knowing it helped stem the tide of her tears. She sat back down, her face in her hands and began to weep without care or control. She cried great groaning sobs for the family pet who never had a chance, for the little gypsy girl not three days dead, for Mike who she could still see in her mind as she left him—who was twice the man her father was—and for the simple hideous fact that David wasn't by her side for this homecoming.

And for the truly terrible mistake she now knew she had made.

Her parents hovered over her helplessly, not actually touching her, but upset and unnerved. Her mother's hands fluttered around Sarah's head and shoulders as she heaved and rocked with her wracking sobs.

"Darling, we are so sorry! I told you, James. I told you we should have found a temporary home for him!"

"Now, now, Rebecca, the girl's just exhausted. God knows what she's endured over there. Probably went to bed hungry a time or two and I can already see she's brown as a berry so I'm sure it was no bed of roses. She'll be fine."

Sarah stood up and bolted for the bathroom. "Please, excuse me," she said over her shoulder, her voice still cracked by the crying jag.

She LAID in the bathtub of her parents' home, the water as hot and high as she could stand it and tried to remember what it took to attempt to get clean back home.

Back in Ireland.

Because she couldn't stop staring at everything, particularly the baristas at the airport coffee kiosks, where her father had bought her a *grande latte* for the car ride back to the upscale, gated neighborhood on the Intracoastal where her parents lived.

The first sip hadn't tasted like she remembered it. The second sip was a little better, but it wasn't half as good as the memory of being wrapped in a thin wool rug watching the starlight over the camp drinking weak tea with goat milk.

Her parents had euthanized her perfectly healthy dog. Sometime in the past two years they'd bought a fancy new coffee maker. One that made steamed milk and kept the cups warm until ready to use. Sarah tried to imagine her mother wandering into a store by the Town Center Mall perusing the shelves, determining which model would best suit her needs. She wondered if she'd been fighting for her life at that moment. Or merely hungry and terrified. She knew it wasn't fair to think like that.

John's school started in three weeks.

THE FOLLOWING DAY, Sarah borrowed her parents' car and went to the house she had shared with David. She cringed when she stepped past the threshold. No dog to greet her. No David calling to her from the kitchen. She entered the family room and walked around, touching her own furnishings as if she were a stranger seeing it all for the first time.

She saw the childish ceramics in the kitchen from John's kindergarten years, the sweater she had tossed on the back of her desk chair. A cereal bowl still sitting on the kitchen counter.

She touched the sheet stuck to the refrigerator with magnets. "A+ Good job, John!" was scrawled across the top in red marker. The child who'd brought that test paper home, so proud and excited...*that* child had gone on vacation to Ireland and had never come home again.

She looked at her kitchen. The stove, the refrigerator, the

shelves still full of canned food. She went to the counter under the kitchen window and threw up in the stainless steel sink.

She let herself out without going upstairs. She locked up and drove away.

The rest of the day she spent getting her smartphone turned back on and updated, and renewing the tags on the Highlander in the garage. She made appointments for the orthodontist for John, and physicals for both of them. She went to the mall and sat by the wheelchairs with the old ones, immobilized and numb, as shoppers scurried around her. Later, she came back to her parents and told her mother she hadn't been able to find anything.

By the end of the first week, John had spent every day, all day, playing *Call of Duty* in his grandparents' guest room. He refused to go to the house with Sarah, refused to call any of his old friends, refused to eat anything but Pop-Tarts and Cokes.

Her mother urged her to be patient.

"You were the same way when you couldn't get your way," her mother said.

"I think we're looking at something a little deeper than teen angst."

"That's probably what he'd like you to think anyway."

"You don't know him, Mom. John doesn't play games."

"Well, whatever it is, I'm sure it'll sort itself out once he gets back in school with all his friends."

"The same friends he refuses to see now?"

"Well, then he'll make new ones. It's a new school year after all. And won't John have stories to tell?"

Oh, yeah, he will. Like how he buried his murdered father in a cow pasture? Or maybe how he gave the order to detonate a bomb that exterminated his father's killer? He'll keep them riveted in the school cafeteria with the stories he has to tell.

The thought occurred to her: along with the dentist and his

pediatrician, should she make an appointment for him to see a psychiatrist?

"Meanwhile, you need to get yourself sorted out, Sarah."

Sarah looked at her mother in surprise. "What do you mean? I'm going back to the mall. I know I need clothes."

"I meant start thinking about your future. You know, dating, again."

Sarah tried to see her mother as if she were seeing her for the first time. A pretty woman, she loved her family and she saw them exactly as she wanted to see them.

Just nothing like they really were.

"I'm nowhere near ready for that," she said.

"Well, David's been gone over a year now."

"It's not that. I'm in love with someone."

Her mother's eyes widened. Up to this moment, she had been trimming a tall bunch of Hydrangea blooms to fit in a wide vase. She laid her scissors down on the hall table and turned to look at Sarah. "Someone you met over there?"

No, Mom, the Air Force transport pilot.

"That's right."

Her mother frowned for a moment and then turned to pick up the scissors again. "Well, all the more reason. Nothing like getting back up on the horse to get someone out of your mind, I always say."

"I think I made a mistake, Mom."

"How so, dear?"

"I shouldn't have left."

"Don't be silly. John will snap out of this. You just need to give him some time." She paused. "Give yourself time. You've been through a lot, I imagine."

No, Mom, you really can't.

"Why don't you help me set the table? I always feel better when I'm busy. Don't you?"

19

The teenager squirmed in the hunched over position that the wooden stocks forced him to conform to. He couldn't stand erect and he couldn't shift his weight to put the bulk of it on his back foot. His face looked bewildered, afraid.

Fiona came away from the window and turned to Declan where he sat on the couch. "Somebody has thrown a tomato at the poor lad."

"I'm not surprised."

Fiona clapped her hands on her hips. "Well, bloody hell, man! Is this new regime okay with wasting food?"

Declan looked at his wife and blinked with surprise. "*That's* what you're upset about? That somebody wasted a tomato?"

Fiona sat down next to Declan and reached for his hand but he pulled it away. "I'm upset about the madness that's taken over our community. Declan, I'm afraid."

"Our people are here."

"*Your* people! Mine just got thrown out on his arse."

"We need to think about the baby," he said, not looking at her.

"I *am* thinking about the baby! I'm thinking the little bugger won't have a da if we stay—nor a mam either with Caitlin gunning for me. Why are we still here?"

"I thought you always said raising bairns takes a village."

"I wasn't talking about *Amityville*. We aren't safe here, Dec."

Declan put a hand to his face. In the three days since Papin's burial and his beating, his cuts and bruises were fading. Jamison had broken two of his ribs but Declan knew it could have been worse.

A lot worse.

"How do you feel?"

He grimaced. He felt like shite. He was sick of hiding and he hated the thought of running. But he didn't see any other way. He glanced at Fiona and felt a wave of amazement that his perfect world could have changed so drastically so quickly.

"The boy out there is a gypsy," Fiona said.

"So?"

"She's targeting them. You see that, right?"

Declan made a noise of disgust. "Is there any tea left?"

Fiona flounced off the couch and stomped into the kitchen. He watched her go. She was already filling out fast with the little one. Christ, he hoped it wasn't twins. He heard voices outside as people gathered by the poor bastard locked in the stocks.

Fiona wasn't wrong. Brian's bitch was targeting the gypsies. This morning while Fi was gathering firewood for the stove, his cousin visited him to complain. The Kelly twins, Colin and Cedric, visited the gypsy section of camp frequently to bed the young teen girls—more than once not by consent. Declan knew it was only a matter of time before some young white stud got his guts rearranged with a skinning knife.

"There's no sugar," Fiona said from the kitchen. Her voice was angry and tight. He knew she just wanted to prod him. Hell, there hadn't been sugar since spring.

"Sure, fine," he said.

He hadn't known what to tell his cousin, except to remind

him that he no longer held any kind of leadership role in the community. Which was when they reminded him the leadership role he had in the family couldn't be shrugged off as easily.

He nearly grinned thinking of it. Here he sat, battered, cowed, a virtual prisoner in his own cottage, and the daft boggers were still coming to him to address their grievances. In their eyes, circumstances didn't dictate who was a leader and who wasn't. Declan was born to lead them and by God, that was that.

Fiona walked back to him holding a steaming mug of tea when Declan heard the heavy foot tread pounding up the porch steps. He waited and the door swung open without knocking.

Iain Jamison stood in the doorway. The Kelly twins stood behind him. One held a truncheon in his hands that he slapped in the other as if in anticipation of using it.

"Oy, Cooper," Jamison said, his eyes flitting briefly to Fiona and then back to Declan.

Declan bit back a venomous retort. *No good could come of baiting this arsehole.* One glance at his companions confirmed that. They *wanted* him to resist.

He kept silent.

"I'll be needing you to vacate the premises effective immediately."

Declan saw one of the twins crane his neck to look around the living room as if ready to move in, himself. Clearly, that's what this was about.

Fiona marched up to Iain, still holding the cup of tea, and Declan forced himself to his feet, his ribs screaming in protest. "Hold on, love," he said, hobbling to reach her to touch her elbow before she did something that got them both a beating. "Is that tea for me?"

She faced Jamison. "You're kicking us out, you useless piece of shite? Does your wife know what depths you've sunk to, Iain? Does *Edie* know you're kicking me, a pregnant woman, out of her home?"

Declan could see that Fiona had unsettled Jamison. He took her arm and, spilling tea on the floor as he did, pulled her gently away from the man. It was Declan's experience that men who feel unsettled quite often did things—bad things—they might not normally do. "Let's go, love," Declan said under his breath. "It is what it is."

All three men entered the cottage now and he could see the twins taking stock of their new quarters.

"How we going to get the stench of wog out of the rafters, eh?" The twin with the club said, smiling nastily at Declan.

"Five minutes to gather what you can carry," Jamison said, his voice strident now with obvious stress. "And be glad for that much. You'll leave your rifle, Cooper. And your horse and cart. There are no personal possessions at *Daoineville*. Everything belongs to the camp."

"How is he supposed to shoot game to provide for his family?" Fiona asked, her hand on her stomach. She looked at Declan as if expecting him to argue. "And you're stealing our horse?"

"Not stealing, as I just explained to you," Jamison said tersely. "You've got five minutes and since none of us has a watch that works, I'll be guessing the time." He looked at Declan who had yet to speak to him. "I'd hurry, you, in case I guess on the short side." His hand dropped to the pistol tucked into his belt.

Declan understood. The bastard just needed a reason to kill him. Being too slow to leave would serve as well as any other. "Come on, Fi," he said, holding a hand out to his wife. "Leave it all. There's bugger all here anyway."

MIKE WATCHED the dust motes dancing in the air of the early morning kitchen. It had been two and a half weeks since they buried little Papin. Two and a half weeks after he left John and Sarah in Limerick. Two weeks after he watched Declan and his pregnant sister trudge up the dusty road to his cottage, the slope of their shoulders, the plodding steps telling everything.

They were outcasts, all of them.

And none of them any too safe.

Mike woke early this morning. Aideen and Taffy had one bedroom and Declan and Fiona in the other, leaving himself and Gavin to bed down on the living room floor. He was grateful for the roof over his head—and that they were all together.

A broken cart axel had delayed them precious days, but he expected they would finally be able to head for the coast tomorrow. He tried to quietly light the cooker to start the water boiling for the tea. He could see that it had done Dec a world of good just to get out of the camp. His injuries had healed—now he just needed to work on his pride.

"Da! I'm going out for a whiz." Gavin stood in the living room and pointed to the front door.

"Grab some more firewood while you're out there and mind you don't piss on it first."

"Let me do that."

He turned to see Aideen moving silently from the second bedroom. She was fully dressed, her hair tied back, and even wore a touch of make up.

He was surprised she still bothered. He handed her the tin of tealeaves. "It's probably the last pot," he said. "We'll find more as we head to the coast."

"It doesn't matter. We'll survive without tea."

"Aye, but it's nice not to have to, you know?"

She didn't answer. He watched her movements as she spooned the tea into the pot and then gave the fire a poke with a long stick. The kettle on top began to steam.

"So will we be leaving tomorrow?"

"Aye. We've stayed too long already," he said.

"Dec said at dinner last night that he knows bugger all about fishing."

"Yeah, well, he knew bugger all about sheriffing, too, but he managed to learn."

"That's true."

"Look, Aideen, I know this has been difficult—"

"Mike, don't. It is what it is. Let's just get where we're going. All right?"

"Aye, sure." He would have liked to put a hand on her shoulder, or even to pull her to him for a hug but he didn't dare. If she was holding it together with spit and a prayer—and the Lord knows he knew how that felt—he didn't want to do anything to make it harder.

Gavin came inside, his arms full of wood, the front door banging loudly behind him.

"Oy, Gav, let yer poor auntie sleep late just one morning, would ya?"

"Don't worry, I'm up," Fiona said, yawning, as she stood in the doorway to the bedroom she shared with Declan. "And from the sounds coming through the wall, so is wee Taffy."

"Mam! I'm hungry!"

Aideen hurried back to her bedroom and her howling daughter. Fiona poured the boiling water into the teapot. "Is there enough for a pot?" she asked.

"Should be," Mike said. He nodded at Declan as his brother-in-law emerged from the bedroom.

"Not used to being idle," Declan said, grimacing. "I bloody hate it."

"Well, you won't be long," Mike assured him. "The life of a fisherman—"

"Stinks to high heaven?" Declan said, a smile twisting the corners of his mouth.

"Very amusing. No, I was going to say, is never dull."

"Da, are we going to get a boat?" Gavin reached out for the cup of tea that Fiona handed him.

"Aye, we'll need a boat."

"I hate the fecking water," Declan said.

"That is a problem," Mike said.

"And I can't fecking swim."

"Go on with you!"

"It's true. It is not a skill I ever thought I'd fecking need."

"Well, shit, Dec. If you're going to be in a boat every day, you need to know how to swim."

"I'll teach you, Uncle Dec!" Gavin said, grinning. "I'll teach you the way my Da taught me."

"Does that involve me knocking a few of your teeth out, because I think I know that method," Declan growled.

Fiona handed her husband his tea and a quick kiss on the cheek. "Whisht!" she said. "Let's all stay positive, why don't we?"

BRIAN WATCHED his wife as she silently crept through the front door. It occurred to him that he should be glad she bothered to sneak. She probably wouldn't for much longer.

Could it be this place that had changed her? He'd seen it the moment they entered camp. The sweetness and compliance shining in her face every day until the moment they rode into Daoineville was gone, replaced by a hardness that now seemed difficult to believe hadn't always been there.

Who are you, Catherine Kelly Gilhooley? He turned his face to the wall, unsure of whether or not he should let her see that he was awake.

It was bad enough that her father knew she'd been out half the night. But Brian had endured the old man's wordless pity all evening.

"You awake then?"

She had a scent like lilacs—although where in the world she'd come by it was beyond him. He turned to face her and she slipped, already naked, into his arms.

"I am," he whispered hoarsely, urgently. His neck reddened with his shame.

"Will you promise me you'll go collect Donovan tomorrow? Me poor father's waited years for the justice denied him. I'll not have the dear man wait any longer."

Brian closed his eyes. Could he really arrest Donovan with no proof but an angry, grief-stricken old man's say-so? What kind of trial could they have that would produce anywhere near the result he knew his wife and her father needed?

"Or," she said, her voice low and seductive, "you could bring him in for springing that murderin' wog. He'll confess to it, I'm sure. He's that arrogant."

Brian's eyes opened and he smiled at her in the dark.

Now *that* he could do.

"Iain and I'll go first thing in the morning," he said, as he stroked her bare hip.

She batted his hand away. "Not first thing," she said. "Iain will want to sleep in a wee bit."

20

L e *Bon Bon* was her favorite middle of the week lunch spot in Jacksonville.

Or at least it had been two years ago.

Sarah looked around at the French décor. A six-foot metal replica of the Eiffel Tower anchored the center of the little restaurant. Nothing seemed changed about the place that she could see. The fragrance of the fresh-baked croissants was as pervasive as ever. The *patisserie* case in the front of the shop was still crammed full of every imaginable kind of *petit four*, tart and *gateau*. The *quiche du jour* was as heavenly as she remembered. But that was the problem, she realized as she held her fork over the delectable golden brown crust, the creamy, cheesy filling nestled perfectly within.

She had imagined it during other times. She had used the memory of this dish to keep herself from eating her leather shoes one day during her trek through the Brecon Beacons in Wales last year. She had kept the texture of its rich custard uppermost in her mind the day she had needed to force down a mouthful of rabbit—raw and still bloody from her slingshot—to keep from starving to death.

She placed her fork back on the plate, noticing her fingers shook as she did.

No. There was no longer a place in her mind for this favorite dish, one that was assembled without effort and very little cost.

Not in her world. Not ever again.

"Is something wrong with your *quiche*?"

Sarah looked up, her mouth smiling before she engaged eye contact—something she had started to do more and more since she'd been home. Her girlfriend, Debbie, sat across from her and frowned.

Debbie looked exactly as she had the last time Sarah had seen her—a steak dinner out with both husbands just before Sarah and David had flown to Ireland for a much-needed vacation. Her nails had been recently gelled, the lines in her forehead recently smoothed, her blonde hair recently highlighted.

She must think I look very different, Sarah thought. She had gotten out of the habit of looking in mirrors while living in Ireland. Involuntarily, Sarah's hand reached up to touch her hair. She'd pulled it back in a rubber band but there was no question of it having any kind of style. She'd bought some makeup at the mall last week but kept forgetting to wear it.

"No, I guess I'm not as hungry as I thought."

"I want to put together a little welcome home party for you," Debbie said. "Will you be up for that? Everybody knows you're back and they're all dying to see you."

Sarah nodded, being careful to keep her smile nailed in place. "Yeah, no, I don't think so, Debbie," she said. "Thank you."

Debbie reached across the table to touch Sarah's hand. "Is it because of David?" she asked earnestly.

Well, it's true that nothing puts a damper on a party like somebody being dead, Sarah thought, forcing herself not to extricate her hand from beneath her friend's touch.

"Partly," she said. "But I just thought I'd get back in touch with everyone in my own time."

"Of course. It's just that everyone so wants to see you."

Sarah didn't answer. She eased her hand away on the pretense of making another try with her *quiche*.

She found it somewhat surprising that Debbie—and Sarah's parents, too—hadn't asked for many details about what her life had been like in Ireland. Sarah assumed it might be too difficult to imagine it hadn't been so bad if they had evidence to counter it.

What they don't know, they don't have to deal with.

That was fine with Sarah. She didn't want to talk about Balinagh, or Mike or Fiona, or where David's grave was, or what happened during her two months in the UK last year. No, their instincts were definitely sound as far as not asking her too many questions, she decided.

If they think I'm awkward to be around now, just imagine if I were to tell them about how seven months ago we took a young, fit and healthy twenty-five year old, put a rope around his neck while he screamed and wept and then...

"Dessert, Sarah?"

The waitress had materialized at their table with a tall blackboard she was settling onto an easel. On the board were dozens of different kinds of desserts. A subhead touted the fact each was made on the premises every day.

How is that possible? Sarah wondered as she craned her neck to look past the waitress in the direction of the kitchen.

"Sarah?"

She looked back at Debbie who was staring at her now with a worried expression.

"I'm so sorry," Sarah said.

"That's okay. Do you—"

"I need to go." She scraped back her chair and grabbed for her purse. "I'm sorry, Debbie. I can't do this."

Without stopping to see the horrified look she knew she

would find on her friend's face, Sarah pushed past the chalkboard easel and ran out of the restaurant into the blinding sunshine of the parking lot. She hurried to her car, slipped inside and blinked at the bright light. She had very few memories of it being sunny in Ireland. Whether that was because she wasn't paying attention or because the sun rarely came out, she wasn't sure.

She put her hands on the steering wheel and stared ahead at the strip mall parking lot, watching people come and go, carrying dry cleaning, entering and leaving the little French restaurant, standing in line holding boxes at the postal store.

She and John had been home for two weeks now. While he still stayed in his room playing video games, after the first week of doing all the responsible things she knew she had to do, Sarah spent this last week holed up in her room. Sometimes she watched the TV that was in there. Sometimes she read or took long blistering hot baths. But always, she wept. Silently, intensely, hopelessly.

I've made a terrible mistake.

This outing with Debbie had been set up by Sarah's mother and she'd only obliged because it was clear to anyone with eyes that Sarah was hell-bent upon descending into a lengthy and nonproductive depression. Not unlike what John was doing.

She bent her forehead to the steering wheel. She had figured out days ago that a depression was just about the only thing that was going to prevent her from thinking about what was happening back in Ireland. She had happily made the self-pact to sink into despair if the alternative was to obsessively wonder what was happening with Mike and Fi and Dec and the camp. It was madness to think Caitlin would let Fiona and Declan live in peace. Or Mike. She tried to envision them all packed up on a big horse cart—not unlike the Okies of the Dust Bowl—and leaving the area for the coast where Mike could fish and help support them all.

Would Declan agree to leave his family? Would the other gypsies come too?

Sarah shook her head. Could she really just force herself to believe that it would all turn out well for them? That Caitlin *wouldn't* catch Fiona alone one night...or that Mike *wouldn't* one day tire of forbidding himself the succor and love of a willing woman?

And what about Siobhan? Who was going to put up with her bullshit and help her with the laundry?

Sarah covered her head with her arms and did what she had done every day since she'd arrived back home— wept without restraint or hope until all her tears were gone and she could only croak in agony. And then when things got as bad as they could get, when she knew she couldn't possibly feel any worse, that was when she called to mind her memory's best snap-shot image of Papin laughing or winking at her—full of life and energy and hope.

And then, and only then, did Sarah feel sufficiently punished for having taken John so far away from home.

THAT NIGHT, after a quiet dinner of roast pork loin and scalloped potatoes, John excused himself and retreated to his bedroom. Sarah watched him go without comment.

"Well, at least he hasn't asked to start taking his meals in there," her father said.

"Or decided he won't eat at all," her mother said as they all heard the bedroom door close firmly.

"I'll help you clear the table in a minute," Sarah said, tossing her napkin down and standing up. "I just need a word with him."

"Now, don't be too hard on the boy," her father said, reaching for another piece of meat. "He'll snap out of it as soon as football season starts. Trust me."

Sarah tapped lightly on John's door and then slipped inside

without waiting for permission to enter. He was lying on the bed, earphones on that were attached to his iPod, an on-demand video playing mutely on his laptop. It occurred to her that he'd missed a great deal as far as technological advances while he was gone.

But he hadn't missed a beat in reconnecting.

She went to his bed and sat down. He didn't look at her. She reached over and gently pulled one earphone bud out of his left ear. He frowned but didn't stop her.

"John."

When he turned to her, she realized his eyes were red. He wrestled his own demons in this room every day and every night.

"I made a mistake."

"I know."

"I'm sorry for not realizing sooner."

"Even though everyone told you."

"*Especially* because everyone told me."

"It's okay, Mom." He reached for the ear bud she still held.

"Not this time it isn't," she said, handing it to him. "Although I appreciate your forgiveness."

He popped the earphone back in and turned his attention to the laptop screen.

"We're going home," she said without thinking.

His head never turned but his eyes flicked in her direction.

"Home *where*?" he asked.

It was right. As soon as she had said the words out loud, she knew it was right.

"You know where."

She watched his eyes light up. He sat up straight, the first unprovoked movement he'd displayed since they returned. "Are you sure? What about college?"

"You've got plenty of time for that. I'll homeschool you." The thoughts came faster and faster. Why hadn't she thought of this before? "We'll bring the books back with us that we'll need. You might not be ready to take your MCATs, but you'll at least get into college."

He launched himself into her arms, wires and earphones springing free as he wrapped his arms around her and hugged her tight. The feeling of connection after so many months of distance was so profound that Sarah laughed out loud. When she pulled back to see her boy's face—his eyes alive for the first time in weeks— mixed with his elation she saw hope and trust.

That he should still believe in me after all I've put him through...

"I'm just sorry it took me so long to figure it out," she whispered, hugging him close.

A tap on the bedroom door made both of them turn. Her mother stood in the opening, beaming broadly at the two of them. "Oh, I'm so happy to see smiles again!" she said, clapping her hands together. "Can I count two more then for rice pudding?"

Sarah looked at John who grinned. "Absolutely, Grandma," he said. "You can count us both in."

THE NEXT MORNING, for the first time since she arrived back in the States, Sarah awoke to a purpose and a full slate of errands— each more pressing and vital than the one before. While she was looking over her to-do list at breakfast, her mother placed a tall stack of blueberry pancakes in front of her.

"I know you said not to, but I made them for John this morning so if you don't want them, you can—"

"No, they're great, Mom. Thanks," Sarah said, pulling the plate closer to her.

Her mother hesitated and then sat down at the table. She slid a small pitcher of warmed maple syrup across the table to Sarah. "John's already up and gone," she said.

Sarah slathered the stack of pancakes with butter and then poured the syrup over the top. "Oh?"

"Which shocked me," her mother said, picking up her coffee mug. "I mean, since the child hasn't left his room in nearly three weeks."

"Did he say where he was going?"

"His friend, Luke, came by with his mother. They picked him up."

"That's nice. I'm glad he's seeing some of his old friends."

"That's what I thought, too. He's really a changed boy since... well, ever since you went into his room last night."

Sarah raised her eyes to her mother's, which were quickly filling with tears.

"Mom..."

"What are you thinking of doing, Sarah?"

"I never should have left, Mom."

"That's ridiculous. This is your home."

"Not anymore it isn't." Sarah put down her fork, the pancakes untasted, and reached out for her mother's hand. "I didn't want to upset you, Mom. Maybe you can pretend we live in Seattle or something and we're just here for our annual visit."

"Seattle."

"I'm sorry, Mom. But this isn't home for us anymore. We have a life we've built back there. I was so focused on...on getting John here and back on track that I didn't think of anything else. I've caused a lot of people a lot of pain because of it."

"You'd rather go back and live in a tent with no electricity than here."

"Yes, but honestly I think I can bring a few things back with me to make it better this time. That's my plan, anyway."

"Eat your pancakes, dear. They're getting cold."

"Mom, are you okay?"

"Yes, of course. When were you thinking of leaving, may I ask?"

"I...I guess there's no real hurry, but probably in the next few weeks."

"Well, then I guess we'll just have to enjoy the two of you as much as we can in the meantime." Sarah watched her mother hold her emotions firmly into place. She stood with her coffee mug and walked into the kitchen without another word.

SARAH DROVE down the residential street feeling the familiarity kick in as her body automatically braked and accelerated to take her to Debbie's comfortable Craftsman-style home in the gated community.

She'd even remembered the gate code.

When she parked her parents' SUV in Debbie's driveway, she noticed that Rick's Honda was in the garage and that surprised her since normally he'd be at work.

Debbie answered the door as if she'd been watching Sarah drive up and was waiting for her. "Sarah!" she said in unconvincing surprise.

"Hey, Debbie, I am so sorry about yesterday. I can't imagine what you must think of me."

"Not at all. Come in. I was just putting the coffee on."

Sarah entered the home and stepped over a large dog toy in the foyer. She had always envied Debbie's home over the older split level that she and David owned. She tried to remember if she'd ever visited unannounced before. The place looked...unlived in.

"Is Rick home? I saw his car in the garage."

"No," Debbie called from the kitchen. "The Honda's mine now. Rick got a Mustang. He'd been wanting one for ages." She handed Sarah the coffee and motioned for her to sit at the kitchen table. "Compliments of the divorce," she said.

Sarah froze. "You and Rick?"

Debbie smiled woodenly. "Yeah, I was going to tell you yesterday but you didn't look like you could handle it. I'm glad to see you're better. You had me worried there."

"What happened? Are the kids okay?"

Sarah sat at the table and looked around the quiet living room from the kitchen. Debbie joined her with her coffee cup.

"Not really. They took it badly." She shrugged. "This is their week with Rick, which is why they aren't here. Is there enough sugar in that?"

"I got used to drinking it black," Sarah murmured. *When I could get it at all.* "I'm just so sorry to hear that, Debbie. I had no idea y'all were in trouble."

"Me, neither."

"I don't know what to say."

"Well, then, let's don't go there. Let's talk about what you're going to do now that you're back. I can't tell you how much I missed you, Sarah. I really needed you."

Sarah nodded. "I'm sorry I wasn't here for you."

"But you are now. The truth is, I've had to go back to work since the divorce and that sucks, but it is what it is. The house goes on the market next month. I waited as long as I could because the kids just had so much to deal with I didn't want to add to it but I can't afford it."

This beautiful house, Sarah thought, glancing around, *that I have coveted every day since she moved into it.* "I can't believe this happened," she said softly.

"Hey! If you're interested in a roommate situation, we could move in together at your place. I know Brady and Jemmy both adore John. Yours is a four bedroom, right?"

Sarah nodded.

"I mean, do you want to think about it? I swear the idea just came to me. But it would be so perfect. Screw men! We could create a good life together for the kids, you know? What do you think?"

Sarah smiled. "Let me sleep on it, okay?"

Now that she looked at Debbie more closely, without the

helpful soft lighting of the restaurant, she could see that the nails were press-ons and the highlights were streaks of gray.

"Where's Brody?" As long as Sarah and David had been friends with Debbie and Rick, they had known the playful Labrador retriever the two had bought as a puppy before their first child was born.

"Rick got him in the settlement," Debbie said, her eyes dull and lifeless. "Which is good. He was a lot of work."

"Oh, wow."

"It worked out."

"Well, that's good then. So, tell me about your job, Debbie. Tell me all about your job."

As a result of her visit with Debbie, the day had been a mixed bag Sarah realized as she hit the garage door opener at her parents' house and guided the large SUV into its interior bay. She'd spent nearly four hours at the warehouse home improvement store near their neighborhood and almost two on the phone at a coffee shop talking with financial planners and professional services people.

If it hadn't been for the necessary stop at Debbie's, which had depressed Sarah for a full thirty minutes before she finally shook it off with images of her homecoming back in Ireland, the day would have ranked as one of her best ever.

One of the main pleasures she was now allowing herself was to think of Mike, to remember how he looked, how he moved, how he laughed and how he looked at her in that special way of his. Until now it had been too painful to do anything but scrub all thoughts of him from her mind. Now she allowed the thought of his arms around her to fill up her day. She envisioned the moment he saw her again—the unbelievably delightful surprise in his eyes when he knew she was back and that they would finally have their time.

She replayed the images of the fantasy in her head over and over in every possible, imaginable form. And she never tired of them.

When she opened the garage door she saw her father was home from whatever recent pleasurable activity he'd taken up— Ma Jong at the clubhouse, golf, or antique hunting. Her father liked to keep busy and his hobbies had always taken first place in his life for as long as Sarah had known him.

She walked into the kitchen and saw him standing up at the counter sorting through mail. "Hey, Dad," she said, giving him a kiss on the cheek. "Mom and John around?"

"No. Perhaps they're together," he said, turning to her and smiling. "You look good. I hope you've just come back from a spa treatment or some other well-deserved pampering?"

"No, just errands." She twisted her neck as if it were stiff. "But after two hours sitting on a wooden chair at the coffee shop making phone calls, I have to say I'm tempted to book a spa day."

"What phone calls?" Her father frowned.

She had hoped to delay this conversation for at least a few days but another part of her wanted it behind her. She took in a deep breath. "I was talking to my financial advisor about cashing out my ROTH and my 401K."

The look on her father's face did not surprise her. His mouth hung open. "You...you cashed out your 401K?"

"And David's."

"Have you lost your mind?"

"I can see how you'd think that, Dad. The fact is I made a mistake coming back."

"What in the world are you talking about?"

When she didn't immediately answer, he tossed down the mail in exasperation and put a hand on her arm to command her complete attention. "You haven't given yourself enough time. Is it John? You've allowed him to manipulate you."

"He's not like that, Dad. If you knew him at all, you'd know that."

"I know he's a teen boy who isn't getting his way and has been acting out for nearly three weeks now."

"You and I see things differently."

"May I be so bold as to inquire what you did with your retirement funds? You know you paid insane fees to cash out early?"

"I bought what I consider necessary items."

"What in the world are you talking about? Has your Irish experience *unhinged* you? What possible *necessary* items do you feel you need?"

"Generators, for one. Seeds. Tools. Guns. Ammunition. Books."

Her father looked at her as if she had just suggested the immediate overthrow of the US government. "And why in the name of all that is holy do you believe you need these items? Are you afraid the US will be under attack like Ireland was? Because I can assure you—"

"These items aren't for here, Dad."

"You think you're going back to Ireland?"

"I *am* going back. John and I both are. I'm going to go out on a limb here and ask you and Mom to come too."

He simply stared at her.

"Well, that last part was a bit of a long shot, I'll admit," Sarah said. "It's not comfortable where I'm going. But you would have family there." She shrugged.

"You would ask your mother—a seventy year old woman—to go live in a post-apocalyptic battleground with no medical facilities and no...amenities, in order that she could see her only grandchild?"

"Yeah, it doesn't sound like a very good deal when you put it like that."

"The idea is not only insane, it's impossible. The fact is, you can't go back."

"I knew you would say that, Dad but I feel very—"

"No, sweetheart. You misunderstand. You will not be *permitted* to go."

"What are you talking about?"

"The US government just announced this morning the immediate cessation of all travel outside the country. Nobody's going anywhere. For *years*."

21

M ike saw them coming on the horizon and felt his stomach twist into a knot. He turned to look at Declan, who was helping Fiona into the wagon. Declan had seen them, too.

"What is it, Mike?" Aideen asked. She was in the back next to Taffy, their few possessions stacked at her feet in the back of the cart. Mike saw her twisting around to try to see what had caught his attention.

Son of a bitch. We were so close. He climbed into the driver seat. Declan and Gavin stood by the small horse wagon and watched the riders approach. This was no message being delivered from Brian cantering down the twisting driveway to where they waited. This was a posse. Iain rode in front next to one of the twins. Behind him were Brian, Archie and the other twin. Even from here Mike could see they were armed.

"Whoa up there, Donovan!" Iain called to them as the five men entered the cottage forecourt.

Mike's glance flitted to his rifle, shoved into its leather holster at his feet. If he was going to use it, he'd have to shoot every one of them. There was no way a heavily loaded wagon was going to outrun even one half decent rider on horseback.

He nodded grimly at Jamison but said nothing.

Fiona stood, but he saw Declan put a hand on her to pull her back to a sitting position.

"I'll be needing you to step out of the wagon," Jamison said. "The women and Gavin can stay where they are."

"What's this about, Iain?" Mike asked, feeling an immediate tightness in his chest.

Gilhooley urged his mount in front of Iain. Mike could see he wasn't comfortable, but he imagined it had more to do with the fact that he was an inexperienced rider than the purpose of his visit.

"Michael Donovan," he intoned, his voice cracking, "you and Declan Cooper have been found implicated in the recent jail-break of one Ollie...Oliver..." He turned to look at Iain who shrugged. Gilhooley turned back to Mike, embarrassed now, his face redder and fiercer. "Our recent prisoner, the gypsy found guilty of murder. You'll come peaceful like."

"And if we don't?"

Archie, silent up to now, pulled out his rifle and jabbed the air with it. "You'll be giving me the chance I've been looking for since the day you murdered my darlin' girl, Ellen," he shouted.

"Too right!" Cedric said, riding up next to his father. "If you can't be gotten for justice for Ellie, then we'll just have to do it another way!"

"Gonna hang your arse, Donovan," the other twin, Colin, snarled. "One way or the other."

Fiona screamed and tried to jump to her feet but Declan held her firmly. Mike could see Aideen was clutching Taffy, who had begun to cry. Her face, twisted in anguish, searched his for reassurance.

Mike knew there was nothing for it. If he didn't have two women and a little girl to worry about he might risk a shoot out with the crazy bastards. As it was, he sighed and raised his hands. "We'll come."

Live to fight another day...

"Da, no!" Gavin ran to the wagon, prompting Brian to bring his handgun out of its holder.

Mike saw Iain lean over and pull Brian's hand down. "Hold on, there, Brian. The lad's not doing anything. Donovan said he'd come."

Fiona was fighting with Declan, trying to prevent him from willingly leaving her. She buried her face in his chest, her hands clamped around his neck. He could hear Declan murmuring reassurances to her.

"We'll get it sorted out, Fi," Mike said to her, but he was looking at Aideen.

"At the end of a fecking rope, you'll get it sorted out!" Cedric yelled.

Mike saw his father-in-law nod grimly but his eyes were on Gavin, his grandson.

Revenge isn't always cut and dried, is it, you old bastard?

Mike dropped the reins and jumped down from the wagon, his eyes landing once more on the rifle.

Gavin grabbed his sleeve. "Da, what do I do? What should I do?"

Mike put a hand on his boy and felt a fissure of defeat. Was this the last time he would touch him? Was this goodbye? He forced himself to shove the thought from him mind.

"Take care of your Auntie Fi and Missus Malone and Taffy, aye?" Mike looked at Fiona, now sobbing in Declan's arms. "In fact, start for the coast today. Dec and I'll catch up with you."

"Da, no," Gavin said. His eyes were red as if he were struggling not to cry. Mike wished he could have all the answers for his son. Especially today.

"No, we will." He spoke under his breath. "Take your auntie, Gav. It's not safe for her here."

"Hey! Hey! There'll be no plotting," Brian called to Mike. "Move away from the lad, Donovan, or we'll bring him, too. In fact, we probably should bring him just to be safe."

"Eh? What?" Archie looked at Brian and frowned. "There's no call for that. But the boy should come with me. I'm his only kin now."

"Fuck that," Gavin said to him and spat in the dirt.

"Steady on, lad," Mike said to him, giving his shoulder a hard squeeze before turning toward where the riders waited.

"Let's go, Cooper. She can visit you at the jail. Start walking." Iain's voice was loud but Mike couldn't help but think there was a forcefulness to it that was missing.

Almost as if he wasn't completely sure.

Declan broke away from Fiona and joined Mike as Iain dismounted and approached the two with strips of leather in his hands. Mike knew it would be next to impossible to get out of leather binds. As soon as his hands started to sweat, they would grow even tighter. He held out his hands, his eyes on Iain's face.

Iain bound Mike's hands in front of him, concentrating on the task and refusing to meet Mike's eyes. The morning air only heard the soft sounds of Fiona and Taffy's weeping as Iain turned to Declan and bound his hands, too.

"Fecking wog," Cedric spat as Declan walked in front of him.

Iain remounted and indicated that Mike and Declan were to walk together behind his horse and in front of the Kellys and Brian.

He forced himself not to look back at Gavin or Aideen. If, God forbid, this really was the last time he saw either of them, he didn't want to remember the look of terror imprinted on both their faces.

CAITLIN STOOD by the empty stocks and watched the men return.

Annoyingly, it appeared that Mike and the filthy knacker hadn't put up any kind of fight. The two looked boringly untouched as they sauntered into camp.

Iain hates that Pikey! And he couldn't find a reason to rearrange the bastard's teeth? And then there was her father. She looked at him with disgust as he rode solemnly by her—*as if he were a part of something momentous. The old tosser. If he really cared about Ellen's murder, Mike would be sporting a black eye or limping at the very least.*

As usual, it was all going to be up to her.

"Hello, love, waiting for us?" Brian appeared from behind Cedric. His face regarded her with eager hope. Did the idiot really think she was out here waiting to greet him?

"The men in camp wouldn't mind me while you were gone," she said petulantly. "They said they don't take orders from me. So now I'd like you to order them for me before you do anything else."

She saw his face fall and his small, beady little eyes flit from side to side as if worried someone might be listening to their conversation.

Gawd! How could I have married such a spineless worm?

Iain rode up to her and swung down from his horse. Her heart beat a little faster to watch the muscles in his arms as he flipped the reins over the animal's neck to hold in his hand.

"Iain," she said to him in acknowledgement, a smile edging at her lips. She didn't care that Brian was staring right at her—probably registering the fact that she was mentally stripping Iain down to his knickers and not stopping there.

Iain put a hand to her chin and frowned. "What happened here, then?" he asked gruffly. She pulled away from him, her mood blackening immediately. The scratch still stung and ruined all the work of dressing so pretty this morning.

As was its intention.

"It is the reason I needed men to act like men and assist me," she said, forcing her eyes to fill with tears. Caitlin would need to make sure Iain saw how brave and injured she was.

Because it was a sure thing his bitch wife would be telling him her side of things fast enough.

She looked over Iain's shoulder where Mike waited patiently, his hands bound and clasped in front of him.

"Iain," Brian said, haltingly. "Go ahead and lock up the prisoners. I'll be along directly."

"Why can't *you* do it?" she said to Brian. "I need Iain to sort out these boggers in camp who think they can ignore what I say."

"Well, because Iain is the camp sheriff," Brian said patiently, a thinly veiled whine fluttering in his voice, as he slid off his horse. "Excuse me, Cedric? Collect the horses, please and take them to the stables. If there's nobody there, if you could untack them and rub them down, I would appreciate it."

Caitlin nearly laughed out loud at the expression on Cedric's face. He made a rude hand gesture to Brian's back and turned away, ignoring the request.

"Cedric? Did you hear me?"

"Never mind, Brian," Iain said. "I'll see it done. But first let's get the prisoners sorted out." He nodded to Caitlin, the message in his eyes direct and clear: *find me and tell me what happened.* He turned away, gesturing to Mike and the gypsy to follow him.

"Now, my dear," Brian said, still holding the reins of his horse. "What was this about the men in camp not minding you?"

Caitlin tore her eyes from Iain's retreating back to look at her husband. "Oh, never mind," she said. "Go untack your horse or something." She turned to follow in the direction that Iain had gone.

THE SUN WAS SETTING EARLIER and earlier, proof that summer was racing away, taking with it the sunny afternoons and easy evenings of plenty to eat. Fiona poured the boiling water into the teapot. The leaves had been used and reused but it was still better to hold a hot cup in your hands that somewhat tasted of tea—than nothing at all.

Aideen came into the room and shut the bedroom door behind her.

"She asleep then?" Fiona asked, setting a mug down for Aideen on the table.

"Finally. Was that Gavin I heard? Did he leave?"

Fiona sighed. "He's just out walking. I reminded him his da said no heroics and no jailbreaks."

"I know he's frustrated and scared."

"As we all are."

"What do you think will happen now?" Aideen sat down heavily in the kitchen chair. Fiona knew how much she loved Mike. Somehow it must be worse, she thought, loving and worrying over someone who wasn't really yours.

"I have no idea." She massaged the small of her back. "But Sarah would have an idea or two. Trust me on that. I know you didn't like her. But she was resourceful as hell."

Aideen nodded and sighed. "I'm sure you miss her."

"It's just, in a situation like this? She was in her element."

"How so?"

"As scared as she might be, when she saw a thing needing doing, she didn't worry about the consequences."

"You *really* think she could do something if she were here? Something we're not doing?"

"I do."

"I think you're just remembering her bigger than she was."

"Maybe. When I first met her, she'd lost both her husband and John and she convinced Mike to go with her and attack a blood-thirsty pack of thirty men with just them and two others."

"She sounds persuasive."

"And then? When Mike got hurt and couldn't go with her? She went anyway."

"That's all very impressive, but there is nothing Sarah Woodson could do any differently than you or I are doing, Fiona, were she here today."

"I don't know if that's true," Fi thought, frowning.

"You're not thinking of doing anything crazy?"

"All I know, Aideen, is that Sarah wouldn't just sit here and wait for word that her brother and husband had been killed by maniacs."

"We don't have a choice, Fi."

"Why should I believe that when I know Sarah wouldn't?"

"Because you want to live to give birth to that little one in there."

Fi hesitated and put her hand on her stomach. She looked at Aideen. "And what will I tell him when he asks where his da is?"

"Don't you even want to hear my side of things?" Caitlin hissed at Iain from where they stood on the perimeter of the north pasture. The edge of the woods was to their backs where the camp—and anyone coming—could be easily seen.

"Did you or did ya not tell my wife I was leaving her to be with you?"

Caitlin stopped. "And is that not true?"

"On what planet do you live where you think it might be true? I'm *married*, Caitlin. Come to that, so are you."

"So what we have is nothing to you?"

"Oh, it's something. Same as for you. Horizontal recreation."

Caitlin felt her anger building in her chest as a rosy flush spread up from her neck to her face. "You have your position in this camp because of me," she said hotly.

"I have this position, as ya put it, because Gilhooley can't stand the thought of working with a Pikey."

"I thought you and I might lead the camp together."

"You're as crazy everyone says you are, Caitlin," Iain said, shaking his head. "I'm not even sure if I'm staying in the camp."

"What are you talking about? You have to stay! What if...what if..." She looked wildly about them as if trying to find the answer in the bushes and the trees. "What if something were to happen to your wife? Would you want to stay then?"

Iain leaned over so close, Caitlin was sure he was going to kiss her.

"If something happens to my wife, you crazy bitch," he snarled, his lips only inches away from her own. "I'll kill you with me bare hands and won't wait for no fecking trial, neither." He roughly pushed her, rocking her back on her heels. She fought not to fall as he abruptly turned and walked away.

She watched him go and ground her nails into the palms of her hands in impotence and frustration. A burning flush of humiliation crept up her neck to her face.

Bastard! He'll pay for this and that bitch wife of his, too. How about if your fecking kiddies are orphans, Iain? How would that work for everyone?

22

Sarah closed the door to John's room. Telling him they were staying after all was absolutely the hardest thing she ever had to do. And she had had to do some very hard things in the last two years. He simply nodded and went back to whatever he'd been doing on his laptop. Sarah could actually see the wall come crashing down between them.

As she stood in the hallway she saw her mother standing by her bedroom door, waiting for her. It was late and her parents had retired hours earlier.

"You okay, Mom?"

Her mother looked every minute her seventy years when the makeup was gone and the shape wear was replaced with a sagging nightgown cinched in the middle by the belt of a favorite robe. She looked frail and vulnerable. Sarah tried to imagine her in the village in Wales where the people chose to kill their elders rather than feed them. She felt a shiver go down both arms.

"A word, darling?"

Sarah wasn't sure she had ever felt more exhausted in her life. The two days of happiness-charged adrenalin had pushed her further and longer than she could possibly have gone on mere drugs or good intentions. But the comedown was a bitch.

"Sure, Mom." Sarah moved to her own bedroom and heard her mother's soft tread behind her.

That afternoon when Sarah's father delivered the terrible news that she wouldn't be able to travel back to Ireland felt like years ago. How she had stumbled through dinner and a mindless evening of TV until she could break the news to John was beyond her. All through the relentless hours of waiting she promised herself a good long cry in the privacy of her bedroom.

The fantasies of running into Mike's open arms dissolved like some taunting, treacherous nightmare where the love of your life turns into a monster before your very eyes. It had taken every ounce of courage and self-control she had not to think of him, not to see his face, remember his laugh...

She sat on her bed, her shoulders slumped in defeat, and waited for her mother to sit down next to her. She was sure to come bearing the wisdom of the world for just this occasion and Sarah needed to be sure and act as if it made a difference.

Her mother took her hand and Sarah braced herself. "You know, darling, how much your father and I love you."

"I do, Mom."

"And how we would do anything for you."

"I know."

Now it was her mother's turn to take in a long breath as if working up the courage to continue. Curious now, Sarah turned her attention away from the carpet beneath her feet, and to her mother's face. *Were her fingers trembling?*

"What is it, Mom?"

"You father wants what's best for you."

"I know."

"And so do I," her mother said quickly. "But..."

Sarah forced herself to be patient. To wait for it.

"But I also want you to be happy."

Sarah felt the pulse in her throat begin to beat in double time. And she couldn't say why, but somehow she knew something was coming. Something big.

"Maybe that is a mother's special difference in the way she loves," her mother said, holding onto Sarah's hand.

"Mom, what is it?"

Her mother turned to look at her and said firmly. "Your father's information about the government closing all travel is accurate," she said. "But…"

"But?" It took everything Sarah had not to stand up and shake the next words out of her mother. "*But?*"

"But," her mother said, her face glowing with pain and sacrifice, "what he didn't mention is that there is a window. A small window. After which time there will be no travel between the US and any other country for at least ten years. Maybe more."

Sarah stared at her mother as if trying to comprehend what she was telling her. "You're saying intercontinental travel isn't restricted *yet*." Sarah said the words slowly to make sure she understood.

"If you leave immediately you can go back, but you won't be able to return, Sarah," her mother said. "Not for at least ten years. Your father and I…" Her mother looked away.

We may not be alive when you return. The unspoken words filled the air between them. Sarah pulled her hand away and drew her mother into her arms and held her closely.

"I love you, Mom," she whispered. "I love you so much."

"I know, dear. And that is why I feel I can ask you, please, *not* to go. Your father's way was to keep the truth from you, but I knew once you found out you'd hate us. I am begging you, Sarah, for John's sake and for your father's and my sake, and yes, even yours…please don't leave."

Sarah held her mother. She could feel her own heart beating and feel it pounding in her throat.

"I know it's a terrible thing to ask," her mother said. "But you are all we have. All *I* have. It has to be your decision. It can't be something that prevents you from going. That much I know. So now you know all the truth. You can leave but you can't come back." She took a long ragged breath and pulled back to look at Sarah's face.

"And I am begging you to stay."

Sarah looked into her mother's eyes and thought of Mike. She thought of her request to meet him in five years. *If I push it to ten, would he still come? Will I even want him to? Will he?*

The tears came then as she thought of the years between now and then. The long years that would spin them forever apart—even further than the miles across the ocean that separated them now. The years of habit and routine and life that would push him to the back of her memory—where David was—until he never really existed at all.

Sarah knew what she had to do. In a way she had probably always known and just refused to see it. As she leaned her head down on the frail shoulder of her now weeping mother, Sarah felt the death of all her dreams in one moment of pure despair.

"I'll stay," she whispered.

23

From where Mike stood in the newly finished jail cell, he had an unobstructed view of the center of camp. He actually took a moment to be impressed with the logic behind this when he saw the construction begin on the stage where three nooses were strung up over a long horizontal beam supported by two pillars. Not only were the stocks in plain view of whatever poor sod happened to be imprisoned at the time, but the gallows were, too.

He had to hand it to Brian. For a sadist, he was very thorough.

"Oy, Mike," Declan called. He was housed in the next room and separated by six inches of stacked log. "You see what I'm seeing?"

"Aye."

"Why are there three?"

"I was just wondering the same thing."

"Do we get a trial at least?"

"Would it matter?"

The two men fell silent as they listened to the ringing of hammers against metal as the men of the community finished up the stage construction.

"If the lazy boggers had put a fourth the energy into securing the perimeter fence that they're putting into creating that trap-door, we'd be totally enclosed by Christmas."

"Jaysus. You're still going on about the fecking perimeter fencing? You really don't quit, do you?"

Mike drew a tired hand across his eyes and took a withered breath. Was it really possible? Was he really going to die tomorrow morning? Was there no one in the community—the community he had created—who would lift a finger to stop it?

"Mike? You still there?"

Mike cleared his throat. "No, I ran out for a pack of fags but I'm back now."

"I'm never gonna see my kid."

"Shut up, Dec," Mike growled. "That's not helping."

"Someone's coming."

Mike heard it too. Voices first and then the distinct sounds of footsteps—several people it sounded like—coming down the gravel path toward the new jail. The sun was setting and shooting off blinding flashes of colored light on the hammers and saws being used on the stage. He squinted to see who was coming.

It was a crowd of four, no five, men. They were backlit against the setting sun but he recognized Jamison's big lope and also the one in the middle. He had the memory of that walk imprinted on his brain.

It was Gavin, walking with his hands bound in front of him.

"Jaysus, Mike! It's Gav."

If Mike could have vomited, he would've. His stomach fought to empty its contents but there was nothing there. He groaned and grabbed the side of the window, the single bar preventing any hope of escape from that area.

He turned as he heard the sound of the men talking and then the rattle of the lock that was on his door. When the door creaked open, Gavin stumbled inside and Mike caught him by the hands so he wouldn't fall.

"Da, I'm so sorry," Gavin said. "I came to talk to Grandda. I was sure he'd listen to me."

"You'll get your chance to talk to Archie," Iain said from the outside. "He'll come after dinner. Mr. Gilhooley didn't want to take the chance ya might have other ideas besides talk on your mind."

Dear God in heaven, Mike thought. *Is that why there are three nooses?*

"Hey, Gav," Declan called from the other room. "You okay, lad? How's your Auntie Fi?"

"She...she's good, Dec," Gavin said, his eyes never leaving Mike's as if he would find the answer to this nightmare written in them.

How did things get so arse over tit? Mike felt a wave of helplessness wash over him. There was nothing he could do to protect his boy—not if that monster Gilhooley had it in his mind to hang him. There was nothing he could do to stop anything from happening to any of them.

Caitlin's strident voice pierced the low rumble of voices that were coming from outside and Mike lifted his head to peer out. She obviously had decided the schoolmarm look wasn't working for her, Mike noted. She was back to wearing her usual low-cut tops and miniskirts. Ridiculous in a community that survived only on the sweat and hard labor of its inhabitants.

She stood between Gilhooley and Jamison. Mike watched her point to the jail in sharp jabbing motions. Behind her, he could see Archie hurrying up the gravel path toward them.

"Him coming here is guilt enough!" Caitlin said, shrilly. "Why else would he come? To break the other two out."

Jamison was shaking his head. "He said he came to talk to your father."

"That's what he *would* say! Don't you see?"

"Jaysus, Caitlin," Iain said. "He's your own fecking nephew."

"He is nothing to me!"

Archie joined the group. "What's going on here?" Mike could see he was out of breath and red in the face. He looked from Brian to Caitlin, his face seared in a permanent grimace.

"Gavin came to break out his da from the jail," Caitlin said. "And Iain here is too weak to do what's needed."

"The lad said he came here to talk to you," Iain said to Archie. "We intercepted him before he could."

Archie nodded. "He'll have come to beg for his father's life."

"You'll not *listen* to him?" Caitlin said to him in outrage and horror.

"What would you have me do, Caitie?" Archie still fought for breath and Mike thought the question was more a stalling tactic than a serious question.

"He is an accomplice to the crime," she said, turning her eyes to Brian. "He needs to hang with them."

Mike felt his stomach grind and then let loose and he turned away to vomit up spume and water into the corner of the cell.

"Da, you okay?" Gavin said, resting a hand on his father's shoulder. "What are they saying out there? It's about me, isn't it?"

Mike's head was spinning and he forced himself to squat down against the wall until he felt steadier. He could still hear their voices but only snatches of the men's words.

Caitlin was clearly audible. "You've got this fantasy that you have a relationship with him and you've met him exactly twice!"

"...matter...still my grandson!"

Mike took a long breath and fought to get back to his feet. The last thing he needed was Gavin listening to this shite.

"Oy! Ye bastards!" he called to the group. "What you're contemplating is murder, plain and simple. The authorities will hunt you down—"

"I am the authorities in this camp, Donovan," Gilhooley screamed at him. Mike could see the man was worked up. Caitlin had reverted to hanging onto him in her appeal. He glanced at

Jamison who had backed away from the group in apparent disgust.

Your tender feelings won't save my lad, Mike thought fiercely. *Step up, man! Or burn in hell.*

"Well, I won't do it," Jamison said loudly. "Gavin is as innocent as anyone could be and it's just....just *sick* to be going after your own kin like that."

"So say I!" Archie yelled, jabbing a finger in Caitlin's face for emphasis. "You'll not kill me grandson! I won't allow it." He turned to Gilhooley and Mike saw the man shrink away from him. "Don't even try it as long as me and me boys are around."

"You're an addle-headed old bastard!" Caitlin snarled and Mike smiled grimly as he saw Gilhooley shudder at her language. *Get a good look, ya daft bugger. Here's your little angel in all her glory.*

"Fine," Gilhooley said, holding up his hands as if to command peace or a cessation of hostilities. "We won't hang the boy." He glanced at Caitlin and cringed when she stared back at him. "But...but..." he said, gathering steam and looking to Jamison to support him, "...we'll hang the other two without benefit of trial at first light tomorrow." He looked at Caitlin to see if this assuaged her at all. She turned away and stomped up the gravel path, leaving the men standing there.

The three dropped their voices and then went their separate ways.

"It doesn't matter," Declan said through the wall. "The trial was only going to be a piece of theatre anyroad."

Mike turned to see the look on Gavin's face, chalk white and stricken with the thought of his father's execution. Mike hated to be the one to cause him such pain, but the relief at Gavin not being hurt was so immense, that, insanely, he thought he'd likely sleep well tonight.

24

The morning brought with it the first hint that fall was coming. A bite to the air sifted between the bars of the jail cell where the three men were just waking. Mike stood by the window to inhale as much of the sweet air from the meadows as he could. Just the week before, members of the community had taken the remaining wheat to the little town of Callan—nearly fifty miles away—to have it ground into flour. Mike was proud that the members had been able to orchestrate such an important task on their own without him holding their hands every step of the way.

There was truth to the idea that he hadn't been good at delegating. He looked over his shoulder at his sleeping son in the hay and felt a debilitating wash of weariness. On the other hand, while it's true they got the wheat milled without buggering it up, they were also going to stand by and watch a public murder and not raise a hand or a voice.

These people who he had laughed with, shared hard times and good times, who he had called his friends as well as his neighbors, were going to watch him hang, and Declan too—the man who risked his life to save their ungrateful arses barely a year ago. He shook his head but deep down, he understood them.

When it comes to sheep, even a shepherd lobbing hand grenades at you is better than no shepherd at all.

"Mike? You up?" Declan's voice was soft and raspy. He'd had a bad night.

Not surprisingly.

"Aye. How you doing?"

"I've been better."

Mike turned his attention to Gavin who was sitting up and rubbing the sleep out of his eyes. He looked so young. Mike remembered the boy as a toddler when Ellen would carry him about the cottage and sing to him. A stone settled on his heart to think of how much she had loved him.

Had loved them both.

"They're coming," Declan said.

Mike turned to see the group walking down from the main camp. It looked like it was Jamison, Gilhooley, Archie and the twins, Cedric and Colin. Five against two, and the two still securely tied.

Nobody spoke until the door to Mike's cell swung open. Jamison filled the doorway. He didn't look at Mike but gestured to Gavin. "Say goodbye to your da,"

"You're a right bastard and I hope you rot in hell, Iain Jamison," Gavin said, tears choking his voice.

Iain backed out of the cell, leaving the door open. "You're likely right, lad."

Mike heard the other cell door opening and he turned to Gavin. He had spent most of last night wondering what in the world he would say to the boy if a miracle didn't happen and they came for him.

He still didn't know what to say. He cleared his throat and held out his hands, still bound. The boy rushed to him, his own hands also tied, and rested his face against Mike's shoulder.

"I love you, lad," Mike said hoarsely. "Mind you take care of your Auntie Fi."

"I will, Da," Gavin said, trying to talk past his tears.

"I'm proud of you, Gav. I've always been proud of you, son."

"I love you, Da."

"I love you, too. And Gavin?"

"Yes?"

"Promise me you won't look."

BRIAN ORDERED every member of the community to watch the hangings. They stood, all sixty of them, shoulder to shoulder in front of the seven-foot high stage. As Mike stood over the secured trap door, the noose tight around his neck, he could see most of the people he knew.

There was Caoimhe Byrne, who Fiona had nursed for a week because the poor bastard had no kin who could or would. There was Cian O'Neill, who Mike carried on his back for three miles across a rocky pasture because he'd turned an ankle out hunting.

If he wouldn't do anything to stop it, he at least, had the decency to stand watching with tears streaming down his face. There was Ciara O'Reilly, shaking her head and mouthing the words *sorry, I'm so sorry.* Mike had rescued her eldest boy, Dan, from a wild boar and still carried the scar on his calf from the beast's tusk to show for it.

"What part of you thinks justice is being done here today?" he shouted at to them.

The crowd murmured. A few looked up at him. Most simply shuffled and looked at the ground.

"There was no trial that brought me and Declan here. Just vengeance and racism. That's all that's being proven today. Every last one of you that stands there and does nothing is a part of it as surely as if you'd put the noose around our necks yourself."

"Well, did you do it, Mike?" Someone yelled out. "Did you let young Ollie go?"

"That's not why I'm here, Jerry," Mike called back. "I'm here because that man has nowhere to go with his grief over his dead daughter but to lay it at my feet."

A few in the crowd turned to look at Archie, who stood glowering at Mike, his arms crossed against his chest, his face purple with hate and, now, embarrassment.

"Shut up. You're not being punished for your wife's death," Archie shouted. "He's being punished for letting Ollie go."

"Yeah, but wasn't he acting leader at the time?" somebody called out.

"That doesn't matter," Gilhooley said. "It was in direct violation of my orders!"

"Cor, sure sounds like you give as many orders as Mike did. And I'm still waiting for my extra ration of sugar to show up."

The voices in the crowd swelled like a wave cresting as more people added their complaints to the growing din.

"This is neither the time nor the place!" Gilhooley yelled, trying to silence the crowd. "After the execution, we'll have a general camp meeting to address all of your concerns. Tell me you ever did that with Mike Donovan?"

Mike saw the crowd consider Gilhooley's words. No, he'd never had a camp meeting to do anything but to tell them what would happen next. A couple of them nodded as if they had to agree with that.

"This is just the vengeance of one old man," Mike said. "This is murder."

"Enough talking!" Archie yelled out. "Jamison, do your job!"

Mike turned to look at Declan who stood impassive and unnerved. He stared straight ahead, not looking around, refusing to look at Mike.

If that's what he needs to do to get through this, Mike thought with resignation, *I'll not fault him.* Mike turned away to close his eyes and pray.

God, please don't let Gav see this to be tortured with it the rest of his days. Please look over Fiona and her bairn and watch over me and Dec as we come to you, please God, this day.

And dear Lord, please have my Sarah finally happy with her life wherever she wants to be.

Into your hands, I commend my soul.

FIONA SAW the two of them as they stood on the stage and forced herself not to react to the sight of it.

She'd been preparing herself for much worse.

The horse she rode was skittish, used to pulling a cart and green under saddle. She knew she telegraphed her nerves to him through her knees and thighs, her hands jerking on the reins.

He didn't so much enter the camp as charge it.

Fiona twisted a handful of his mane into her hands and hung on as he galloped through the gate and straight down the main pathway to the center campfire and the staging area. She saw Mike standing with his head down, his hands in front of him as if praying. Her own husband watched her come, his eyes growing larger as she neared.

She was grateful no one was directly in her path. The few who were too close had only a moment to jump out of the way before she barreled on through and up to the foot of the stage. Her chest heaving with fear and anticipation, she watched Gilhooley and Jamison stare at her with open-mouthed shock. But neither went for their pistols.

Sarah was right about that, Fiona thought, with breathless satisfaction, feeling the strength she needed well up in her chest. *If the bastards think you're weak, you can catch 'em off guard.* She pulled out the handgun and pointed it at Iain Jamison's head.

She could hear the members of the community gasp but she wasn't worried. With her back to them any one of them could approach her from behind and pull her down from her horse—even now dancing about as if his feet were on fire. But she knew they wouldn't. They weren't participants in this nightmare. They were only watchers.

Her gun arm wobbled and she fought to keep it aimed at Iain. Instead of reaching for his gun, Iain raised his hands in surrender. It was then she knew he didn't want to go forward with any of this. He had been waiting for an opportunity to back out of it.

"Declan, Mike, back away from the trap doors," she said, hating her voice for sounding so shrill and feminine.

"Are you going to just let her do this?" Another female voice punctured the air, rising several decibels with each word.

Fiona didn't bother to look at Caitlin. She cocked her semiautomatic with one hand and struggled to keep control of her mount with the other. "We're leaving the way we came in," she said, panting and trying not to think about what she was doing or how she was going to get Mike and Dec out of the camp.

Thinking too much was never good.

If she'd heard Sarah say that once, she'd heard it a hundred times.

She was amazed that still nobody moved. To Fiona, it was almost as if the crowd was waiting for the show to start. Which is why, when she heard the rustling and murmuring grow louder—yet nothing on stage had happened to warrant it—she turned to see what was happening.

Behind her, a stream of men and women poured into the staging area from all sides of the camp. The gypsies who normally kept to themselves pushed to the front of crowd. Fiona could see they were armed and that they held their weapons in their hands ready to use. Still pointing her gun at Iain, Fiona shifted in her saddle to see that the three largest gypsies stood at the foot of the stage in front of Declan.

But they were looking at her.

She directed her attention back to the stage and steadied her aim. "Untie them."

Iain moved quickly to Declan and jerked his hands free of the leather thong. He turned and did the same for Mike and then stepped away, his hands held up.

"You coward!" Gilhooley shouted at him. "Nobody move! This execution will go on as planned!"

Fiona saw him grope for the gun he had jammed in his belt loop, but before he could reach it Caitlin jerked it from him and pointed it at Mike.

Instantly, Fiona corrected her aim and pulled the trigger. She watched Caitlin jerk backward as the bullet punched into her chest at the same time Fiona's horse screamed and wheeled away at the loud report. As she grabbed at the saddle to stay upright, the gun slipped from her fingers. A roar from the crowd engulfed her and she felt rough, harsh hands grabbing at her and pulling her to the ground.

She hit the earth hard and felt the air punch out of her lungs in a violent expulsion. When she opened her eyes, Archie Kelly was standing over her. He held her by her jacket in one hand, and drew his other back in a large meaty fist aimed for her face. Before she could bring her hands up to protect her face—or the baby—hands reached out and grabbed Archie, yanking him away. Fiona scrambled to her feet and felt herself being pulled to the perimeter of the melee. Siobhan Murray, with a bloody lip, held her tightly by the elbow and pushed them both to the outskirts.

"Watch yourself now, darlin'," Siobhan said soothingly. "We'll not let the bastards have their way this day!"

Did...did I just shoot Caitlin?

Fiona turned to see the gypsies ripping down the stage with their bare hands. Some of them were running after the Kelly twins, chasing them with planks of wood with jagged nails sticking out of them.

"Where...can you see Dec and Mike?"

"Oh, they're fine now, lass. Don't you worry. Let's just get you and the little one somewhere safe while we wait out the row, aye?"

"Siobhan...did...did I...is Caitlin dead?"

"Well, I don't rightly know. Seeing as how she was spawned from the depths of hell, we probably won't know for certain if she's really dead. But we can hope!"

Fiona allowed Siobhan to take her to the porch of her old cottage and sat with her on the bench and watched the battle as the members of Daoineville took back its community with a two by four to the head.

She could see Gilhooley bending over Caitlin's body on the stage and her stomach lurched to see it. *Demon from hell or not,* she thought, trying to swallow past her bile, *did I kill her?*

"Hello, my beauty."

She snapped her head to the other side of where she was sitting with Siobhan to find Declan—a fresh cut over his right eye —and a broad grin on his face. "Oh, Dec!" She launched herself into his arms. "I can't believe you're here. I can't believe it."

"Nor me, darlin'," he said laughing. "Did you really decide to spring me and your brother all by your lonesome?"

She looked at him with wonder. Hearing him say the words made her realize how mad the idea had been. "I guess I did. But oh, Dec! Your family came! At just the right moment!"

"Aye, they said they went to find you at the cottage and Aideen told them what you were up to. You know they've decided you're their new Gypsy Queen? My wonderful Fiona—mad, beautiful and brave as any gypsy goddess you could hope for." He kissed her.

Siobhan leaned in to speak over the fighting still going on. "Not to take anything away from the gypsies, mind," she said pointedly to Declan, "but the people of Daoineville are finishing the job they started. Let's don't leave that part out of the story when it gets told around the campfire."

"It's true," Dec said, putting his arm around Fiona. "When that nutter Kelly went for you—a pregnant woman, no less—it finally stirred something in the crowd."

"The very idea—attacking a woman with child!" Siobhan said. "What are they, *English*?"

A shadow descended across the front porch and Fiona looked up to see Mike and Gavin walking away from the dismantled stage.

"Mind if I kiss my rescuer?" Mike said, leaning in to kiss Fiona on the cheek. "Sure, I never imagined in my wildest days that it would be you, Fi. And six months pregnant to boot!"

"I know," Fi said, feeling the glow of his praise and the pure joy that he and Declan were safe. "Sarah always said a woman's best weapon was a man's blatant disrespect of her abilities. 'You can always take 'em by surprise,' she said."

Fiona saw Mike's face soften as he brought Sarah to mind. "Aye," he said. "I can just hear her." He leaned in and kissed her again and then slapped Declan on the knee. "Come on, mate. Let's mop up what's left of this mess."

Declan gave her a last squeeze before bounding down the stairs to join the gypsies and the cleanup of the melee.

Fiona watched him go and realized that the day that had started so poorly—so full of terror and hopelessness—was ending with a happiness she had no right to ever imagine or hope for.

And all it took was riding into an armed camp with one gun on an unreliable horse and a determination not to accept failure.

Fiona placed her hand on her swollen tummy and leaned back against the house and watched the activity before her. Archie and Gilhooley were both on their knees weeping by Caitlin's body, but being watched closely by Declan, who stood near them with a gun in his hand. The stage was now a pile of splintered wood and Fiona watched two gypsies dragging pieces of board to the main cook fire.

Women walked by with babies on their hips as if today were no different than the last time a stage was constructed—at the Harvest Festival. A few of the gypsy women smiled shyly at Fiona as they passed. One waved.

As Fiona watched the camp right itself, she slipped her hand into Siobhan's without speaking. The old woman turned to look at her and Fiona watched her face visibly ease.

"You all right?" Siobhan asked. "Quite a bit of excitement for so early in the morning."

"I'm good," Fiona said. "I'm real good." She beamed and let the glory of the morning—and what she had done—wash over her.

She had changed the tide. She, Fiona, had turned it all around when no one else could. And now Mike was back bossing people around with Declan, his best mate, at his side just as before.

And on top of it all, she was home again. She was sitting on her own front porch, safely reinstated in her own tiny corner of the world. Fiona smiled and closed her eyes, feeling the sun break through the thick morning clouds to caress her upturned face.

Sarah, darling, you would've been proud of me today.

25

T he walk back from the village graveyard was a somber one. Fiona drove the cart with a few of the children from the village, including Taffy, while Declan walked along side. The morning was chilly, wet and gray.

Perfect for a funeral. Even better for three.

Caitlin and her brothers, the only fatalities from the fight the day before, were buried together in the Ballinagh kirkyard with the sun struggling to peek through the clouds that hung low in the sky before finally giving up the effort.

When Mike asked Declan to find out how the twins had died, his brother-in-law only shrugged. It appeared the gypsy fathers and brothers of the raped girls of the camp were not able to tell Cedric from Colin, nor did they care to. Justice was justice. Sometimes slow in coming, but always coming.

Gilhooley and Archie trudged side by side to the funeral, although Mike never saw them exchange a word. The fight seemed to have gone out of both of them during the long day and night since the three Kelly siblings had been slain. Even so, Mike locked them both up in the newly built jail so that the rest of the camp might sleep without worry.

Both would leave immediately following the burial with whatever belongings they came with—except for their weapons.

Mike drove the cart from the burial with Aideen and some of the older women of the camp, including Iain's wife, Edie, who sat in front with Mike and Aideen. Iain walked behind, dishonored and dejected. Because he refused to hang Gavin, Mike allowed him to keep his weapons.

But he too would have to leave.

Mike looked over at Edie sitting rigidly next to Aideen, her face impassive and unreadable. He kept his voice low although the children in back were too young to understand.

"I'm happy for you to stay, Edie," he said. "You don't have to go with him."

Edie gave a snort of derision, but whether it was intended for Mike or the situation, Mike didn't know. "He's my husband," she said. "For better or feckin' worse."

"If you ever want to return, you are welcome any time."

"Thank you, Mike," she said, not looking at him. "And..." She fumbled for a tissue in the sleeve of her cardigan and Mike felt Aideen stiffen. "And I'm sorry for everything he did."

"No need to apologize for him..."

"You mean for him nearly hanging you? I'd say there is."

"It wasn't you."

"No, but I married him."

Mike didn't speak after that. It had been hard enough to watch the three young people lowered into the grave. His eyes kept straying to the grave close by that they had just dug three weeks before.

Sleep well, little Papin, he thought sadly. *We miss you, girl.*

WHEN THEY REACHED THE CAMP, Mike helped the two women down, but before Aideen turned away she held onto his arm. "A word, Mike?"

Nodding, he followed her away from the cart to stand in front of his hut. He and Gavin had moved back in the night before.

"I don't suppose there's any way you'll reconsider and let Iain stay?"

He looked at her with surprise, but before he could speak she hurried on.

"It's just that we all make mistakes and everyone knows that as soon as Fiona showed up, Iain was fighting on *our* side...on the side of the camp, I mean, not Brian's."

"I'm aware of that."

"He told Edie he's sorry about all of it. You can't see it in your heart to let him stay? I mean, it means Edie and the babies are out in the cold, too."

"I said they could stay. But it's her decision."

"I know, but won't you reconsider?"

"You've become friendly with Edie."

"We have a lot in common. I adore her little boys and Taffy gets on well with them, too."

"Did she ask you to talk to me?"

Aideen laughed without humor. "As if I had any special influence over you."

"Of course you do," Mike said, resisting the impulse to touch her shoulder to assure her. "But I can't let him stay. Gilhooly was barking mad about a lot of things, but on that he wasn't wrong." Mike shrugged. "I was soft. I nearly paid the ultimate price for that. I won't soon do it again. I'm sorry, Aideen. He needs to go."

She nodded and looked down at her feet. "In that case," she said, "I think I'll likely go with them."

"Are you serious?" He was stunned. "Why would you do that?"

"I don't know, Mike," she said brightly. "Maybe because I'm in love with someone who every time I see him tears my heart right out of my chest and I think I stand some chance of being happy if I'm away from him?"

He blinked at her as if she had started speaking a foreign language. He couldn't believe she would leave the safety and comfort of an established community just to save herself the discomfort of laying eyes on him. "Is it that bad, then?"

She laughed and shook her head. "You really are clueless, aren't you? Yes. Yes, it's that bad."

"Where will you go?"

"Iain says he's heard of a place over on the coast. He's learned a lot, Mike. He's learned what not to do. And he's learned all he has to lose, too. We're all going to start over. I'm not sad about it. I don't want you to be either."

He shook his head and this time he did give in to the urge to touch her. He put his head next to hers and they stood quietly for a moment. "If you're sure," he said.

"I am."

"I'm as sorry as I can be."

"Don't be. It is what it is, as a wise man once told me." She lifted her face to him and kissed him on the mouth. "Take care of yourself, Mike Donovan," she said. "I wish you happiness."

"And me, you."

She turned and he watched her walk to where Fiona stood waiting for her on her porch, her arms open, ready to take her in. And say goodbye.

GILHOOLEY SLUMPED on his horse like a man who'd had his spine surgically removed, Mike thought as he approached him from his hut. The rain had started sometime in the night and had kept steady all though the morning and the burials. It was only getting worse as the day wore on.

You wouldn't send a dog out in this shite, Mike thought. He turned to look at Archie sitting in the driver's seat of the wagon he'd arrived in. The bed was nearly empty except for the saddles that belonged to the two riderless horses tied to the back of the wagon. Archie wore a baseball cap that did nothing to prevent the rain from sluicing down the front of his face and across his chest. He stared down at his hands holding the reins as if he didn't see them.

Mike took the bridle of the horse in harness and patted his neck. He didn't look at Gilhooley or his father-in-law. "Got everything then?" he asked gruffly.

Neither man answered him.

Out of the corner of his eye, he saw Gavin walk up to the wagon where Archie sat. Gavin stood for a moment as if unsure of what to do, then stuck out his hand to the older man. Mike watched Archie hesitate for a moment and then unclench from the reins to take his grandson's hand.

"Take care of yourself, Grandda," Gavin said. "I hope you stay well."

Archie nodded but didn't let go of Gavin's hand. Mike watched him put his head close to Gavin's to speak privately to him. Mike let them have their moment. He turned his attention to Gilhooley.

"You know how to get back to Dublin?"

Gilhooley shifted his eyes from his pommel to Mike's face. His eyes were bloodshot and dazed, his face a picture of heartbreak.

"Don't know that I'm going to Dublin," he said.

"Well," Mike said, "wherever you go, mind you never find your way back this way again."

"I would rather die than revisit this godforsaken den of death and abomination."

"Well, good. That works out for both of us then, since if you ever come back I'll shoot you."

Brian ground his teeth and looked at Mike through narrowed eyes but didn't respond.

Mike turned his collar up against the rain and hunched into

his jacket as he turned back to Archie's wagon. Gavin untied the two horses and was leading them away to the stable.

"What's going on here, then?" Mike asked as he walked over to the wagon.

"I gave the boy the horses," Archie said. "I don't need them."

Mike nodded. Horses—even elderly plow horses—were extremely valuable during these times. And the twins' mounts were good horses. "You'll go back to Dublin?"

Archie shrugged. "I dunno. Me family's all dead, aren't they?" He stared down at his hands on the reins, his voice flat and low.

Mike nodded. "All but one."

Archie didn't answer.

"I never hurt Ellen," Mike said. "I loved her."

Archie's face crumpled into ugly tears, his shoulders heaving under the rain as it came down even heavier. "I know," he said softly. "I was just so...so..." He brought his hands up to cover his face. Mike resisted the impulse to touch him. With the rain had come an early advent of autumn's chill. He shivered in his cotton jacket.

He tried to imagine how the poor bastard could be feeling—could even be sitting upright—after having buried three of his four children this morning.

It was unimaginable.

"I'm sorry."

The words caught Mike by surprise and when he looked up, he saw the tears coursing down the old man's face. Mike cleared his throat and forced himself not to look away from the man's agony.

"I forgive you," Mike said. He patted the rump of the horse in the harness. "You'd best get going if you want to find a place for the night before you drown," he said.

"Aye." Archie wiped his tears with a sodden jacket sleeve and looked around as if trying to decide how to maneuver the horses for the best exit from camp.

"And, Arch," Mike said, "once you've had some time to think on everything and know how you feel...if you were ever to want to come back to Daoineville, you'll have a place."

Archie's eyes grew round with the shock of Mike's words and his lips trembled as his eyes strayed in the direction where Caitlin and the twins were buried. He hesitated and then nodded, not looking at Mike. "Thank you," he said in a low voice. "I think I'd like that."

MIKE SAT at the dinner table, thunderstruck by his wealth of blessings. He watched Fiona—surely showing her pregnancy more than she had even this morning—set down steaming bowls of mash with creamery butter, the last of the fresh corn, and a roast chicken, the fragrance of which had tormented him for the better part of an hour as it baked. Siobhan Murray was running her fingers through Gavin's hair in an obviously futile attempt to eliminate the snarls from it and the lad was doing his best to escape her by scooting his chair closer to Declan.

It appeared that somehow the old widow had touched a nerve with Fiona. In the space of a day, she'd been granted official granny status. Mike shook his head and grinned.

A day that had begun with a noose around me neck.

"I'll be saying grace tonight if there's no objection," Mike intoned seriously.

"Well, saints be praised," Siobhan said. "If nearly killing you is what it takes to bring you back onto the path, then I'll be sharpening me dirk."

The table laughed.

"Thank you, Lord," Mike said, "for this meal made by the hands of me own personal savior, Fiona Cooper..."

"All right, now," Fiona said, wagging a spoon at Mike. "Say it proper or let me take over."

Mike clasped his hands together and bowed his head. "Thank you, Lord, for this meal made possible by your bounty and the good weather you gave us to grow it. Thank you for letting us live another day to eat it—"

"You are terrible at this," Declan said, shaking his head.

"And thank you for all of us together and well."

The sounds of the rain hitting the wooden roof and shutters underscored his words with an image of safety and protection.

"Amen."

"Amen," everyone repeated.

As Fiona began passing the bowls, Declan turned to Mike. "So, no election to have you formally reinstated as Camp Commandant?"

Mike frowned. "It's still not a democracy. I think we showed today that if people don't want me as their leader, they don't have to kill me to get rid of me. They can just tell me."

Gavin spoke up. "But they voted you back in anyway, Da. They had the election while you were in the stables with the horses this afternoon."

"Oh, well, then," Mike said. "Good to know everyone was working as hard as I was this afternoon."

"You'll do it then?" Fiona asked. "Take over as leader?"

"He kind of already has," Gavin said, grinning. "It's like nothing's changed."

"Except everything has," Mike said. He looked at Declan. "The loyalty of your people coming to defend you..." He shook his head. "This community could learn from them."

"Well," Declan said, plucking a large corn muffin from a basket. "They're family. That's the difference."

"Aye. I can see that."

"You can't expect your neighbors to act like family," Siobhan said. "Even if nowadays they're really more than neighbors."

"Wise words, Siobhan," Mike said, grinning at her. "And may I say, I'm happy to see you at our table?"

"It's permanent," Fiona said, spooning into her mashed pota-toes. "I've asked her to come live with us." She looked at Declan but he only smiled. Asking a gypsy if he minded living in close quarters with family was like asking if he cared that rain was wet.

"You'll be needing help with the bairn," Siobhan said. "And the lad's not grown yet. Not by a long shot." She gave Gavin a pointed look and the table laughed again.

As soon as everyone turned their attention to their meals, a low-grade humming sound became instantly noticeable. Mike and Declan stood at the same time, but Gavin was faster than both of them. He was at the window looking out, but before he could even give the yelp that brought the women out of their chairs Mike saw the light in the dark as a twin pair of headlights pierced the window.

"What the feck...? Gavin, no!"

But Gavin was out the door before Mike could drop his napkin on the table. Whatever it was he'd seen, he obviously wasn't afraid of it.

Which didn't mean he shouldn't be.

Mike lurched for his handgun on the side table by the couch and ran out the open door into the dark and the rain behind Gavin and Declan, who now stood stock still in front of him in the forecourt of the cottage.

Sitting before them was a large transport truck, its high beams stabbing the little cottage like aliens preparing to beam down. The engine was thrumming loudly in the quiet of the camp.

Mike squinted to see if it was another US military vehicle. He held his gun by his side. By God, US military or not, he'd not lose his camp after he'd just gotten it back. He strode purposely to the truck, blinded the whole way by the headlights until he reached the driver's side door.

"May I help you?" he asked loudly, feeling much less sure than he sounded.

"Well, yes, as a matter of fact," a familiar female voice said, "you can help me unload the groceries."

THE MINUTE SARAH SAW HIM, it was all she could do not to pop the clutch and lose control of the truck. John was out of his seat belt and the passenger's seat before Mike had finished walking up to her window.

The look on Mike's face was one she would never forget. His mouth was open, his eyes large and unbelieving. He stood there staring at her. Over his shoulder, she saw Fiona and Declan running up to them. Gavin was swinging John in a wide hug and pounding on his back in greeting. She could see lanterns turning on one by one as more and more of the community members came to investigate.

Sarah unfastened her seatbelt.

"I brought a few things," she said, her voice shaking. "I got wine, sugar, guns, bullets. There's a generator in the back for the refrigerator Fi's always wanted...and a refrigerator, of course. In fact, four of them."

And still Mike just stood there, a gun hanging from his hand, his mouth agape.

"I couldn't remember everything you said we needed. I guess I should've listened better. But I got peanut butter, seeds, wool blankets, baby shoes, petrol...oh! And a satellite phone. John tried to talk me into bringing his iPod but I said no. You would've been proud of me, Mike, for acting the firm parent." She watched him drag his eyes away from her to look at the seven thousand pound capacity truck. She could already hear the sounds of John and Gavin opening the back hatch.

"I've arranged for a small air-lift of a few more things I thought we might need, but that'll be coming next week. Mike? It would really help if you would say something about now."

"You brought wool blankets to a country that's four-fifth's

sheep?" Mike's gaze returned to her, and when it did, she grinned with relief.

"That would be an affirmative."

Mike dropped his gun on the ground and jumped onto the truck's running board, where he gripped the rim of the driver's window and looked at her with wonder in his eyes.

"Sarah Woodson, I know you're not telling me you willing left the world of hot baths and fast food restaurants to come back here and plant pole beans with us." He reached through the window to unlock her door and jerk open her door.

"Crazy, huh?" she said, her eyes shining with unshed tears. To see him again, to hear his voice after so many weeks...she was sure her legs wouldn't hold her. "I wonder if there's any way I might get a commitment from you somewhere *near* the same scale?"

He pulled her into his arms. "Marry me."

Her heart felt so full she could barely breathe. "That'll work," she said, gasping. She turned her face to his and felt his mouth insistent and probing, sending tingles of heat through her limbs. Then he stepped back to the ground with her still wrapped in his arms and swung her wide off the ground. She hugged him tight, not wanting to disentangle from him even for a moment—she had waited so long to feel his arms around her again.

She had given up so much to have it.

Somewhere in the background, she heard the sounds of Gavin and John unloading the truck. Squeals of delight from the growing crowd wafted back to her where she stood with Mike.

"So you're back, are you?" Fiona said, throwing her arms around her. "I can't wait to tell you how you helped me save the camp today."

"Is it anything like how the Irish saved civilization?" Sarah asked, laughing and hugging her back. "Oh, my God! You're huge! How is it possible for the baby to have grown so much in just three weeks?"

"Enough of that," Fiona said. "For the love of God, did you bring chocolate?"

"I did! Barrels of it."

Someone in the gathering crowd yelled out, "So you're staying then?"

"Hell, yes, I'm staying," she called back, then turned to Mike and spoke just to him. "It's my home, isn't it?"

He put his hand to her cheek and she could have sworn he had tears in his eyes. "Welcome home, darlin,'" he said.

"By the way," she said, "did something happened here? What is that big pile of boards for in the middle of camp?"

"*That* is a long story, which I'll tell you later when I've given you time to climb back into your clothes again."

"Mike!" Sarah laughed. "John will hear you."

"He's too busy playing Santa to care about what his old da is getting up to with his mum."

"Where's Caitlin?" Sarah craned her neck to look past him. "And Aideen?"

"Everything in due time. I cannot believe you're here. I cannot believe you're standing right in front of me."

"I almost wasn't. They closed the window for travel back to the States, Mike. I can't go back now even if I wanted to."

"I'll make you happy, Sarah. I swear on me mother's grave I will."

"Just you being alive makes me happy, Mike. Knowing you're finally mine puts my happiness into orbit." Sarah grinned at him, her hands still on his arms. She realized for the first time that she could touch him now whenever she wanted. There finally was no one to be hurt or to care.

"How did you come to buy all these things? Were you rich back in America and I never knew it?"

"I cashed out my retirement fund. And the US government gave me a cash award for agreeing not to sue them. Now we'll be able to build a mill and grind our own flour. Plus, with the generators we'll have lights for the perimeter watchtowers. I put the bulk of my funds in a US-secured bank in Dublin, so we should be able to buy more petrol as we need it."

"I can't believe any of this."

"The airlift will bring solar panels in case the sun ever shines in Ireland. John said not, but I'm an optimist. And I loaded up with antibiotics, aspirin and basic veterinarian medicines, too. Oh! And there's fifty miles of barbed wire in the truck for reinforcing the camp perimeter. That's an early Christmas present for you. John said it would probably be enough."

"I...I just don't know what to say."

Sarah stood on tiptoe and kissed him. "That, my darling, is a first," she said in a low, velvety voice, moving his hand to her waist. "And we'll drink to that and many other firsts just as soon as I unpack the Bushmills."

"Oh, dear God in heaven," he said, drawing her closer to him, "Irish whiskey? I really am going to cry now."

EPILOGUE

There had been no reason anyone could think of to wait any longer. While Sarah wanted to ride to Limerick to shop for Irish lace to wear on her special day, Mike made it clear he'd rather marry her in a burlap bag than wait another day longer than necessary.

And as it appeared that wearing a burlap bag was becoming increasingly likely the longer she talked of Limerick, she soon gave it up and found herself standing in the little chapel in Ballinagh in Fiona's mother's wedding dress, altered to fit, with every single person from Daoineville in attendance. In the end, the community opted to stick with the name Daoineville and hoped to erase all prior connotations in time.

There would be no aisle–walking or giving away the bride today. Mike and Sarah had both done all that once before. Sarah was glad that both their prior marriages had been happy, loving ones. As she stood now in the cold little chapel, she felt the approving presence of Ellen and David. As much as the two had loved her and Mike, she couldn't imagine them feeling any other way about their union.

She held Mike's hand in her own while clutching a nosegay of late summer blooms. He was handsome in his tweed jacket and Fair Isle vest. She knew she probably wouldn't see him dressed so smartly any time soon, so she would enjoy every minute of him wearing it today.

It had not been two weeks since she'd returned to camp. In the interim, the airlift of supplies had arrived and the whole of Daoineville had been thrown into a whirl of ebullient productivity and vitality. They were now the only town outside of Limerick for over five hundred miles that behaved almost as much as any town in pre-Crisis times did. They had working electric interior lights, motion-activated flood lights, a satellite phone for emergency contact with the outside world, a small pick-up truck in addition to the larger one, C4 explosives, a cache of semi-automatic weapons, and enough medical supplies to outfit a small clinic.

Not all the camp's changes were because of her. Mike had assigned a small group of men to patrol the perimeter, much like Brian Gilhooley had envisioned. The wolf puppies, while still not effective as guard dogs, at least hadn't started eating the chickens and so judgment—and their fate—was reserved.

In the silk purse that lay in the pew behind her was the letter her mother had slipped into her bag before she left America. Sarah's eyes stung with tears remembering her mother's face when she told her she would go back to Ireland after all. In the letter, her mother forgave her with love.

"I understand your decision and I applaud you for doing it, my brave, brave girl," her mother wrote. *"You have always given so much of yourself to others. I know I couldn't be truly happy knowing you walked away from this chance to be happy with Mike. We'll see you and John again one day, darling girl, I swear we will. Until then, stay well, stay strong and know that you go forward with all my love, Mom."*

The priest cleared his throat and nodded at the gypsy standing behind him to begin the Irish wedding march. The older cleric living in the Ballinagh rectory had been replaced by Jamie Riley, a younger man sent by the Vatican to do missionary work in the field which, of course, both Ballinagh and Daoineville now definitely qualified as.

Father Riley nodded at Mike and Sarah as they stood before him. Gavin and John, dressed in their finest and stiff as starch, flanked them, proud and nervous, as if all four were about to be joined together.

Behind them sat Fiona, Declan, Siobhan and the rest of the community, gypsies included. When Sarah saw so many of the women crowding the little chapel with tears in their eyes to watch her marry Mike, she knew it was more than just baby shoes and peanut butter that had softened their hearts toward her.

Coming back when she didn't have to had bridged the gap.

Mike looked down at her and smiled. The sight of him made her breath catch. He was so handsome she sometimes had to force herself not to look at him for fear she'd otherwise get nothing done in her day.

Today, their wedding day, she looked at him and felt her world fill with the pure joyous wonder of him.

"Are you ready, then, Sarah?" Father Riley asked softly.

Sarah tore her gaze away from Mike's face and nodded, finding her voice strong and clear.

"Yes, Father," she said. "I'm ready. With bells on."

ABOUT THE AUTHOR

USA TODAY Bestselling Author Susan Kiernan-Lewis is the author of *The Maggie Newberry Mysteries,* the post-apocalyptic thriller series *The Irish End Games, The Mia Kazmaroff Mysteries, The Stranded in Provence Mysteries,* and *An American in Paris Mysteries.*

Visit www.susankiernanlewis.com or follow Author Susan Kiernan-Lewis on Facebook.

Manufactured by Amazon.ca
Bolton, ON